MAFIA KING

DIRTY MAFIA KINGDOM BOOK ONE

MICHELE MANNON

DIRTY MAFIA KING

I must be a mermaid; I have no fear of depths and a great fear of shallow living. ~ Anaïs Nin

Bastian

NO ONE EXPECTED me to drag a hooded man out of a rental car trunk.

Silence descends over the mafiosi circled beneath the abandoned interstate bridge on the outskirts of Rome.

My father was the Beneventi with the hard-on for blood. A cold-hearted bastard who killed first, then asked questions. I'm the fucking visionary. The no-bullshit, no-mercy businessman who's made the Twelve Famiglie rich. Still, every now and then, I'll snap a man's neck and remind these pricks whose blood runs through my veins.

"What is this about, Sebastiano?" Don Lucchese, our capo di tutti capi, demands.

"Securing our investments."

Everyone waits for Don Lucchese to lose his shit. The old-timer prefers we air our grievances his way, with the Twelve Famiglie assembling in neutral territory abroad to discuss issues calmly, with minimal violence or surprises. Everything laid out on the table, all diplomatic and shit. As if there isn't a man present without a gun locked, loaded, and tucked inside a waistband, waiting for the slightest provocation to fire.

I shove the man into the circle, and he falls to his knees as my gaze roams over the faces of the most dominant capos besides myself: a smirking Luca Ricci, Vegas, my closest ally; an expressionless Xavier Moretti, Chicago, whip smart yet young; a scowling Matteo

Lombardi, West Coast, a capo with a temper and money trouble; Roberto Ferrara, St. Louis, my biggest rival, and a wide-eyed Bible Belt Benny Manocchio, *guilty* as all fuck.

I skip over the lesser men, and my sons, Alessandro and Lorenzo, to the reason we've assembled—Emilio Conti, the low-ranking capo who runs Atlanta.

Or rather *used* to run the region. As soon as the new East Coast Gaming Commission begins overseeing gambling regulations up and down the East Coast, I'll be controlling the territory.

A fact no one but Don Lucchese is aware of yet.

Tempo scaduto, segaioli.

"I don't have all day, Sebastiano," Don Lucchese grinds out. "Who is he?"

I free the pillowcase and expose the man's terrified face. "Don Lucchese, meet the newly appointed head of the soon-to-be-defunct Atlanta Gaming Board."

"Hell yes, it's on," Luca murmurs.

Bible Belt Benny stares at his feet. Confirmation Emilio Conti isn't acting alone.

Don Lucchese scowls. "What did you say?"

"This ..." I slap the man on the back of the head. "... is the Atlanta Gaming Board's new chairman."

Conti's uncle. His fishing trip buddy. An ace in the two-on-one poker match he and Manocchio believe is being played out between us.

Did they believe I was off fiddling my dick and unaware the former chairman had been shot? His corpse was still warm when I heard the not-so-surprising news. I anticipated pushback on the new East Coast Gaming Commission's formation. Once it's operating, the Atlanta Gaming Board becomes irrelevant, and the Beneventi holdings can shift south.

Most present are invested in casino expansion. Others, like Manocchio and Conti, turned down my offer. That conniving little worm Conti should kiss my dirt-crusted shoes for extending an invitation for him to play with the big boys. What does he do instead? He sabotages me by killing my man and replacing him with his uncle.

How stupid can these stronzi be?

I've waited a long time for this day. This isn't a poker game, it's a game of chess.

Checkmate, motherfuckers.

"This man's been vocal about the new commission," I continue. "Thinks the Atlanta Gaming Board is enough."

"Do I need to draw you a map?" Conti bursts out. "Atlanta is Conti territory. And Georgia is—"

Manocchio territory.

Don Lucchese holds up his hand. "Emilio, you know this man?"

The blood drains from Conti's face.

And then Sandro snickers.

Ma che cazzo?

Manocchio seizes the opportunity. "Just look at them." He gestures at Sandro, then quickly moves on to Renzo, with his busted face and bloodshot eyes, looking like he had his ass handed to him. "So squeaky clean, I can polish my shoes with them. Atlanta's a big market with a lot of competition. Think they can front a successful multicasino operation? They've no credibility."

Sandro stares daggers at him.

And Renzo ...

"As clean as that fat ass you've been thumbing. Che palle!"

"Che palle?" Manocchio turns bright red. "What balls? You dare speak to me this way?"

Don Lucchese's lips draw tight. Renzo might be his godson, but he's not a made man.

Brain dulled by liquor and drugs, the little shit opens his mouth again.

Sandro slams a hard elbow into his side and knocks the breath out of him.

"I've a business meeting this afternoon," I inform the old man, "and a man I'd like you to meet."

"I've an appointment." His gaze is locked on Renzo, his head shaking in disgust.

"She'll wait."

That gets his lips twitching. The old bastard loves compliments about his virility. Yet he'll have a raging hard-on after my meeting. Because nothing gets him off more than a corrupt politician. He's fucking obsessed with the idea of indoctrinating one into the famiglie. We have strong ties with local commissioners and assemblymen but never anyone with significant power.

That's about to change.

I'm about to invest in the shittiest, shadiest, and savviest politician around. He'll be perfectly positioned to become chairman of the East Coast Gaming Commission, once I help him win the New York gubernatorial race. He becomes governor. I have a mouthpiece. Don Lucchese gets his politician. A win-win-win situation. I'll decide, once I meet New York's next great governor, if I'll sweeten the pot with more than money.

Conti's uncle whimpers.

I lock eyes on Don Lucchese and wait. Relishing the moment my patience and hard work become reality.

Don Lucchese wiggles a crooked finger at Conti. "Instead of killing you for making a move without my permission and compromising my goddamn investments—"

"I've never seen him before ..."

"I'm giving Sebastiano Atlanta."

Silence descends like a gavel.

Manocchio's face turns red. Moretti and Lombardi remain impassive, untouched by the decision. Luca Ricci stares at me with newfound respect. And Conti looks stupefied, still processing he's been outplayed.

I'd laugh, except I've a problem that can no longer be ignored.

The twins are twenty-three. Sheltered little shits. Sandro, so fucking serious he can dry fresh wallpaper with a single look. And Renzo, who'd likely be snorting the wallpaper glue as fast as it's rolled onto the sheets. He showed up in my hotel room this morning bloody, beaten, and as high as a goddamn kite. I'm no saint, but something needs to be done about him.

Renzo wants to run his mouth like a made man?

Let's make him one.

A first kill will sober him up.

I shove a gun muzzle into Renzo's chest. "Ask Don Lucchese if you can shoot him in the throat?"

Next to him, Sandro stares his brother down until Renzo finally speaks. "Do I have your permission?"

"Permission granted."

"When he bleeds," I lock eyes with Renzo, "make sure it soaks through your and your brother's squeaky-clean shoes."

He stares, his expression blank.

It'll be my son who brings about our downfall.

Sandro snatches the gun from his grasp. "I'll do the honors." He steps forward and aims, his thumb on the trigger. "Don't know this man, eh?"

"Wait, I—" Conti sputters.

The man's head explodes, blood splattering everywhere.

"Meeting concluded," Don Lucchese comments, like this is another day at the office. "Bury the body."

Renzo and Sandro look at each other as they wipe the blood from their faces.

Benny exposed a weakness—these little shits are soft. I killed my first man, someone twice my size and using a Swiss Army Knife, when I was eight years old. I've coddled them.

Both will pay for Renzo's hesitation. But not in a way either will anticipate.

Alessia

SIENNA and I curl up on a window cushion in an alcove a floor above Villa di Cesare's foyer and watch our father's guests file into a limousine below.

"What was the point in dressing up if his associates leave before dinner?" My sister sounds disappointed, although nothing she says or does anymore should surprise me.

I touch an ice cube to my throat, savoring the cold respite. Central air-conditioning and ice cubes are the two things I miss most while attending school in Rome. Even here, on the Amalfi Coast, where our father's hosting a campaign fundraiser, the ocean breeze feels like a warm huff. The quaint old villa does have an ice machine on my floor, a surprise I eagerly took advantage of, filling a bucket and appeasing my sister's worries about contracting heatstroke. I'm highly sensitive to touch and gliding the ice cube across certain trigger points—throat, back of the neck, behind the ear—has an immediate soothing effect.

Sienna mimics my movements as we stare out the window, the nearly empty bucket perched on the seat between us as the last of the half-melted cubes offer us relief.

Not nearly the monumental relief I feel after having avoided playing hostess for Father's mafiosi friends. I'd take heatstroke over rubbing elbows with cold-blooded criminals any day.

"Don't tell me you hoped to meet those men?" I know how Sienna will answer yet ask anyway.

"Frankie says Don Lucchese is a big deal."

I struggle not to cringe. My sister's new boyfriend is also fond of saying, "Tutti colpevoli, nessuno colpevole." *If everyone is guilty, no one is guilty.* If he drinks too much, so must my sister. If he's doing Lord-knows-what at ungodly hours of the morning, so must Sienna. Con, thieve, murder—who knows what a low-level mafioso who brags about his "big Glock and big cock" does. Like my father, Frankie has no moral compass, so naturally my wild, carefree sister is drawn to him.

She rolled in six weeks ago like a thunderstorm and took up residence on my sofa, sleeping all day, partying all night, and having loud sex with Frankie. I warned her he's trouble. She laughed it off, then called me sheltered. As if I don't recognize how dangerous Frankie is. As if I'm naive to Father's duplicities and how our family's falling apart. My sister's as foreign to me as the country I'm studying in.

"Don Lucchese's headed the Twelve Famiglie for years," she says with awe. "Wonder how Father managed a meeting?"

I swallow hard. How can she accept the fact our father is horribly, unspeakably corrupt? Winning the election and becoming New York's next governor, by any means possible including *mafioso* involvement, is exactly what today was about. A secret meeting Father hosted at an exquisite Italian villa on the Amalfi Coast, under the guise of visiting his youngest daughter. Far away from suspicious eyes looking for a scandal to exploit. I don't want to know what Father's offered these men in exchange for their financing his election. If Don Lucchese's such a big deal, what favors must the head of a criminal network be demanding in return?

The limousine taillights fade as the car pulls away, and I turn to look at Sienna. She reminds me so much of our mother, who often dressed for Father's events in a similar fashion, in a sleek black off-the-shoulder dinner dress that complemented her shapely figure. My stomach knots, and I squeeze the ice cube a bit harder.

"You should pop a few buttons. Live a little." She rakes eyes over me. "You look stifled."

My dress is preppy pink, with little pearl buttons leading from collarbone to waist. The hem skims my knees, and the material flows freely. It's classic and conservative, perfect for a hot day, and not something my sister would wear.

What's hidden *beneath* this dress would shock her.

"You look beautiful." I draw the cube across the back of my neck. "The ice helps, right?"

"I suppose."

I sigh. Does she even realize she's not the only one who's changed? "Ever wonder what life would be like if Mama hadn't died?"

Sienna replies without hesitation. "Less chaotic. More stable. *Happier.*"

Nothing has been the same since our mother's death. Grief guides our lives now. My sister and I stumble along, tripping and falling until we're so banged up and numb we reach for any lightness, any shadow, to pull us through. We lost our mother and our security blanket. And every day since is a fight not to lose our souls to our father's ambitions or our own reckless stupidity.

Guilt washes over me. Sienna may be older by two years, but I've always looked out for her. My decision to study abroad shocked her and my father. But I had to get away from the chaos, away from playing sister-keeper to someone whose new self-proclaimed mission in life is to paint every city shades of red. I had to escape Father's ridiculous demands. There was a life all my own I was eager to discover, far away and free from the drama always encircling my family.

I had to escape, though heartbreak will always accompany me.

I wipe wet fingers across my skirt. "Do you think he loves us?"

Her ice cube falls to the floor. Like my questions knocked it free. Like she feels the same loss, the same desperation.

"Of course he does," she snaps. A safe answer. Because an honest response might crumble the cage she's constructed around her heart. She's locked everyone out, including me.

Daddy Dearest loves three things: money, power, and himself. Deep down, Sienna recognizes it. It's why she does the crazy shit she does—for attention. Anyone's attention. And, it appears, she'll do anything to get it.

I remove the last half-melted cube from the bucket and pass it to her as a peace offering.

"Thanks," she begrudgingly says.

If anyone discovers what Sienna's done, it'll destroy Daddy Dearest's plans and the remnants of whatever family ties exist.

If she doesn't want to discuss Father, fine by me. We've more pressing business that can't be ignored.

"What were you thinking?" I softly ask.

"About?" she challenges, as if I don't know what she's done.

I shake my head. "If Father's political rivals find out ..."

"You're always such a scared little bunny." She glares, then looks away. "I knew you wouldn't let this slide."

Lord, she's selfish, like our father. And drinking out of the same poisoned glass, from a brew that breeds assholery. Still, I try. "I love you. You know that, right?"

She flinches, and then looks three seconds from crying.

"I'm not judging you."

"Of course you are. You, a timid wallflower who wouldn't know what to do with a dick even if one hit you in the face. Let me guess, still a virgin, right?" Her sneer echoes around the window alcove as her words cut deep. If there was a medal for judging people, she'd win gold.

How can she not notice I've evolved? Or wonder who I am now or what makes me tick? True, I suffer from infinite shyness. Also true, I've never had sex. But what's false is this—if a dick slapped me in the face, I'd know exactly what to do with it. Because I'm drawn to the shadows as much as the light. I'm as wild as she is, I simply don't act on it in any obvious way.

Obvious being the key word.

"You filmed a sex tape with that criminal Frankie."

"So what?" she says, defensive.

I stare at her in disbelief. "So what?"

She slides to her feet. "Mind your own business."

"Look. We crave security after the instability in our lives. It's natural to be attracted to powerful men." I gesture to the empty driveway below. "We're both searching for a protector. But Frankie's not it."

"We?" She laughs unpleasantly. "A meek bunny like you would get eaten alive by someone like him."

"Better a meek bunny than a reckless fool. You made porn with a lowlife mafioso."

She flinches. Gullible, and lost. And, like me, broken, so, so broken.

"He'll probably sell it," I stress.

"Frankie wanted it for his own use. A memory of our time together. He said it fulfilled his biggest fantasy of filming himself having sex with a hot girl."

"Let's hope it's not the gift that keeps giving."

Her spine straightens. "Maybe we'll watch it later."

She says it to shock me.

If she took the time to meet the new me, she'd know better. Because, deep within and locked away with a hidden key, I harbor a secret. A highly guarded *obsession*.

With art films ... Okay, woman porn.

Featuring Roman gladiators, pirates, billionaires, mafia bosses—any dominant alpha male, really. Dark romance novels translated to film. *Fifty Shades of Grey*, but kinkier and more graphic. It's my secret thrill. What fires up my mind, feeds my active imagination, and gets me off.

That's right.

Me, a twenty-year-old woman too shy to even kiss a man.

"A prude like you wouldn't know this, but thousands of new

videos circulate every day. Even if he publishes it, what does it matter? The video shows my face, like, three times. I'm an anonymous woman in a foreign country. I could be anyone." She prepares to charge off. "Trust me, no one will care."

"You're the daughter of the future governor of New York. Dignity. Decorum. And beyond reproach—remember what Father said?"

"Potato, potahto."

"Burnt potatoes, after Father's political rivals discover a way to fry him—"

She cuts me off. "What are your plans for tonight?"

I frown. "Um ..."

"Exactly."

"What?"

"Frankie's on his way." Her expression changes to a vicious look I recognize. "You're pathetic, you know that?"

I draw in an angry breath. "Nothing good can come of that video. Make him delete it."

Her jaw tightens, and in that moment, not a trace of our mother can be found. I've lost my sister, too, haven't I?

"Have fun watching paint peel off the villa walls." She spins on her heel and stalks away. But not before snickering a parting blow.

"Stay out of trouble tonight, Sissy."

3

Alessia

I HEAD down the hallway with a full ice bucket and a heavy heart, to a room with walls covered with decorative wallpaper, and with so very little paint to occupy my time.

As if.

With a sigh, I raise my key to the door.

"Spread your legs."

The man's sharp order stops me short. My key tumbles to the carpet as my grip slips on the bucket, though I catch it before it falls. Ice cubes clatter as silence descends over the room across from mine. Did I imagine it? The whiskey-toned timbre intertwining with each word, the sinful seduction sharpening the edges? Is heatstroke wreaking havoc on my mind?

Breathlessly, I wait, until a woman groans.

The door is half-open. *Anyone* could hear them.

Swallowing hard, I crouch to scoop up my room key.

His voice rolls over me once more, a hushed, indecipherable rumble. Warmth doesn't just fill me, it sets me on fire. I wobble on my heels, my position awkward; the wicked depravity within the man's dirty promises *exhilarating*.

I place an unsteady hand on the carpet and strain my ears.

"Chiudi gli occhi e piegati." His cold tone cuts through ice. *Close your eyes and bend over.*

My lower lip actually trembles.

Oh Lord. This is a test, right? Not divine intervention but a force pulling me in another direction, toward hellish temptation.

"Stay out of trouble tonight, Sissy."

I squeeze my eyes shut and ignore the impulse to do something I really, really shouldn't do.

"Facciamo un gioco?"

Want to play a game?

Yes. Please.

Crippling shyness will disarm the most courageous women. Forcing you to retreat from danger and sheltering you from less sensitive people. Protection from advantage-seeking bullies. Safety, with sacrifice. It doesn't mean you're cowardly or lack gumption. It doesn't mean you resist being drawn to the occasional guilty pleasure.

Do it, Sissy. Live a little.

I'm compelled toward their room, and although I can recite one hundred and one reasons why this is a bad idea, I ignore each and every one of them. Ever so carefully, I peer around the door. Then blink, and blink again.

Oh. Sweet. Lord.

Not one. Not two. But three women are bent over a massage table. On their toes, maid uniforms raised to their waists, and bare bottoms lined up and presented to a tall man in a suit. His broad back is to me, so my attention shifts to the women; a brunette, a redhead, a blonde. Coincidence? Or is it intentional? A needy hum rumbles from the brunette's throat. A handprint marks the redhead's pale cheek. The blonde waits in anticipation.

They're not really maids, right? This is a *scene*.

My eyes dart back to the man. His stance oozes power and harsh, sexual energy. His presence is dangerous and undeniable. They don't stand a chance against this big beast. He'd ravish any woman—*women*, more viking plunderer than billionaire playboy.

The brunette parts her thighs. "Vieni e accarezzamimio."

Come and caress me.

"Do gli ordini, piccolo troia." Hand drawing high, he smacks her hard. *I give the orders, you little slut.*

My breath hitches in my throat.

And then, he turns.

My lips part on a long exhale as my eyes feast on him with a slow upward drag.

Big bare feet. Dress pants hanging from his hip bones. Deliciously wicked V-cut accentuated by fine black hair rises from the material. Eight-pack abs. Massive muscular chest. Long, large fingers wrapped around a black leather flogger. Corded arms. Thick neck. And ... *oh ... wow.*

His handsome face defines temptation. Perfect Roman nose. High cheekbones. Midnight stubble on his jawline and chin. Lips drawn tight. And he's older—likely in his thirties. A man, through and through. Cocky and self-assured. Confident in his power. I grip the ice bucket tighter as butterflies dance in my stomach.

God help me, he's sexy. In a dirty, animalistic way. Like he'd mount you from behind and bite your neck as he pounds into you.

This stranger's every dirty fantasy rolled into one human being.

From my safe position by the door, I can only guess his eye color —probably dark chocolate or midnight black to match his hair. He studies the women, his aura cold and calculating.

Unyielding.

The women wiggle and shift, impatient.

Is this the game? Deny them control? Make them beg for their pleasure?

"Please." The redhead switches from Italian to English. "Your mouth."

I squeeze my thighs together as my skimpy underwear grows wet.

He jerks his hand, like he's been waiting for someone to speak, then snaps the flogger.

The leather licks the redhead's private area. "Cavolo," she screeches.

Sweet hell. That. Was. Hot. Did it hurt? Did it feel as wicked as it looked?

"I don't kiss." His growl is like the strum of a chord on a bass guitar and penetrates deep. "And I sure as fuck don't eat pussy. Capisci?"

So selfish. So cruel.

"Otherwise ... puoi avere qualsiasi modo si desidera." *You can have it any way you want.*

My skin burns. I'll need multiple ice buckets when this is over.

I'm not ready for it to be over.

Slowly, ever so slowly, he rolls up his sleeves. Lord, even his forearms are massive. Prowling forward, he drags the flogger in a line across their backsides. Deciding which woman to begin with? Showing them he's built to pleasure them all?

I can almost feel the leather graze my tender skin. Would a sensualist like me writhe beneath those lashes? Yes, my inner voice answers. It's why my undergarments are silk or light cotton. My French hairbrush made of the finest boar bristle. I swear even making pasta, digging my hands into moistened flour and shaping dough between my fingers, arouses my nervous system. Would I enjoy being tied up in silk? How would I respond to being flogged?

"Quale di voi troie sarà la prima?" *Which of you sluts is first?*

Oh. My. God. *Me, please.*

My body trembles, and the ice bucket slips in my arms. Cubes crash and the plastic lining crackles as I struggle to right the bucket. My stomach drops, the weight of what's happened paralyzing me with fear. I stand half-hidden by the door and pray I wasn't too loud.

Seconds that feel like hours tick by as the women beg for his attention.

"Lo sono la prima." *I'm first.*

"La seconda." *Second.*

"Non è giusto." *That's not fair.*

Goose bumps prick my skin. I'm flushed and skittish. Disaster averted, true—but do I stay?

Slowly, with great care and as silently as possible, I shift backward. One step. Two.

Thr—

The door's ripped open, and his massive frame fills the space. His presence overwhelms my senses, and like a deer caught in headlights, I freeze. He's ten times *everything* up this close.

Handsome—like, drop-dead gorgeous—with tousled jet-black hair and dark drawn eyebrows, lusciously plump lips he never pleases a woman with, and a small, faded scar on his right cheek from the violent lifestyle he must lead.

Powerful, like he'd snap you in two without hesitation, his chest a wall of muscles, his broad body leaving little room in the doorframe.

Sinful, like he'd make you come in unimaginably inventive ways, at his command, at his mercy, before slitting your throat and burying you in his backyard. Women all over the world have likely sacrificed their bodies for the thrill of his wicked presence.

Our eyes connect.

Blue—his eyes are blue. I was wrong.

Wrong to believe I could spy on a man of his ilk and get out alive.

"What the fuck do we have here?"

Blue eyes narrow. Heartless. Cruel.

I flush from toes to head.

He notices, his gaze shifting from my kitten heels to the top button of my pink dress, to my anxious expression. His eyebrows pinch, and he shakes his head. Like he didn't expect someone like me to be spying on someone like him.

His massive form looms over my smaller one.

Alarm bells ring in my mind, too late to do any good. Isn't there a hidden alcove or a hole in the hall floor, anywhere that can swallow me up—before he devours me whole?

"You get off being a kinky little voyeur?"

His husky tone wraps around my core like the lick of his flogger. Everything inside me quivers.

"Answer me."

My response gets trapped inside my throat. With enormous willpower, three words finally slip out. "I ... um ... sorry."

He pokes a finger onto the pearl button between my breasts, and I nearly drop the bucket. With slow, calculated movements, he continues the journey upward, tapping each pearl like he's keeping count until he reaches the top button. Round and round he goes, rolling the pearl between his fingers, briefly, before plucking it free from the material and tossing it over his shoulder.

My breath catches, but he ignores my surprise, drawing his finger upward across my throat to rest beneath my chin. I'm startled by his actions and my reaction. Captured and enraptured by his presence.

With a steel-like push, he angles my chin up. Forcing me to look at him once again.

"Dressed for church, yet at my door, spying."

This is what a tornado feels like, wild and surreal, destructive and deadly. I'm trapped, and spiraling, round and round.

"How old are you?"

"Twenty," I murmur.

"Twenty," he repeats, like it's his least favorite number. A *V* mars his forehead as he considers me.

I blush beneath his intense scrutiny, and at the vivid memory of his other *V*. My gaze falters, and then drops.

Holy sweet Mary. If I make an upside-down peace sign, I can trace it with my fingers. No, you can't ... *won't*. No. No. No. My eyes snap up to reconnect with his.

"You like what you see?" He smirks.

No, no, no, no, no.

Yes, hell yes.

I swallow hard.

"I respect honesty above all else, so be careful how you answer." His tone is honey, his words fire. "You a little perv who gets her thrills from watching me?"

How do I answer? How can I explain? Swallowing hard, I decide on the simple truth. "I think so."

"You think so?"

"Yes."

Gorgeous blue eyes flash with surprise. "Huh."

I stare at him, mortified. Wishing I could take my admission back. His stare feels like he can see straight through me.

Then he steps closer.

It takes all my willpower not to run as he lifts the ice bucket lid, tosses it aside, and plucks an ice cube out. Slowly, ever so slowly, he presses it to my lips. The cube feels ten times colder, probably due to how the rest of me burns from his proximity.

"I'd ruin a kinky little voyeur like you."

Everything stills except my racing heart.

"Get lost, before I change my mind. I'm not a man who indulges curious little sluts in pure pink dresses, no matter how ripe they are for the plucking."

He pops the ice cube into his mouth.

Then the door slams in my face.

4

Alessia

MISERY COMES in many shapes and forms. A teeth cleaning that morphs into a root canal. The New York City subway system. Being forced into the spotlight at social events, such as Father's gubernatorial gala or like now, Sienna's engagement announcement.

I'd prefer a subway ride to the Beneventi estate *after* a root canal if hopping a flight back to Rome afterward were an option.

It's not.

Father canceled my tuition payments, broke my lease, and ordered me home. When I protested, he callously informed me, "You can make spaghetti in New York."

I was flourishing in Rome. Making new friends. Nights out dining and dancing. Even dating, first a sweet, sensitive Italian boy who brought me flowers and held my hand and then a naughtier boy who liked to push me into dark corners and steal kisses from my lips. I changed after the risky encounter on the Amalfi Coast. Like two hot wires, the stranger's words and my reaction sparked life into me.

"I'd ruin a kinky little voyeur like you."

God, how I crave to be ruined by an older man like him. Ravished. Violated.

It's ridiculous, really. Dangerous men in powerful positions devour innocents like me. As if I'd find the courage to be with someone like that.

Baby steps until I'm ready, I kept reminding myself.

Except my dreams are on hold while I'm stuck stateside and forced to play dutiful daughter and sister-keeper.

Dangerous men, like mafioso capo Sebastiano Beneventi, haven't given Father pause. No, Daddy Dearest's jumped headfirst into a political arrangement with him and offered Sienna up like a gourmet feast. Father's wedded and bedded the mafiosi, and now Sienna will, too, in a marriage between my sister and Alessandro Beneventi. Guests are gathered in the Beneventi estate outside Providence, Rhode Island, for the surprise announcement. We mingle inside a great room while waiting for Sebastiano Beneventi's arrival, though an hour's passed without sign of him. Speculation about the reason everyone is here has Beneventi's associates abuzz. They don't know what's coming. Only my family and my future in-laws are aware of the pending union.

Father says Sebastiano Beneventi will kill him if the news is leaked.

If I don't do the job first.

"For Christ's sake, Alessia, pretend you're excited for your sister." Father's hiss is low, his demeanor relaxed.

"Don't you feel the slightest remorse for selling your daughter for political gain?" My spine straightens. He's ruining my sister's life. Upended mine. All because of his twisted ambition.

He has the audacity to gasp. "Jesus, Alessia. For a shrinking violet, you've sharp teeth."

"For an overrated politician with no morals, you've nerve." Until recently, I never talked back. But I can't stay silent anymore. "Mother would be proud."

"Don't you dare bring her up." His cheeks flush, his fingers clench. "One more comment, and you'll be studying art history from a coloring book."

"You canceled my tuition payments."

"Next step is to unenroll you from that ridiculous program you were so hell-bent on majoring in."

Like his love and affection, it's clear—Italy's lost to me too.

Scowl deepening, he pauses, and I brace myself. Unfortunately, he never disappoints.

"Can't you be more like your sister?"

You'd think the constant comparisons wouldn't hurt as much. That I'm used to falling short in his eyes. That nothing I've said or done after Mama's death means anything. Sienna stepped into her role, and I took to the shadows.

"Be like Sienna? And be manipulated by you? Forced into marrying a stranger?"

"You're jealous."

This is his response? Stick a label on it and call it a day. How convenient. How wrong. I'm appalled, and sick to my stomach.

"Look at her." He gestures to Sienna, who is across the room, surrounded by mafiosi, and laughing like she's having the time of her life. Reckless and carefree.

Foolish.

"Her fiancé isn't even in the room. Maybe Alessandro has cold feet."

"He's by the bar."

Sienna might not realize it, but she needs me in her corner. It's what Mama would want. I glare. "That's Lorenzo Beneventi."

"You don't say?" Daddy Dearest shakes his head. "Hell if I can tell them apart."

"Does it even matter which son she marries?"

Silence.

My heart dips deep inside my chest.

"What if Alessandro doesn't want this marriage?"

We met him shortly after our arrival. Alessandro Beneventi was cordial, polite, *indifferent*, with a strong arrogance about him. He shook our hands, directed us to the bar, then disappeared.

As for Lorenzo Beneventi, he's been propped against the bar and drinking straight from a bottle the entire time. I wonder if he's even aware of this arrangement. Is he even curious as to why we're here?

"Alessandro will do whatever Sebastiano asks. We've a verbal agreement."

My eyes widen. "His word? What kind of man hosts a party without making an appearance? Maybe he doesn't view your verbal agreement in the same light?"

Maybe there's hope for Sienna yet.

Her laughter filters across the room. My beautiful sister is wearing a curve-hugging white gown that barely contains her willful soul.

"Sebastiano Beneventi's a busy man, is all. Now, shut up about this and go mingle. If you behave, and once you've served your purpose, I'll consider your returning to Rome."

Serve my purpose? Do I mean nothing to this man besides Sienna's sister-keeper? I bow my head, choking back tears as I move away. Mingling will never be an option, so I position myself in a corner near a tall potted plant.

Father makes the rounds, shaking hands with anyone who notices him. Are the mafiosi aware he's the New York governor? If not, they are now. Do they wonder why we're here?

Sienna seems ecstatic. Alessandro is an enormous step up from Frankie DiCapitano. She's likely thrilled to marry into such a powerful and wealthy mafioso family.

My attention pivots from face to face, and then lands on an enormous painting across the hall. A king sits on a gilded throne, head bent and thighs parted. A woman wearing a stark white nightgown is curled up at his feet, her cheek pressed against his thigh as she gazes hungrily up at him.

The dramatic dark background contrasts beautifully with the light reflecting across the woman's expression. Very Caravaggio in style. Very 1600s Italian Baroque. I exhale sharply, the fight going out of me.

It's a sign, a signal all will be right. Survive the next few weeks, lie low, and bite my tongue, until my usefulness peaks. And perhaps, for once in recent years, Father will honor his promise.

I slip through a side door into a hallway, then pop two buttons at the throat of my dress before making my escape. Sunlight on my face will soothe my aching heart, right? Not mend it—that's impossible with a family who only knows how to rip it apart.

Halfway down the hallway, I stop short, blocked by an enormous palm toppled into my path. "Poor baby," I murmur, the urge to do something, anything—even righting a bit of vegetation—strong. "Let me help you."

I grasp the trunk and lift ... and fingers wrap around my ankle.

"Holy hell." I jerk my foot free and step back.

The palm topples.

And then laughter rings out from somewhere beneath it.

<hr>

"YOU'RE WEARING RED."

I look wildly about for a way to escape as the lunatic beneath the houseplant rolls into a seated position.

"What?"

He snatches my ankle once more. "Your underwear is red."

"Remove your hand," I order in a shaky voice, "or I'll kick you."

He *laughs*.

Leaving me no choice. I kick him in the kidney, forcing him to release me.

"Ah, the angel has some devil in her?" He falls back onto the floor, arms and legs in an X, like I actually injured him. In that moment, I recognize him.

Lorenzo Beneventi.

I step away with a gasp.

He rolls to a seated position again, then runs fingers through his jet-black hair. "How long was I out for?"

Passed out behind a house palm, he means?

This is Sienna's soon-to-be brother-in-law? I'm at a loss what to do.

Voices echo from down the hallway.

He nudges my thigh. "Help me up, will you?"

I'm three seconds from bolting. Yet there's something familiar about him …

"Please."

I stare at him, and at the hand offered.

"Hurry. Before they find us."

"You. *I'll* be long gone."

"Ah, she speaks."

Our eyes lock. Mine, full of wonder at the impression we've met before. His, bloodshot.

"You'd leave me like this?" He grins a grin that's for sure charmed a woman or two. What is it about Lorenzo Beneventi that invites a response?

"The pervert who looked up my dress? Let me think about it— yes."

He attempts to rise but falls onto his ass.

How drunk *is* he?

"You promised."

"I did not." God help me, he's surprising, even endearing.

"Poor baby. Let me help you," he repeats my words.

"I was talking to the palm."

"Right. I opened my eyes to discover you basically straddling my face."

My cheeks warm.

The voices grow closer.

"You know who I am?" he asks.

"No." I don't know why I lie. Maybe because he's drunk? Maybe because he's a Beneventi? Maybe because I'm frightened about the future and angry that my dreams have been interrupted by a nightmare.

Maybe because Lorenzo's Armani suit's wrinkled? Because a palm frond sticks out of a buttonhole? A bruise mars his right cheek?

He's a beautiful disaster. I should say goodbye and make my escape.

"Is that you, Alessandro?" a woman calls out.

"Ah, fuck." He's on his feet in a heartbeat. "Can you run in heels?"

"Um ..."

He sways, in no condition to walk, let alone run.

With a sigh, I weave an arm around his waist. "Where to?"

"The kitchen door. Follow the hall to the end."

We stumble-run toward the kitchen and pass through it toward another door. Awkwardly, like partners in a potato sack race. Outside, we cross an elevated veranda paved with grey stone slate and stop at steps leading down to a sprawling lawn. A few yards ahead is an enormous pool with a stone waterfall feature at one end and a large casita at the other.

"Thank fuck." Lorenzo drops the arm anchored around my waist. "I need a drink."

I *snort*. I never snort.

"Judgmental much?"

"Ass-drunk at your father's parties much?" I shoot back. Shocking him, and myself.

"Ah, so you do know who I am." He grins. "An angel with a mouth. Heaven's dream. What's your name?"

"Sheila." The lie rolls off my tongue. We spent an hour in the same room, yet he has no clue who I am? How quickly can I make it across the grass and around the side of the house in heels?

"My friends call me Renzo."

"Okay, Lorenzo."

His phone chings, startling him. I study him as he checks his messages, sadness creeping into his blue eyes. His manner reads disappointment. It's like witnessing someone who believed he found his lost puppy only to receive bad news. His skin pales, and then turns a greenish hue.

Oh no. "Are you going to throw up?"

"Not right this second." He offers me a fake smile.

How many times have I done the same? How many times has disappointment nearly destroyed me?

"I'm in the mood to sober up."

Like with the potted plant, the overwhelming urge to help him spurs me on. My pity and judgment won't distract him from whoever is causing him pain. So, I settle on snark.

"Should I clap my hands or something?"

His smile steals my breath. Not because it's winsome or beautiful. Renzo Beneventi's smile's heartbreaking.

Who would have thought, on a horrible day such as this, I'd meet someone whose soul is as lost as my own? And he feels it too, doesn't he?

For a brief moment, we stare at each other.

Until our protective masks slip back into place.

"So, Sassy Sheila, my angel from above," he says, the joking jester reappearing, "want to see the golf course?"

5

—

Bastian

GOVERNOR AMATO'S butchered corpse is about to stink up my dungeon.

I swirl the whiskey around my glass, seconds away from trashing my office. I've a houseful of guests waiting for a big announcement. The Great Room is abuzz with speculation. And, with one email, everything's shot to shit.

I don't lose face, *ever*.

The Amatos are going to pay dearly.

Twenty years ago, my father beat me senseless, called me worthless, and told me I'd never amount to anything, that I'd never be capo. Not only did I become head of the Beneventis after his murder, I've surpassed everything he dreamed of achieving.

The Twelve Famiglie's businesses are thriving. Thanks to my investments, money rains down on us like a ticker-tape parade. Our combined stock portfolios are in the trillions. We're fucking drowning in cash. I spent years proving my worth. Now I handle everything—even some of that penny-pinching punk Benny's investments—while they sit back and collect.

And what do I get in return, besides luxurious Maseratis and a lifetime pass to fucking Disneyland? Something my old man strived for but never earned—respect.

Still, it's not enough.

I want the motherfucking kingdom.

Murdering my way into power won't get me there. We mafiosi operate in the twenty-first century now. The world's changed, and the Twelve have had to adapt. Don Lucchese recognizes this. Wars caused Rome to fall, so what makes us believe we're any different? Famiglie who work together, flourish together, right? And while I may have built a financial powerhouse, the sly, chain-smoking ball-buster has united us into a finely tuned subversive empire.

All twelve capos signed off on the new rules of succession. No more wars, but instead elections. The Twelve vote between two men to become the next capo di tutti capi. Don Lucchese decides who's earned the right to be nominated, and their names are recorded on a notarized and sealed legal document that's then secured inside a vault.

Everyone talks about it being all democratic and shit. Except there's a hitch—Dante Lucchese. He's part of the package. The Veep, if you will. Dante won't step into his father's shoes. Yet by being assigned to a lesser role, he's less likely to be murdered in his sleep because of cries of foul play.

I've mentored Dante for years. No one likes it, but too fucking bad. I earned the old man's respect a long time ago and continue to do so.

Everyone knows the biggest crooks operate from white dome buildings within every state capital, with the largest cluster located in Washington, D.C.

I promised Don Lucchese the sleaziest and most influential of them all.

And the Amatos have made me a chump.

Heat radiates off my laptop, and I contemplate smashing it into the wall.

The only saving grace is that Dante is in Vegas to negotiate a new joint venture with Luca Ricci on my behalf. Translation: Don Lucchese won't hear about my being screwed six ways to Sunday from him.

I can hear Xavier Moretti's laughter all the way from Chicago.

I hurl the glass at the wall.

If only I'd kept my mouth shut.

If only she'd kept her thighs closed.

If only Amato weren't a disloyal motherfucker.

I scratch the back of my neck. Think, Bastian. What's the next step? What needs to happen to fix this before word gets out?

My mind calms yet remains blank. Some Molly and three mouths on my dick will take the edge off. Then perhaps I'll see things clearer.

But not before I settle on an explanation to feed Don Lucchese as to why I murdered the politician we've courted for months.

Alessia

RENZO BENEVENTI IS the sunshine on a snowy day that gives you sunburn when you least expect it. Playful and hilarious, with an inner darkness that cuts through his give-no-fucks bravado. He's so charismatic, I forget my shyness.

"You've got a grass stain on your breast."

I glance down and grimace. Regretting driving a golf cart across the expansive lawns of the Beneventi estate, then caving into Renzo's heckling by taking a few swings on the family golf course.

My first drive landed halfway down the green, and Renzo danced around like I was the next Tiger Woods. Ten strokes later, I sank my first ball, and he pulled me in for a hug. Turns out, I am a *natural* at golf.

Problem was ... is, I'm wearing a white Tom Ford dress.

I look down once again, the green stain marking one breast unmistakable.

From the golf cart seat beside me, Renzo catches my dismay. "Martian tit."

"This isn't funny."

"I fucked a girl dressed up like a martian once." My eyes widen as he winks at me. "The sex was out of this world."

I burst into laughter. How can I not? His wicked humor puts me at ease. If Sandro's anything like his twin, Sienna's marriage may not be so horrible. Relief for my sister washes over me, but it's sprinkled with hope. With Sienna successfully married and Father's dealings with Mr. Beneventi concluded, I'll find a way to make my escape—with Father's support or not. If I can drive a tiny white ball one hundred and forty yards with a club, I can attend art classes in Italy on my terms.

"Do you have a passport?" Despite knowing Renzo for just over an hour, I'd like to keep in touch with him. It's strange how quickly our friendship's formed. How comfortable he is joking with me. How free I feel in his presence. We're opposites, yet we gel.

Besides, the Roman streets would look different with him by my side.

He gestures toward the Beneventi mansion in the distance. "My passport's inside a drawer beside my bed. Why? Thinking we should run off and elope?"

Um, awkward. My sister marrying his twin and us running off to get hitched. My brows draw tight. What kind of friendship is built on a lie?

"Am I that deplorable, Sheila?"

"What? No. It's just ... I have a confession—"

"Watch out!" he bellows at the same time.

The cart hits a speed bump and lands hard. My fingers tighten around the steering wheel as Renzo pitches sideways. I lift my bare foot from the flattened pedal, and the golf cart lurches to a stop.

Seconds pass as we both readjust ourselves.

"You, my friend, drive like a lead-footed martian after several martinis."

I laugh until my stomach hurts.

"Save your confessions for Sunday, and tell me what exotic locale you propose we escape to?"

Escape, for sure. "I know we just met …"

"Don't chicken out now."

"I'm on a short break from studying Art History in Italy." Like me, he's curious. Unlike me, he's a risk-taker. Renzo would be the perfect person to explore places I wouldn't dare venture with anyone else.

"Florence?"

I shake my head. "Rome."

"Rome."

The light fades within his eyes quicker than a storm cloud swallowing the sunshine. I've upset him. "Are you okay?" I hastily ask.

"Define okay."

I blink.

"Okay, fucked up? Okay, broken beyond repair?"

"Renzo—"

"Okay, being a constant disappointment to my family?"

His raw honesty is startling. God, he's beautiful, even when consumed by so much pain.

"I understand," I whisper. "I really, really do." I nudge him with my elbow. "The only person whose expectations you need to live up to are your own."

"You read that on a coffee mug?"

I stiffen.

"I'm the Beneventi fuck-up. The son who stumbled where everyone could see. I never asked for the Life, but choice doesn't exist in this family. My father dangled time like a leash, then yanked it back the second I faltered. One hesitation—that's all it took. My twin swooped in, snatched my shot, and left me looking like the weak one. My old man barely looks at me now. My brother gloats like a smug son of a bitch."

He leans in, teeth bared, voice rough as gravel. "And me? I'm jagged, broken. You want the filth under my skin? My grandfather should've drowned us both in the cradle like he threatened."

What?

"That's right. My grandfather said we'd be a distraction, a liability." Renzo looks off into the distance. "Turns out, he was right."

"I don't know what to say."

"Nothing to say. That mean bastard's dead now. Buried somewhere near the ninth hole."

I choke on thin air.

Renzo snorts. "Or so my father's fond of saying."

If Sebastiano Beneventi's jokes are as frightening as his reputation, I want nothing to do with the man.

"Sandro cried when our mother dropped us on the doorstep then fled. Know what I did?"

My throat's tight. "What did you do?" Poor Renzo.

"I rang the doorbell. Luckily, our father answered. He whisked us away to Italy to meet our godfather before his old man returned to follow through with his death threats. We're alive because of our godfather's blessing."

"That's ... horrible."

Renzo quiets for a few seconds. "He took a beating for us."

"Your father did?"

"Spent a week in the family dungeon with three cracked ribs, two blackened eyes, and a bottle of water. Almost died. Yet no one dared lay a hand on us."

I hit the gas and the cart takes off once more while I sit beside him, horrified. What kind of family is this?

A notorious mafioso family, Alessia. Did you expect all rainbows and sunshine?

"In the famiglie, weakness isn't about truth, it's about perception. And that perception can be a death sentence. That's the lesson I've learned since returning from Rome."

"Your father's an important man," I offer. "Expectations are high."

"The highest." Renzo grimaces. "He's set to become the next capo di tutti capi—the leader of all the mafioso famiglie. Sometimes, I think it's all he wants."

"But he didn't abandon you. He went behind his father's back to keep you."

Renzo grunts.

I look around the ridiculously expansive course more fit for professional players than for private use in someone's backyard. And suddenly, it dawns on me.

"He built a golf course in his backyard for you, didn't he?"

Silence.

"He and your brother don't love golf. You do. Why else would he do such a thing?"

"To bury the bodies."

The cart stops with a lurch once more, and Renzo lunges forward in his seat. "Jesus." He readjusts himself, then emits a drawn-out sigh. "Look, Sheila. My father's never hidden who he is from us—hell, he's more older brother than father. One day, school sent us home early due to a power outage. We walked in on our father and two gorgeous women. He had them bent over our kitchen barstools with coke lines dusted across their asses." Renzo chuckles. "Sandro asked him what he was doing. Know what he said?"

Any form of response is stuck in my throat.

"They were baking."

My eyes widen.

"My brother believed him, like it was perfectly normal to have flour on your ass while baking cakes naked." He pauses, then continues in a softer voice. "My father's calmed down, now that he's older."

A similar scene flashes across my mind, featuring a sinfully wicked man spanking three women under his command. What did he promise them? *You can have it any way you want.*

Why does the thought of being at a man's complete and total mercy excite me so much?

"I've shocked you."

"You haven't," I admit. But do I really want to admit to my future brother-in-law that I'm a closet kinkster?

"But want to know what's even worst?" He stares off into the distance, and I'm convinced he's not going to continue. "Because of everything happened, I'm forced to break a promise."

I wait for him to say more, but he doesn't. Lord, he's passionate ... and deeply, deeply troubled.

His smartwatch buzzes, and we both freeze on the seat.

"We have to get back." Renzo jumps out of the cart and runs around to my side. "Scoot over." There's an unfamiliar urgency about him that's unsettling.

My stomach drops. Mr. Beneventi must be home, and the announcement about to happen.

We cross the lawn at a breakneck speed, airborne most of the time.

"You sure you're sober enough to drive?" I yell out at one point.

"Too fucking sober. I'll need another drink to get through this."

Seconds turn into minutes until we're off-roading across the perfectly landscaped back lawn. The cart stops at the steps leading up to the stone veranda, and I quickly slip my kitten heels on.

"Before you head inside," I say in a rush, "there's something I need to tell you."

"Before *we* go inside," Renzo replies, jumping out of the cart. "Come on."

For the briefest second, I contemplate escaping. But, if Sandro's anything like his brother, everything will be okay. Sienna will live her life, Father his, and I'll finally be free from them and the burden I always carry. I exit the cart with shaky legs.

"Hurry. Or do you want to get me killed?"

"Killed?" Dread sinks in. Because he's *serious*.

"No one keeps my father waiting."

He stops long enough to clasp hands and together we climb the stone stairs.

"Wait." My toe snags on a stone and I stumble.

He catches me before I fall.

"I'm frightened," I confess.

"You should be. My father locks himself inside his office for two hours, and now calls a meeting?" His fingers tighten around my hand.

"Everyone present should be afraid."

Bastian

JOSEPH AMATO ENTERS my office with a confident swagger.

His daughter follows behind him, her laughter designed to draw attention.

Sandro comes to stand in front of my desk, his eyes locked on mine in complete understanding that shit's about to go down.

"Where's your brother?" I demand.

Amato's grin slips, and his daughter chokes on air.

"On his way."

"What's this about?" Amato inquires, offering me a politician's smile to hide his unease. By the time I'm done with him, he'll wish unease were the only emotion he's feeling.

"Family meeting." I gesture to the chairs in front of my desk. "Take a seat."

They sit while Sandro drags three more chairs before my desk.

"About the announcement?"

"We'll wait for my other son."

Amato offers me a broader smile, meant to charm. What I'd find charming right now is his broken body swinging from the meat hook in my dungeon.

Silence spreads across the office.

"Without fear, you're weak," my old man liked to say. I don't disagree, but fear doesn't always have to be provoked through violence. What would devastate a politician like Amato? A tarnished reputation? Financial ruin?

After I work him over within an inch of his miserable life?

I killed my first man at eight. My father's friend, who cornered me in our barn and thought he'd force a blow job. I waited until he had his dick out before driving my Swiss Army Knife into his kidney.

My father was so pissed he beat me, and then tossed me into the family dungeon. Not because I'd killed the fucking predator, but because he had to come up with an explanation for the circumstances surrounding the mafioso's murder. I survived a week belowground, with several broken ribs and a bottle of water.

It didn't stop me from going behind his back over my sons, and knowingly facing the same consequences.

Now, given the situation I'm in, I understand my old man's predicament. A brutal ass whupping and the dungeon won't resolve the position the Amato's placed me in.

What am I supposed to tell Don Lucchese? I've been duped first by our favorite politician, and then his daughter? We'll no longer have a man heading the new commission? Our casino expansions are on hold? The old man bought a yacht. Hates flying but sails around the Mediterranean like an NBA All-Star. Trusted me when I assured him the deal was done.

I grab the whiskey bottle and pour another drink. Amato and his daughter exchange glances.

"Sandro, ask your fiancée if she's been to Rome."

My son searches my expression, then his lip curls. Without words, the little shit recognizes the engagement's off. As for his brother ... Where *in fuck's name is Renzo?*

"I love Italy," Amato's daughter exclaims. "My sister attended school in Rome, and I spent a few weeks visiting her. The museums, the food—"

"The nightlife," I deadpan.

She forces a laugh. "Yes. It rivals New York." She turns to Sandro and offers him a bright smile. "Do you like to go out?"

"No."

She flinches.

"Like her sister," Amato interrupts, "Sienna's more of a homebody ..." He drones on and on with his lies, praising his fallen apple. I lean back and let him talk. Soon, we'll get to the point of what really needs to be said.

Did he think I wouldn't learn of the deal he made with Conti? How he's been double-dipping in the mafioso pool? How he represented a rival famiglie to the commission in a territory I'm about to take over?

A commotion outside the office announces Renzo's arrival. Two knocks, and in he bursts, dragging a young woman in a conservative yet classy white dress behind him.

"I'll meet you in the great room," she argues with my son. Renzo has that effect. He can draw the devil out of a saint with a single word.

"I need you beside me."

"I've grass stains—"

"No one will be looking at your tit. Not with that angel face of yours."

Sandro makes a noise in his throat. I raise my eyes from her gorgeous full tits to her face.

Well, surprise, surprise. As if this day hasn't already rolled me over and fucked me hard.

I scowl, and study her more closely.

She's pretty. Lean with big tits and a tight ass. Blond, with soft pouty lips, high cheekbones, and big expressive eyes. They widen as they land on me, and then dart away. Cheeks flushed, she tucks in closer to Renzo.

"Father." Renzo nudges her forward. "This is Sheila."

"No, Renzo ..." she gasps, but it's too late.

"Who the hell is Sheila?" Amato's tone is incredulous. "Alessia, is that what you told your soon-to-be brother-in-law?"

Sandro guffaws.

Renzo frowns in disappointment.

And I grow impatient. "We've a family of liars in our home."

Everyone freezes. The room's so quiet, you can hear a pin drop. Amato's screams will be all the more memorable in comparison. I gesture to the two vacant chairs. "Sit down."

Alessia turns, about to bolt. Renzo throws an arm around her shoulder. "I've got you, Sheil—Alessia."

Chivalrous. Kind. Ready for another taste of Miss Innocence's sweet pussy after their romp in the grass? My eyes dip. The grass stain on her breast only enhances her hard nipple. Another Amato who can't keep her thighs closed?

I smash my clenched fist on the desk.

Everyone jumps.

What the fuck? Am I attracted to a little baby like her? I track their progress toward the chairs. Judging by her flushed state, she's well aware of who I am.

"There seems to be some sort of misunderstanding," her father says, drawing my attention back to the matter—or rather *matters*—at hand.

"Then how about you explain this to me?" I flip open the file on my desk, push it toward him, and point to the letter he wrote to the local Atlanta gambling commission on Conti's behalf, introducing himself as the future East Coast Gaming Commissioner. News I didn't want announced yet. Not until everything was in place.

His eyes widen, and he shifts in his seat. "Um ..."

"Isn't this your signature?"

He stares at his name scribbled in ink on the paper before him. I've a shitload of other signed documents with this exact signature.

"Yes or no?"

His Adam's apple bobs as he swallows hard. "Yes."

I lurch across the desk, grab him by both arms, and flip him onto my desk. Face up because I want to see his lying mug as I rain punches down on it.

His nose breaks. Blood sprays everywhere.

His daughters scream, their white dresses soiled by their father's stupidity. Then Miss Innocent slumps in her seat, passed out cold.

"Did Conti approach you or you him?" I demand.

"He came to me."

"He know who you are?"

Amato nods, then winces. "Yes. He told me you sent him. He said you asked for me to introduce myself to the local committee who oversees the extensive sports gambling operations around the Atlanta metro area."

"He lied." I punch his kidney, and his face turns green. "He pay you?"

Amato doesn't answer, which is answer enough. I crawl off him and, with a hard shove, send him flying off the desk. I slam my fist onto the laptop he almost takes with him.

Conti's never been the sharpest tool in the shed. Murdering Amato would have hurt me more than Conti paying him off. Announcing Amato as chairman was a hand I wasn't ready to play, not before my men were in place to report back Bible Belt Benny's response to the news. I've been patient. Atlanta is mine, and I'm almost prepared to move on it. The South will be mine eventually, a fact Benny will recognize.

I could kill Amato, and find a replacement. No one is irreplaceable. But any delays will fuck up investments already made.

I could turn him into my puppet and marry Sandro off to another greedy politician's daughter. But I had to go and run my mouth to Don Lucchese about bringing Amato into the famiglie, didn't I? The sly old bloodhound will wonder why the Amato girl was no longer in the picture and start digging around. If the video of her surfaces, I'll become a laughingstock.

There's no way out of this unscathed.

Fuck, I put all my eggs on the Amatos, and they turned up rotten.

I hurl my new whiskey glass at the wall. At this rate, I'll need to replace the fucking set.

Even Sandro looks alarmed.

"If I were Conti, you'd be dead. And if you don't do as I say, you will be."

"Please," Sleeping Beauty whimpers, once more awake. Good. She's not going to want to miss this. "He saw the money in his bank account and nothing else. Don't hurt him."

The little liar believes she can save him, does she? "There's more."

Amato staggers to his feet, and then falls into the chair. "I swear on my dead wife's soul, that was the extent of it."

"Her soul?" Alessia rises and turns to him. "How dare you."

She's going to need that spine by the time I'm done here.

"Sit," I snap.

She obeys without hesitation, then clasps her hands on her lap and, lip quivering, studies the floor.

Good girl.

The wayward thought makes my blood boil. I address her father. "You've two choices: I ruin you politically and financially, and you're obedient. Or I ruin you politically and financially, and you die."

"I don't want to die," he bursts out. "If I'd known Conti wasn't who he said he was—"

I hold up a hand and silence him. "If the trouble you Amatos have caused me isn't resolved quickly and quietly..."

"Let his daughters go," Renzo speaks up. Then, reading my thunderous expression, adds, "And I'll guarantee they disappear."

Alessia gasps.

He touches her hand in reassurance. If his interruption wasn't enough to piss me off, that compassionate little gesture is.

"Sandro will guarantee they disappear."

Renzo stiffens.

His twin smiles.

"It was a mistake," Amato pleads. "I'll make it up to you. I'll do anything you ask."

"Perfect. You have a week to find your replacement—if you survive my dungeon and fists. He must meet three requirements: be loyal to me and only me, be in position to step into your place as the head of the new East Coast Gaming Commission, and have a daughter Sandro can marry."

Amato sputters incoherently.

Sienna looks like someone snatched away her designer purse.

Renzo's frowning.

Sandro's goddamn elated, knowing it's unlikely Amato will succeed within the necessary timeframe.

And the little voyeur is frozen, staring at the laptop like she knows exactly how easy it'll be to ruin her father.

I flip it open, spin it around, hit unmute, and then play.

Sienna's lusty groan fills the room, while that Italian punk, Frankie DiCapitano, drills her from behind.

7

Alessia

MONSTERS ARE SUPPOSED to live in closets or beneath beds. They're not supposed to be the porn star in your darkest, dirtiest fantasies. In reality, Sebastiano Beneventi is both a disrupter of dreams and my worst living nightmare.

I blink back tears and stare at my father asleep in the hospital bed. Alive, barely. Beaten, brutally. Deserving of punishment, undoubtedly. I blame him entirely for the chaos he caused. Yet I understand the power Sebastiano Beneventi has over others, having experienced it myself.

That man's magnetism draws you in so quickly, you forget to run. Is this how my father was lured in? Why he agreed to a marriage? Why he indulged a mafioso capo who could make life hell?

I recognized Sebastiano Beneventi immediately. His finely muscled body is branded in my mind. How many times have I relived our exchange? Replayed his gruff warning, how I'm ripe fruit begging to be plucked. Coming face-to-face with him, and realizing he's exactly everything that terrifies me and absolutely not a man I should fantasize about, is like ice water to the face.

Sure, he's undeniably sexy.

But dangerous.

And so very, very vindictive.

He didn't recognize you. At least there's that.

When you're a little kid, you fear things like spiders and ghosts, a bad report card and not being invited to the It-Girl's birthday party. I never understood what true fear is until now.

His wrath descended upon my family like an iron fist.

He promised financial ruin and delivered with astonishing speed. One by one, Father's bank accounts have been frozen. Notices confirming stock sales fill his email. The ruthless capo must have compiled a list of our family's assets well before that horrible day. But he didn't stop there.

A huge "Building Code Violation" sign now decorates the entrance to our Tribeca loft, warning that an investigation into the building's elevators is being conducted and prohibiting residents from using them until the matter is resolved. The only way to access the loft is by using the stairwell. And with my father hospitalized, the trek up and down the stairs is unavoidable.

Even the soft hum of the IV machine feels like an attack, my anxious thoughts keeping tempo with the machine while the same question spirals on repeat: What next?

What next?

What next?

Because there will be a next.

Sebastiano Beneventi wants names. A ridiculous, impossible list of corrupt politicians who'd be loyal to the mafioso, powerful and politically savvy enough to be elected chairman of the new East Coast Gaming Commission, and have a sacrificial daughter of marriageable age. Naming corrupt politicians is easy. But none are in the perfect position to satisfy all the requirements.

Hello needle, meet haystack.

Lord, what are we going to do? The beating was a warning—he'll kill my father.

Daddy Dearest shifts his head on his pillow, yet his eyes remain closed.

Just like his eyes were closed when he approached Mr. Beneventi about financing his campaign.

Look what you've done—the price your family is paying because you did business with the mafia.

"You should get some sleep," the private nurse I hired, who has just entered the room, informs me. If it wasn't for her, I'd be completely lost. "Recovery takes time, especially after the vicious attack he received. His broken ribs will take time to heal. But he's lucky. These days muggings don't end as well."

"When can he return home?" The nurse will be moving into our loft and providing around-the-clock care, paid for by healthcare insurance and subsidized by the money from the envelope Sandro gave me—though money isn't my only concern.

"Tomorrow. But he'll be bedridden for a while."

Bedridden in his own bed, inside a loft that may still be inaccessible. I pray the elevator situation's resolved beforehand. How the hell am I supposed to get him upstairs otherwise? Or arrange other accommodations in such a limited timeframe?

Exhaustion sets in. Without a way out of this horrific situation, I can't sleep.

The nurse touches my arm. "Leave using the rear exit, honey. Reporters are waiting at the main entrance."

"Thank you," I murmur, grasping hold of her kindness with both hands. Seconds later, I exit through the back and walk a block to the waiting Uber.

Everyone believes their governor was mugged, and Father will be thrilled by the attention. He'll point the finger at someone other than Sebastiano Beneventi and spin this to his advantage. The headline will read: Fearless New York Governor Takes a Stance on Crime. Because that's what he does.

There'll be no headlines if the mafioso kills him first.

There must be another solution, something more easily accomplished than this ridiculous list.

But as nighttime creeps into our Tribeca loft, I become more and more frantic.

I crave a few things in life: security, stability, and love. A normal life, where I feel protected and understood.

But my well-being never mattered. And, although this isn't a new revelation, it still hurts.

I pack my suitcase, remembering Sandro's warning. "Get lost," he snarled at Sienna and me when the town car pulled up to the curb. "If you ever come back here, you will fucking disappear." He tossed two thick envelopes at us, and then left.

Mean and rude, *nothing* like his brother.

Sienna took his warning to heart and caught a flight the next morning to Tokyo. Freedom from my sister was never a permanent goal. She wasn't supposed to be ripped from my life like a page torn from a book. Was it fear that made her flee, forgetting to ask if I'd be okay? Or was it the hundreds stuffed inside the envelope? For once, my sister took something seriously.

And what did I do?

I'm my mother's daughter. Leaving my father isn't an option. Not until I do something he's never done for me and make certain he's safe and cared for before I say goodbye for good.

My throat hitches tight. So alone. So uncertain what to do. I close my packed suitcase, just as my phone chimes.

I hesitate, fearing reporters discovered my number. But then it could be Sienna—maybe she's checking in on us? I hit the message button and find a name I never expected to see.

Renzo?

He added my phone number to his cell, and vice versa, the day on the golf course but up until today never contacted me. And now I've a series of texts ... all bloodcurdling.

> He's out for blood.
>
> Fuck, ur still in NYC!!!
>
> On my way. Plz. Answer me.
>
> Lessie, come on. This is urgent.

Oh, God. There's a six-hour gap between these texts and the next.

I'm here.

My hand shakes as I quickly type.

Where?

Dots appear as he replies.

Be at Magnum on Bowery and East Hudson
at 9 p.m. I've a plan. Capisci?

No, I don't understand.

I wait, but no response.

What's happening?

You're scaring me.

Renzo???

His messages stop, as does my heart, now positioned in my throat.

The clock reads eight thirty. I grab my purse, a raincoat, and a handful of bills from the envelope.

Please, be there, Renzo.

Please help us.

8

Alessia

RAIN POURS down in buckets as I hurry north on Broadway. Catching a cab now is impossible, yet walking beats taking the subway. I checked my phone a few moments ago but Renzo hasn't responded to my additional texts, most a variation of the same messages: "What's happening?" and "What plan?"

Outside Magnum, I encounter a large man who's straightening the garbage bins outside. Italian curse words flood the street, and I wonder who poked the bear in him. I walk in a wide arc around him and enter the bar.

I bite my lip and anxiously search for Renzo.

"The Bowery Bar is up the road." A dark-haired waitress approaches.

"I'm meeting someone."

"Up the road," she grumbles. "This place is for a certain kind ..."

"Angel, baby."

Renzo's voice rings out from deep inside the bar, and the server's eyes grow wide.

"You made it."

I rush by her and follow the aisle dividing the bar and the tall built-in booths to the back. Renzo sprawled across a bench in a booth.

"Be careful where you step." He gestures toward an enormous wet spot on the floor.

I step over it, slide into the bench across from him, then take off my raincoat, fold it, and set it beside me.

When I finally look at him, my stomach drops.

He looks *terrible*. His face is puffy, pupils dilated, and hair a matted mess. Like he hasn't slept in a while. Like he's strung out.

"Miss the good-looking fella, huh?"

"Renzo, what happened?"

"I had a run-in with a puddle. The puddle won."

My eyes trace over him in alarm. His clothes are soaked. A cut mars his cheek. A glossy emptiness fills his eyes. Blood drips from his forehead.

"A puddle did this? You're bleeding."

"I am?" He dips a coffee-stained napkin into a water glass and presses it to his cheek.

"Your forehead, Renzo."

He flashes me a smile before bringing the dirty napkin to the correct spot. He dabs it three times, and then stuffs the napkin in the half-empty glass. "I forgot how sweet you are."

"Are you drunk?" I frown. Only the one glass is on the table.

He offers me a sheepish look. "Just coke and pot. No heroin this time."

I stare in shock. "This time?"

"Joking," he mumbles, yet I wonder if he really is. What demons drive him to self-medicate? What troubles him so much he's so reckless with his life? These aren't questions I can ask him. Hell, I barely know him.

And Lord knows, I've my own problems to deal with.

Still, I reach across the table, take his free hand, and squeeze, before releasing it. "Friends, remember?"

His eyes soften. "You make me want to get clean."

I try not to wince. "You might need professional help getting there." Marijuana and coke are one thing, heroin another.

"Or an angel by my side."

"I'm serious."

"You talk to my father?"

His father. Sebastiano Beneventi. The reason I'm here right now. The last person I want to talk to.

"He spanked then fucked three women silly yesterday morning, yet evidently, *I'm* out of control."

I gasp.

"Always three. Sometimes two. Never one."

The scene at the villa flashes across my mind. My life hangs by a thread, and he holds the knife. Kinky as fuck. Sexy or not. He's not a man you fantasize about.

"You look like hell, angel."

Says the lost and bleeding soul high on Lord knows what. "I've been through hell."

"Same." He reaches across the table and takes my hand, but then draws my fingers to his lips and bites the tips.

"Stop that." I snatch my hand away.

"Just a lesson on how hell can be enjoyable ..." He smirks. "... under the right circumstances."

Oh, God. He's as kinky as his father, isn't he? Yet, I'm more horrified than enraptured.

"Fuck. I'm sorry. I forgot how inexperienced you are."

I bristle at his assumption, despite it being accurate.

"I'm screwing this up, aren't I?" he whispers, his expression sobering. This is the Renzo I'm familiar with, the one with his heart on his sleeve. "I've a plan to get us both out of hell. My father will save face. Your father won't be killed. Or you, and your sister, hunted. With you by my side, I'll get sober—"

"Hunted!" The room swirls. I steady myself with both hands. "What?" I squeak. My throat's too tight for anything more.

"Just say yes."

"Yes."

Quicker than I believe him capable of in his condition, he snatches my hand. But this time what follows floors me.

A ring. Made from a biodegradable paper straw.

Renzo slipped it on my finger.

"Marry me."

Shock isn't the right word to describe my reaction. My mother's cancer diagnosis was shocking. Father's emotional abandonment caught Sienna and me unprepared. Hell, the worst mindfuck, up until Renzo's proposal, was discovering the star hero in my wicked fantasies is really the villain of my worst nightmare.

"You said yes."

"Yes. To marrying you?"

He nods. "My godfather's expecting a wedding. A Beneventi son marrying Governor Amato's daughter. The old man won't give two shits which son or which daughter. It's the perfect solution."

"But don't you have a girlfriend?" I murmur. "I find it hard to believe you've no one. Won't she be upset?"

His beautiful blue eyes are troubled, his damaged soul struggling with demons no one but he can fix. "I'm incapable of love. All I offer is pain and disappointment."

My heart breaks, and guilt consumes me. How can I expect him to help me when he clearly needs help himself? "I'm not your concern." I attempt a smile. "I'll figure something out."

"He'll kill your father, Lessie." He snaps a finger. "Just like that. Marrying me is the only solution."

I frown in confusion. "Your father's furious over my father's disloyalty ... and my sister's video. My marrying you won't change that."

He leans in. "What if I told you I've the perfect way for your father to get back in my old man's good graces?"

"How?" I whisper.

"He's going to ruin Emilio Conti's sports gambling franchise."

I can't believe I'm suddenly entertaining Renzo's idea, though what choice do I have? Lord, his father should be thrilled by that. "What does my father have to do?"

Renzo smirks. "Rumor has it that Conti's laundering money for Bible Belt Benny through his venues. As chairman of the East Coast

Gaming Commission, your father can close operations while an investigation is underway."

"*Is* Conti laundering money?"

"Who isn't?"

I stifle a gasp.

He stands and then sways on his feet. "Come on. We should hurry."

"What? Where?"

"To Providence. To approach my father before he sends men to New York."

I'm frozen in my seat. Like the sticky remnants of a sugary drink hold me in place.

Renzo's lost his mind. But this might work ... It has to work.

"I'll ask to handle the Beneventi business in Italy—my godfather would love that. We can live in Rome. You can go to school. We'll make it work, Angel. You'll see." He pauses as doubt fills his tone. "Ready?"

Ready to face Sebastiano Beneventi?

No.

I'll never be ready for that.

Alessia

RUTHLESS. Terrifying. *Vindictive*. Sebastiano Beneventi is this and more.

What he *isn't* is father-in-law material.

Mr. Beneventi entered his office moments ago, his formidable presence setting us on edge. The air's thinned. The room temperature swings like a pendulum, from air-conditioning cold to furious, capo-fueled hot. I feel his gaze rake over me as he walks around the desk, yet I don't … can't … make eye contact.

"We're asking permission to marry." Renzo gets straight to the point. He's seated next to me in a chair in front of his father's desk, holding my hand in reassurance and trying not to lose his nerve.

"Not this shit again."

Renzo squeezes my hand a little too hard.

"You. And Alessia."

He remembers my name.

"Don Lucchese is going to love her." Renzo squeezes my hand. "We've a solution to our other problem, as well."

"That right?" Mr. Beneventi's whiskey-raw rasp makes my body tingle and my mind go places it shouldn't. *Puoi avere qualsiasi modo si desidera*—you can have it any way you want.

No, you can't. Remember who Sebastiano Beneventi is, or you won't survive this.

"Lessie will tell you."

An awkward silence spreads.

"Look at me."

My eyes snap up at Mr. Beneventi's command. Our eyes lock, and I'm helpless to do anything but stare into deep, blue eyes accentuated by long ink-stained lashes. Hard, calculating eyes that miss nothing.

I pray he doesn't remember me.

"Drink?"

Renzo responds. "It's fucking nine in the morning—"

"Okay," I interrupt.

Mr. Beneventi moves to the bar behind his desk as Renzo shakes his head at me. I'm surprised his father hasn't commented on his appearance. Renzo looks better than he did last night but he's still pale and jittery.

His father returns with a bottle of imported whiskey and two crystal glasses. Silently, he pours a drink for me, which he slides across his desk before serving himself. He's even more handsome up close. Hair a bit too long, with a lock curling into his face. Sharp cheekbones. A nose slightly bent at the ridge like it's been broken a time or two. The sprinkle of five o'clock shadow on his jawline. And his lips ... his full, plump lips ...

My hand shakes too much to drink, so I leave the whiskey on the desk.

Blue eyes pierce into my own. I can't read him, and don't know how to react. Does he recognize me? Surely, he'd say something if he did?

"A picture of innocence, aren't you?"

"Stop fucking with her." Renzo sits up taller in his seat. "Lessie's not like her sister."

Mr. Beneventi arches an eyebrow. "Is that so?" The full force of his attention turns to Renzo. "Don't ever tell me what to do. Not until you've earned the right."

Renzo exhales sharply.

I roll my fingers into a fist. I can't allow him to make Renzo feel inadequate, especially not when he expected his father's praise for this brilliant plan. We've that in common—the inability to live up to our fathers' expectations.

"Mr. Beneventi," I murmur. Too softly. Too meekly. "My father will prove his loyalty."

"Dead men are always loyal." His statement is meant to intimidate, and it does just that.

My voice quivers. "As chairman of the gaming commission, my father can sway the committee to close Emilio Conti's venues if there's a suspicion of criminal activity."

"Money laundering," Renzo interrupts. "Conti will piss himself when the feds investigate."

Sebastiano rolls back in his seat and clasps his hands. Never once touching his whiskey.

"Conti won't see it coming," Renzo continues. "And that big baboon, Bible Belt Benny, will shit himself over lost revenue streams."

Sebastiano's expression remains blank as he considers our plan.

Finally, he speaks. "Tell me, Sheila, can the Amatos be trusted?"

My stomach drops.

"It's a nickname." Renzo covers for me. "Sheila, Angel ..."

"You haven't touched your drink."

My head spins beneath his intense scrutiny. I can't swallow, so how can I sip whiskey?

"Too lukewarm for you? Perhaps you'd like ice."

Oh, no, no, no. He *does* recognize me, and acting like we've never met has likely fueled his distrust.

His smug smile doesn't reach his eyes. "No? Nothing to say?"

I flush, embarrassed to the core. What can I say? Yes, I spied on you. Yes, I admitted to being curious.

Yes, your cruel, handsome face has played a starring role in getting me off at night.

Renzo jumps to his feet. "Don't fuck with her. I told you, she's not like her father or sister. She's sweet and innocent."

"You think I'm a goddamn fool?" He slams his fist on the desk, and we jump. "If I allow a marriage, what guarantee is there another video won't surface?"

I squeeze my eyes shut. He hates me, doesn't he? And it hurts. I prefer his praise to his anger.

"Lessie's a virgin," Renzo blurts out.

Complete, utter mortification consumes me. His father has no right to such personal information. What does it matter if I'm a virgin or not? I swipe away frustrated tears and brace for more accusations.

"A virgin?" Sebastiano's whiskey-laced voice hits deep. There's an edge to it this time, that tempts me to look.

His nostrils flare, and I'm caught unprepared. A tic dents his jaw, and a charged energy fills the space between us.

He's pleased.

Something stirs within me. Like a secret door's been unlocked and I'm invited to pass through. I've given him a gift wrapped with great care, one he *adores*. And pleasing him gets me off.

By nature, is this who I am? Submissive and eager to fulfill his every wish? Sebastiano Beneventi's the wrong man to spark this revelation, but in many twisted and disturbing ways, he's exactly right. What's the expression? Out of the frying pan and into the fire? But what happens when you crave being burned?

"Do we have your permission to marry?" Renzo's question jolts me from my thoughts.

"Sit."

Renzo hesitates. Such a kind man. Such a troubled soul. He's no match for his father. I tug his hand, and he finally takes a seat.

Sebastiano's attention shifts between us, the mafioso not missing a thing.

"Alessia's answer will decide what happens next."

Okay. He's actually considering it.

Renzo arrives at the same conclusion and relaxes.

"He calls you his angel?"

I frown, confused. This is what he needs clarification on? "Yes."

"He believes you can fix him."

I don't dare glance at Renzo. "I have Renzo's back. The best marriages are based on friendship."

"Friendship. Not sex?" He flashes me a wicked smile, and my throat hitches. Marriage to *him* would involve sex, all kinds of wild, mind-blowing sex.

He's toying with me. The virgin. The shy, fun-to-manipulate young woman. And suddenly, call it this new revelation I've had, call it an insane desire to please him, call it every dirty thought I've had about this man—whatever it is, I test the waters.

"Both."

There. It. Is. The flare. The tic. He *likes* my boldness.

We stare at each other for a moment. Connecting in a way that doesn't require words. For a second, I forget to be shy or afraid. It's a strange feeling, being so attracted to a man that you can barely breathe. A primal urge that stirs my deepest desires. A reckless rush tempting me to act. Even beneath his stern regard, even despite the danger he presents, I feel his pull.

"I'll consider you marrying my son." His low, seductive tone elicits a shiver, and I'm slow to process his words.

I stare at my lap as reality settles in. He'll allow Renzo and me to marry. So why do I feel so unsettled? Is it because, despite my best efforts, I keep having dirty thoughts about my future father-in-law?

"Look at me."

My eyes snap up.

"But only if you're honest. Capisci?"

"I swear it. I'll do whatever you say."

His eyes flash.

When I was a little girl, our family vacationed in a quaint cabin on a farm in upstate New York. A metal fence surrounded the property. One day, a horrible storm thundered in. My mother and I were on the porch when lightning struck, hitting the fence and sending a fireball spiraling around the top. With a loud boom, the fireball crashed into an old barn out back, igniting a blistering inferno that consumed the barn within minutes.

That's how his piercing blue eyes feel. Like he's about to set me on fire and consume me.

My reaction hits me straight between the thighs, and hot, wet need soaks my underwear. I squirm in my seat, struggling for control.

God help me. How could something this wrong feel so right?

His lips curl. He knows.

Then, like a sledgehammer, like the dangerous man he is, his smile disappears and he hurls another fireball into the room.

"Is Renzo an addict?"

10

Bastian

RENZO ANSWERS FOR HER. "It's under control."

As if word of his exploits in New York City never got back to me. As if the little shit didn't show up trashed at my bar, vomit his guts out, and piss off Big Tony. My threats are landing on deaf ears.

And I'm not a man you ignore.

"Speak out of turn again, and I'll shoot you in the leg."

Alessia gasps.

Renzo shuts the fuck up.

And I raise an eyebrow, signaling for her to answer.

"Does Renzo have a drug problem?" she whispers. Buying time to construct a lie? Giving me another reason to distrust her?

She struggles to answer but surprises me when she does.

"Yes. He has issues."

"Let me guess; coke, pills, booze, wet paint chips—anything else?"

"Don't," Renzo begs.

She swallows hard. "Heroin."

Goddamn it. It's exactly what Sandro suspects.

"And you, being his angel, can cure an addict?"

Renzo shoots to his feet. "What the hell? Lessie, please. Don't fucking answer him. Don't you see what he's doing?"

Her eyes fill with apology. "He's your father."

"Don't you have any sense of self-preservation? You're going to ruin our plan."

"He cares. He built you a golf course, remember?"

I scowl at how perceptive she is. About the golf course—it can't be any more obvious that Renzo needs rehab.

"With professional guidance ..." she murmurs.

Professional guidance inside a military-like rehab facility with guards patrolling the grounds. Making escape, this time, impossible.

Renzo throws his hands up. "He'll never approve the marriage now."

Her throat bobs as she turns to me. "Any more questions?" So nervous. So curious. Begging to be corrupted, isn't she?

Don Lucchese would love her.

I never gave the old man a name. Amato's daughter—that's how I referred to her. And as much as I'm itching to end the governor's life, their plan makes sense. Ruin Conti. Give Bible Belt Benny the Italian salute without acknowledging his dick's been all up in Conti's soon-to-be lackluster business. Make Amato my puppet.

Yeah. It'll tidy this clusterfuck up nicely.

But if she's to become a Beneventi, can I trust the little voyeur? Kinky *virgin* voyeur—or so she claims.

I take my first sip of whiskey as a thought settles in.

You can demand proof. Whether little Lessie's innocent won't be difficult to determine. You can catch her in a lie or be given evidence she's trustworthy.

You can make her come as a reward.

My cock swells with blood.

What did she say to me back in Italy when I asked her if she got off on watching me?

"I think so."

I understand my effect on women. I'm the big bad bull, dangerous and uncontrollable. Women don't want to tame me. Women want a wild fucking ride with a beast. The little kinkster thinks I'm unaware of her interest? Like her curiosity doesn't shine through?

Fuck it. When I'm done with her—if she is who she says she is—there won't be an *I think so* left in her pretty head.

Just this once. To satisfy my own curiosity.

One shot for her to earn my trust.

I pick up my cell and text Sandro. *Come to my office asap.*

Then I get straight to business. "Your father will provide daily updates. If he misses one or neglects to disclose information, you'll be held accountable. Capisci?"

"Yes, sir."

My cock jerks.

Renzo lights up. "Thank you ..."

A knock interrupts him, and Sandro enters. Renzo's twin quickly assesses the situation, but when his attention lands on Alessia, his face reddens.

Doesn't trust her? Or doesn't like her? Or perhaps both?

My sons will lose their shit when I break the news. Before I become capo di tutti capi, the protective Band-Aid I've secured over them must be ripped off. It'll sting. But this life isn't for the weak.

"Sit."

"What's he doing here?" Renzo demands.

"Stepping in for you. I won't be embarrassed or ignored."

He flinches.

But the gloves are off, so no sense in being less than brutally honest. "Three different facilities. Three fucking times. Will there ever be an end? You're a liability."

"Stepping in *how?*"

Sandro studies me, not yet aware there's a puzzle he's a piece of.

But the little voyeur's caught on, if her death grip on the chair is any indication. Like she's on a roller-coaster ride and holding on for dear life.

Better hold on because I'm not done with her yet.

"You'll get clean this time, or I'll disown you. Capisci?"

His head jerks back like I slapped him.

Alessia grabs his arm and squeezes it, then casts her eyes at me like I'm a monster.

That's right, baby. You'll soon learn how ruthless I can be.

"So you'll delay my proposal ..."

I shake my head. "No time for delays."

He looks at Alessia, and then Sandro.

"Enjoy rehab, Bro." Sandro snickers. "Hear heroin withdrawal's a bitch."

Alessia glares at him.

I press the buzzer beneath my desk before Renzo opens his mouth, and summon my man, Freido.

"Think this is funny, asshat? I'd pay money to see your expression when he presents the groom to Don Lucchese." Renzo slaps his twin on the back. "Thanks for stepping in."

Sandro's smile disappears. "What are you saying?"

I stand, place both hands on my desk, and lean toward them.

"You'll marry Sandro ..." I lock eyes with Alessia. "... once you prove you're not a liar."

Blood drains from her face.

Sandro rises, one fist clenched.

And Renzo sways on his feet, looking like his brother stole his puppy.

As for me? I learned a long time ago that feelings are best suppressed when it comes to famiglia business. A lesson this trio will need to learn to survive.

Sandro escapes the office, brushing by Freido on the way out.

"You bastard." Renzo shouts at me.

"Five months."

He sputters, rising up and out of his seat. "You can't do this."

"Six."

Renzo's attention swings to Freido, knowing what's coming, yet he still attempts to sprint by my man—who is inescapable. He charges Renzo, tackles him to the floor, then jams a needle into his neck, injecting enough tranquilizer that Renzo won't wake up until he's safely locked away in Maine.

Catching Alessia out of the corner of my eye as she races toward them, I stiffen.

"What are you doing to him?" she cries out, then hurls herself at Freido, knocking him off my son.

A shy thing like her.

I didn't see that coming.

She'd be good for Renzo. If time weren't an issue, I'd allow their marriage.

Freido raises a hand, prepared to strike.

"No," I snap.

He immediately stops.

"Alessia. Come here."

"I'm sorry, Angel," Renzo chokes out before going limp. Her eyes fill with tears as Freido hauls him from the office.

"Don't make me ask twice."

She hesitates still, deciding whether to stay or run.

Head bowed, she shuffles toward me.

If she knew what I have in store for her, she'd be halfway down the hall.

11

Alessia

I ROUND his desk to stand before him, my legs nearly brushing his knees as he spins his chair to face me.

My bottom lip trembles.

"I'm sorry I spied on you." There, I said it. Our history is acknowledged. With Renzo hauled off to rehab, it's up to me to convince Sebastiano our plan is in his best interests. I can't think of anyone who'd make a worse husband than Sandro. Except what choice do I have? If I had doubts that Sebastiano Beneventi would kill my father, they vanished after witnessing the harsh treatment Renzo just received.

But I don't stand a chance without his trust. I hope this embarrassing admission's enough.

Without a word, he reclines in his chair, sips his whiskey, and studies me.

The air charges.

His pull powerful.

I swallow hard. "Your door was open ..."

He snorts. "That's not what this is about."

"It's not?"

With lightning quick movements, he snatches my wrist and tugs me between his thighs. His drink sloshes over the glass rim, but that doesn't stop him from raising my hand to his cheek. "Feel this?" He drags my fingers across his scar. "Six months after my father died and I became capo, my father's right-hand man tried to kill me in my sleep. I woke up when the knife sliced my face. He died a slow death in the dungeon. The capo who paid him off is buried beneath the state capitol. Point is, I trusted the wrong man. Now I'm not the trusting sort."

He drops my hand, but the warmth of his skin still lingers on my fingers.

"I'm sorry." I bite my lip and stare at his handsome face, the scar only adding to his rugged appeal.

"Save your sorrys. You'll need them."

A chill runs up my spine. "What do I have to do to prove my loyalty?"

"Use your imagination."

My heart thunders so loudly my ears ring. "I don't understand," I sputter. But it's a lie, and he knows it.

He drains his drink, and then sets the glass on his desk. "Need me to spell it out for you?"

I don't respond. I can't—my lips won't move.

"What could a kinky little voyeur who claims she's a virgin do to prove she's being honest?"

His tone is from my darkest fantasies. One part question. Two parts order. Three parts *dare*.

But do I dare?

I squeeze my thighs together. Because I'm wet, so freaking wet.

His eyes narrow, tracking the movement. God created man, but the devil's responsible for this sexy beast.

Do I test temptation? Or do I flee and pretend this never happened.

Like he'd allow me to escape unscathed.

"If I wanted to pop your cherry, I could do it. Better me than Sandro—I'd be doing you a favor."

I blink. Imagining him over me. Imagining his big body overpowering me. "So you believe me?" I blurt.

"Part of me wants to believe you." His finger brushes the inside of my thigh, and I shift away in surprise. "And part of me doesn't."

His smirk hits me like a thunderbolt, reducing me to a puddle rippling with nervous excitement.

I *want* him to unlock the secrets within.

Despite who he is.

Despite who I'm going to be.

Despite this being wrong.

"All buttoned up." He flicks a button just below my navel. "All pretty and perfect." His fingertip retraces its path on my thigh. "All twisted and turned around up here." He taps his temple. "I see what you are."

"What am I?" My pulse races. He's older, experienced. How do I appear in his eyes? What does he see in me?

"You get off on watching me spank those women?"

Words come out in a whisper. "I think so."

His eyebrows arch. "You think so."

"It was my first ... only time ..." I blush. "I never—"

"But you liked it."

I nod.

"You play with yourself afterward? Fiddle with your young pussy and wish it were you?"

My eyes grow wide. Dare I answer him truthfully?

His lips curl. Oh, sweet Lord. He *knows*.

"Prove to me what a good girl you are, and I'll give you a taste of what you're so sweetly begging me for." He snatches my wrist, and I'm falling forward, my hand landing on his broad shoulders and my head stopping within an inch of his own. His breath warms my ear. "Be a good girl, and I'll show you what a kinky bastard can do."

"Okay," I murmur.

Oh Lord. He's seductive. Addictive.

I push away to stand. "Tell me what you like."

Eyes flash. Nostrils flare. Cheek tics. And I'm overcome by blinding, reckless lust.

He doesn't hesitate. "Take off your underwear."

I shimmy them off, and the material pools at my feet.

"Pick them up."

Lord, he's bossy. A wicked thrill races up my spine as I crouch.

"No."

I straighten.

"Turn around, and bend forward."

"Oh," I gasp with understanding. I do what he demands, and then some, raising my skirt and slowly presenting him with my ass as I retrieve the underwear. I anticipate his touch. And, when it doesn't come, fill with disappointment.

"Hand them to me."

I spin around and pass my underwear to him.

He stares down at the red silk thong like I handed him a grenade, or something equally unexpected.

My eyes go wide when I notice the wet patch on my panties' crotch in the exact same moment he does.

"Basta," he snarls, thumbing the wet patch. My breath catches as his eyes lift to mine. "You playing me for a fool?"

"What? No."

"Get. On. The. Fucking. Desk."

I hurry to obey, and hoist myself into a seated position with legs dangling before him. The light goes out of his eyes, and all semblance of playfulness disappears. I bite my lip, worried by the change. Worried I've gotten myself in way over my head.

His chair spins, and I glare at his angry face.

Disappointment sinks in, when all I hoped to do was please him. "Did I do something to upset you?"

"Pull your skirt up and place your feet on the desk."

Eyes closed, I raise my bottom, wiggle my skirt free, and lift the material to my waist. My hands shake. I've never felt so powerless. So vulnerable.

"Do it. Or I'll take you across my knee and paddle your ass."

I shift back and place my feet on his desk.

"You get filmed having sex?"

"No." My eyes flash open. What? He doesn't believe me? "I've never had sex."

"Show me that virgin pussy."

Something in me stirs. He wants proof? I'll show him proof. I've come this far—so what if anger drives my recklessness instead of desire?

I unclench my thighs and, shifting my feet, broaden my position. My pussy on full display like a prize jewel.

Except he doesn't recognize its value.

I run a hand down my abdomen to my wet core.

His eyes track the movement, giving nothing away.

How can I reach him? What would please him?

With an uncharacteristic brazenness, I fork my finger over my lips and spread them.

His hiss fills the office.

But I'm not done. I crook my middle finger of my other hand and then, locking eyes with his, dip it into my channel.

"See?" I cock my head. "I can barely take a finger."

His eyes darken an impossible shade of blue, and his gaze immediately drops.

Time stands still.

"How far?"

"Never more than half an inch. When I play with myself, I touch my clit."

It's embarrassing offering up something so personal. But trust goes two ways. Mine, in exchange for his.

I reach out, palm up. "Give me your hand."

His head snaps up.

"But promise me you'll leave me intact."

His expression's blank, and I can't get a read. But then he places his hand in mine.

I tug and wheel him in closer.

"Madonna mia. Look at this sweet little pussy." He brushes my hands aside. "Weeping with need."

My body wants what it wants, despite the risk. And right now, it wants his finger.

"Ever let a man lick your pussy?"

I gasp. "No."

"Play with it?" His whiskey-laced tone has returned. He likes this, doesn't he?

"Answer me."

I shake my head.

"Spank it with his palm?"

"Never." My voice drops. *Just you in my dreams.*

If I couldn't read his expression before, I can now. Lust. Pure, unadulterated lust emanates from him. Like he's half a second from fulfilling all my erotic fantasies. Like he's hell-bent on breaking me in, on ruining me.

He surges from his chair so fast it falls over. Coming in close, he touches his middle finger to my mouth.

"You want to play, little girl? Let's play. Suck."

I draw his digit in and do as he demands. Watching him watch me. Loving his power he over me.

"This is what's going to happen. I'm going to stuff my fat finger into your tight channel, and you're going to take it like a good girl. And if you're really good, I'm going to finger-fuck you until you scream my name. Capisci?"

I nod, and choke on his digit. My eyes water.

"Never suck cock before?"

I don't respond, don't risk choking again.

"You've got me rock hard, you filthy little virgin. If I could defile you, I'd start with your mouth. I bet you'd get off on how deep you take me. I'd shoot a load down your throat that you'd taste for weeks."

He's dirty. And the picture he paints has me shaking with need.

A finger glides across my folds.

"Fucking hell, you're soaking wet. You like this, don't you?"

I nod.

He withdraws his finger with a sexy smirk. Then, with a shove, pushes me back onto my elbows.

My hips lift as he drags the same digit between my lips. "Say my name," he rasps.

"Sebastiano."

"Bastian. Say it again."

"Bastian ... ahhh!"

He feeds his finger inside me until it bottoms out. Doing exactly what he promised yet still surprising me.

I feel full.

It feels strange.

But as he begins to thrust, mostly what I feel is bliss.

"Look at the pretty little virgin getting fucked by her first finger."

I begin panting in rhythm with his movements.

"That's right. Your greedy cunt knows what you need. Milk it, baby."

Every emotion—fear, worry, panic, confusion, excitement, anger—converges into one until the tension becomes so intense I combust.

I shatter hard, and cry out his name. "Bastian. Oh, yes. Yes. Yes."

His name on my lips is the last thing I remember as I pass out.

I'm disoriented when I recover, and embarrassed. Who faints from an orgasm? Me, evidently. But when I catch my breath, harsh, cruel reality is there to greet me.

"You'll move into the casita tomorrow. I'll call Don Lucchese and invite him to the engagement party." He stands before me, already a troublesome memory. All business, with little mercy. "Don't fuck this up, or you'll regret it."

His back's to me.

Like nothing happened.

Like I'm a discarded toy he's already forgotten.

I roll to sit.

His final command is a slap in the face.

"Get out."

I'VE BEEN TRAPPED, in one form or another, since my mother's death. A bird in flight, passing from one not-so-gilded cage to another. But my new prison is pure gold, a place you'd find in *Architectural Digest*.

A few yards from the main house and opposite the pool, the casita belongs in a high-end resort instead of on a mafioso's estate. Floor-to-ceiling accordion doors lead into an enormous great room, with beautifully crafted wooden accents and a highly polished floor.

The space is open concept. A state-of-the-art kitchen occupies the back wall, and a dining area is off to its right. Two bedroom suites bookend the main living space.

And the enormous master shower is unlike any I've seen before, with its Bluetooth connectivity. You can set the lighting, water temperature, and tunes with a few clicks of a remote. For my first shower, I pressed disco moodlighting, cranked up Harry Styles's "Watermelon Sugar," and danced in the hot jet spray like a fool.

None of this disguises the fact I'm a prisoner. The guards patrolling the grounds confirm it.

I sigh and step into the vegetable garden behind the casita. An older Italian woman, Nonna Rosa, arrives at the estate every afternoon at four o'clock to stock the refrigerator and cook dinner. She buys me groceries from a list I compile, and the mafioso guards bring them inside. Except nothing tastes better than fresh produce, so the garden's a delight. I pass time cooking and reading, and *not* dwelling on Sebastiano Beneventi's finger-fuck.

Do I regret insisting he touch me?

Regret is a troublesome word. You regret eating that extra slice of chocolate cake. You regret not telling your mother you loved her enough while she was alive. You're not supposed to regret your first non-self-induced orgasm.

But I do—except for the wrong reason. I've relived the experience, over and over, despite his cruelty and the way it ended. If anything, the experience has awakened this craving inside me. Like the first taste of ice cream with ten times the sweet rush.

He comes and goes without the slightest acknowledgment. I'm as insignificant as the tomato I'm about to pluck off a vine.

Do I still fear him? Yes.

Do I trust him? Sort of—he's a man of his word. My father's alive and flourishing; his bank accounts reinstated, his new role as chairman of the East Coast Gaming Commission giving him the ego boost he craves. And his popularity's at an all-time high as the "mugging" earned him voter sympathy. Daddy Dearest's back in Bastian's good graces, and I still bear the consequences of my family's actions.

And now ... my own.

Do I regret encouraging Bastian?

I sigh. That's the problem, isn't it?

I wish Sienna would resurface so I could talk to her. I haven't heard from my sister. Truth is, I'm envious. Because she succeeded where I failed.

She *escaped.*

I sigh, and then begin selecting the ripest tomatoes. They're perfect for the homemade sauce I'm preparing. At least I've cooking to help pass the time.

You can take online classes. Finish your degree. Add some normalcy to your life. But who do I ask for permission?

Sandro? No thank you.

Bastian?

The sun hangs low, the warm rays soothing my soul. I'm a survivor. I'll find a way to make the best out of this situation. Haven't I already taken a tiny step?

It's almost time.

I rearrange the tomatoes in my makeshift apron with shaky hands. Busying myself.

I hear them before they break through the tree line.

Runners following the golf path that connects to a larger path toward the main house. The larger path winds behind the casita and, at its closest point, is about three yards away.

I spy Bastian immediately. Shirtless. Sweat defining his muscular torso. Flat abs. Thin grey shorts clinging to his hip bones.

His head turns as they race by.

My heart flutters as I avert my own, and pretend I didn't catch him looking.

Mission accomplished, I head back inside.

13

Bastian

"WHY DID you let him hit you like that?" Dante asks in awe.

I touch my swollen cheek. A reminder that pain often accompanies glory. I knocked out a notoriously fierce fighter during today's brawl. I host no-holds-barred fights inside a barn on my property whenever I need to take the edge off. Street fights, where few rules apply. We Beneventis have our vices, and the challenge invigorates me as much as it grounds me.

Overall, it's been a fucking celebratory week. Conti's sports racket's ruined. Benny's scratching his head, wondering what the fuck happened. Amato's swift, effective, and does as commanded. The East Coast Gaming Commission has given the green light on Atlanta along with another expansion project: building the Riverview Casino in New York City. Don Lucchese booked a flight to Providence to bless his godson's engagement, and no doubt interrogate me about the next steps toward making the famiglie rich.

I'm a fucking mafioso king.

"Or are you simply a sadist?" Dante continues. "You've scratches on your neck."

"Says the son of a man whose vineyard is watered with his enemies' blood." Rumor or truth, it's hard to fucking say. I hate wine, anyway. "Nothing better than pain mixed with pleasure. You should try it. Or are you too afraid of damaging that pretty face?"

He smirks. "Don't tell my father, but I'm a lover, not a fighter."

"You speak to the old man?"

His scowl says it all. "Tomorrow."

I smirk. "He has you dragging your ass out of bed at an ungodly hour?"

"Goddamn time change. He likes to talk over morning coffee."

"And a cigarette."

Dante grunts. "That, too."

We enter the kitchen. My cook, Nonna Rosa, hovers in front of the refrigerator, rolling pin in hand. Homemade pasta fills a plate on the island, and my stomach growls with pleasure.

"Buon pomeriggio, Nonna," Dante greets her. "Diventi più bella ogni volta che ti vedo."

The manwhore. Complimenting Nonna on how she grows more beautiful each time he sees her is expected. Dante flirts with anyone with two legs. He can wear a woman down like a new pair of sneakers, slowly and methodically, no matter the age. Once he fucks them, he moves on.

"Who's that behind you, Nonna?"

My head snaps back to my cook.

Miss Not-So-Innocent-Anymore steps into view. Cheeks flushed and body covered in flour. Pretty little thing, with the sweetest pussy I've ever touched. Just thinking about her clenched around my finger —like she hoped I'd never stop—makes me hard.

The kinky slut took a digit so well, imagine her stuffed full of cock? She's begging to be broken in.

Sandro's a lucky little shit.

I scowl.

Dante shoots me an expectant look.

"This is Sandro's fiancée, Alessia Amato." I wave her forward, and she reluctantly obeys.

"She's young."

"Twenty," I reply.

Her eyebrows lift like she's surprised I remember her age.

"She's living at the estate?"

What the fuck? "We have her set up in the casita."

"How didn't I know this?"

I shrug. The asshole thinks he's privy to everything, doesn't he?

"Where's Sandro?"

"Sardinia."

"Italy? Now?"

My lips thin as I grow impatient with his questions. "He'll be home for the announcement."

Dante ignores my mounting frustration. Or is he too stupid to recognize it? "Come to think of it, where the hell did Renzo disappear to?"

My eyes lock on Alessia. "My sons aren't dogs on a leash. Renzo does whatever the fuck he wants."

She bites her lip yet gives nothing away. She struggles for a few seconds, then steps forward and offers him her hand. "Nice to meet you, Dante. Mr. Beneventi kindly offered me use of his casita."

"Kindly," he snorts, and accepts her handshake. Yet when he withdraws his hand, his expression's comical. His palm is white, and coated with flour.

Alessia's cheeks flush pink. "I'll bring you a wet towel."

"We don't have time," I snap. "My office, now." I stalk from the kitchen with Dante on my tail.

"I thought we were done with business?" he gripes.

I don't even grace his question with a lie.

NONNA APPROACHES me at the kitchen island as I help myself to a second serving of fresh pasta with meatballs. I dislike interruptions, so this must be important.

"What is it?"

"La dolce ragazza ... Alessia."

I pause, serving spoon in the air. "What about her?"

"È sola."

"Lonely?"

Nonna nods.

Madonna mia. "Sandro returns in a few days. She'll get over it." I turn back to my plate, but the old woman still hovers.

"Yes?"

"Ti stai godendo il tuo pasto, signore?"

What the hell? I had an easier time taking a face-punch from a killing machine than surviving first Dante's and now Nonna's interrogation. "The sauce is fucking excellent, and you changed the meatball recipe. They're spicier. I like it."

"La ragazza preparò i cavatelli e la salsa di pomodoro."

"Did she?" The image of little Alessia—barefoot, naked, covered in flour, and preparing *my* dinner—elicits a grin.

"Ha chiesto di aiutarmi a cucinare," Nonna requests with hesitation.

"I've no issue with her helping you cook."

"Possiamo acquirstare un forno per la pizza, signore?"

A goddamn pizza oven? Next Nonna will be demanding, on behalf of her little protégée, the keys to my Maserati. My stomach rumbles. Fuck it, I like pizza.

"Purchase whatever is necessary."

"Grazie, signor Beneventi." Nonna gathers her bag and leaves. And I pile my plate full of food, wondering what other surprises Miss Amato has in store.

14

Alessia

ITALIAN CUISINE'S a labor of love, with simple ingredients that take patience and care. And making pasta by hand is an art form.

I spend late afternoons cooking with Nonna, her presence as comforting as the dough in my hands.

This afternoon, with Don Lucchese's arrival a few days away, Nonna's left me to prepare dinner while she shops for the best ingredients in Rhode Island. It's my first time inside the main house alone, and I'm filled with nervous energy. What if I'm *discovered*?

I brush aside my twisted thoughts and focus on what brings me instantaneous pleasure. Dough warmed by my own hands as I knead the dough. Poached plump tomatoes crushed between my fingers and into a sauce bowl. Freshly picked parsley and oregano wafting through the kitchen. This is therapy, Italian style.

I'm wiping flour from my forehead when a small group passes through the kitchen and exits the door.

Shock rolls over me as I count.

Not one. Not two. But three women.

A brunette. A redhead. And a blonde.

They appear and disappear in a blink. But their perfume lingers, poisoning my joy.

I'm not curious or aroused.

I'm livid.

I slam a fist into dough. Flour clouds the air and makes my eyes water. I grab the rolling pin, then beat the perfectly formed mixture as hard as I can. Flattening it into an unmanageable mess.

I imagine the scene, the trio bent over and him behind them. Spanking them barehanded. Flogging their asses. Taking turns finger-fucking them, and more.

It's not even four o'clock.

Tears form, but I force them back. He's not the sort of man you play games with. He'd steal an orgasm, snap my neck, then bury me beneath the ninth hole without remorse. Why tempt the beast? Why feed this twisted yearning for his attention? Do I have a death wish?

With a sniffle, I pick up the knife and cut the dough into large strips, and then into smaller ones. The dough's released too much gluten, which will cause the pasta to break between my fingers. I've ruined it.

What does it matter? Any satisfaction in cooking this meal's exited through the kitchen door along with the happy trio.

"Where's Nonna?"

I nearly jump out of my skin. Spinning, I gasp at his appearance.

He's barefoot. In grey running shorts that dangle precariously from his hip bones. Water beads across his muscular chest. Curls, damp from a shower, frame his handsome face. My eyes narrow—scratches run down his neck.

He arches an eyebrow.

"Shopping," I grind out, having forgotten he asked me a question. My response is quiet yet packs a punch. Like I've substituted sinning or murdering for "shopping".

"I'm fucking starving. What's for dinner?" He stalks by me to the stovetop. Stirring spoon in hand, he dips it into the white clam sauce and brings it to his lips. Blowing first, he then takes a mouthful.

His eyes close as he savors it.

So sexy.

So selfish.

Don't do it. Don't take pleasure in his pleasure.

I turn away as he licks his lips.

Several seconds pass. I feel him studying me. Feel the energy his presence emanates. My throat hitches while my heart squeezes tight.

"I'd like you to prepare a special dish for Don Lucchese."

"Nonna's compiled a menu."

He's silent.

I'm close, so close, to telling him where he can stick Don Lucchese's meal. Except he scares me shitless.

What's he thinking? Punish me for my subtle defiance? Spank me—like he likely spanked those women this afternoon?

His sharp sigh makes me jump. He charges by me and offers a low-pitched warning. "Just fucking do what I ask."

15

Alessia

THE ESTATE BUZZES with excitement as preparations for Don Lucchese's arrival get underway. I've overheard the guards talking. The elderly mafioso's in poor health and rarely travels. His attendance is an honor, and a sign my father-in-law will assume power after Don Lucchese's death.

They say it's a done deal.

Part of me recognizes his need to be merciless, even to his own sons—though that needle plunged into Renzo's neck still horrifies me. Foolish men—like Frankie DiCapitano—don't become capos. Weak men certainly don't become capo di tutti capi.

Sebastiano—*Bastian*—isn't foolish or weak.

A lesson I should take to heart if I hope to survive this life.

Avoiding Bastian as much as possible is my new objective. So, while chaos overtakes the estate, I hide away inside the casita.

For Don Lucchese's visit two days away, I've decided on lamb stuffed with homemade ricotta. It's risky—a lot could go wrong with the preparations. But I'm aiming for the wow factor. If Don Lucchese loves it, so will Bastian.

I toss the cheesecloth into the trash bin beneath the casita kitchen counter, and then place the cheese inside the refrigerator. It has to chill for twelve hours before I can add lemon and oregano.

I glance down at my shirt. I'll never be Martha Stewart neat. They say the best cooks put themselves into their food. No one tells you it's a mutual arrangement, that food has a mind of its own and often ends up all over you. Unless you're Martha, damn her. I believe the sticky, wet cheese creation covering me means I'm simply a passionate cook. You can't touch food without getting your hands dirty.

I chuckle, then head into the bathroom to clean up. Mission accomplished, I return to the great room.

"Hellooo?"

I freeze just as I'm entering the room, the unfamiliar voice startling me.

No one aside from my father and the Beneventi mafiosi know I live on the estate. Aside from Nonna, Freido, and a few guards, I've had no contact with anyone else. I could disappear, and few would miss me. And, of those few, who'd care?

"Alessia, are you here?"

A young woman, with blue-tipped brunette hair, a pierced nose, bright red lipstick, and a warm smile, stands in the great room.

"Wow. This place is something. I expected you'd be set up inside Sandro's suite, but instead Mr. Beneventi's given you these sweet digs."

I stare at her.

She rushes toward me and sticks out her hand. "I'm the martian."

"Who?"

Her nail polish is neon yellow, bold and glaring. Colorful, like her personality. She's the antithesis of me; a person who thrives on attention.

She snatches my hand and shakes. "He said he told you."

"Who? Told me what?"

"Renzo. About the Halloween party?" She huffs. "I'm not explaining myself too well, am I?"

No, though she's said enough to spark my hope. "You know Renzo?"

"Yep. He asked I introduce myself as the martian—guess I should have known better than to listen to a serial rehabber." With a hasty glance over her shoulder, she continues while my thoughts hurry to catch up. "I've five minutes before Freido charges in here and hauls me out, and I'm making a mess of it."

"Escorts you out?"

Her sigh is Broadway-worthy. "I'm banned from the Beneventi estate."

Now *I'm* anxiously looking toward the accordion door.

"My vape canister exploded and set a small fire in the East Wing. Sandro's Halloween party had to be evacuated. He's convinced I'm a train wreck—his words, not mine. Didn't mind my adventurous nature in bed—he loved doing all sorts of crazy shit to me."

Whoa. And wait just a minute. Martian sex with Renzo? Jungle gymnastics with Sandro? She nearly burned Bastian's home to the ground?

A rumble bubbles up from deep within, like it's been waiting for the perfect moment to break free. For the first time in weeks, I laugh.

She also cracks up, while gasping, "Renzo was sure we'd hit it off."

Renzo, my angel with broken black wings.

"I can't believe you're living here. Mr. Beneventi's picky about who he invites over."

"Unless you're brunette, redhead, or blond." I clasp a hand over my mouth, but the words have already escaped, complete with mocking tone.

Her eyebrows rise to the rafters, like I've shocked *her*. When I can recount intimate details about her sex life despite not knowing her name.

"Fucks them like a bull, or so rumor says."

Lord, I regret mentioning those women. Who or how my father-in-law fucks isn't my concern.

I feel compelled to warn her. "We should be careful, so let's not discuss him."

"Believe me. I get it. My father works for Sebastiano Beneventi. I've been around the famiglia my entire life."

I have a million questions I shouldn't ask, so instead I land on a safer one. "You mentioned Renzo thought we'd get along. Have you spoken to him?"

"Yep." She sighs with great exaggeration. "He stole a nurse's phone to call me. That was the last I heard from him."

"Can I have that number?" Lord, I'd feel better about everything if I could speak with him. Reassure myself he's okay. Get reassurance I'll be okay. I hurry to the kitchen island to retrieve my phone. She reads off the nurse's number, and I save it to my contacts.

"You've been warned, Zoey." Freido steps through the open door.

"Oh, shit," she exclaims.

"Hurry. Enter your number." I toss her my cell before Freido can reach her. I've a new friend. Someone who understands this world, and the Beneventi men. Someone who can help me navigate.

She frantically types, and then tosses it back to me just as Freido grabs her arm. His threat rings out. "Jump me again, and you'll be sorry."

"You're marrying a heartless son of a bitch. A total control freak," Zoey hollers. "Renzo thought you should know."

"Zip it, Zoey," Freido barks.

"Be prepared for some major passive-aggressive bullshit. Chin up, Alessia, or he'll eat you alive."

Freido forces her toward the door, and the air goes out of me. A second friend met by happenstance. A second time they've been literally dragged off.

"Oh, I almost forgot. One more thing I think you should know." Zoey grabs the accordion doorframe. "If Sandro's ice, Mr. Beneventi's fire. Avoid the bull at all costs."

She releases her grip, then makes a call-me gesture, before Freido drags her away.

Alessia

"DID ZOEY MAKE IT HOME?" I demand the next morning when Freido appears at the accordion door.

"Yes." He scowls. "She's not permitted on the grounds without Sebastiano's permission."

"So, I'll get his permission."

Freido looks doubtful. "Mr. Beneventi requests you join him for lunch at noon."

I anticipated this moment. Don Lucchese arrives tomorrow, and Bastian has trust issues. He likely needs reassurance I won't fuck things up.

If I impress Don Lucchese, it'll go a long way toward earning Bastian's trust. Without it, my new life as a Beneventi will be miserable. This isn't a coin flip; I understand which side I must be on. I'm nothing if not a survivor.

"The food will get cold." Freido looks me up and down, from my tank top and shorts to my daisy flip-flops.

"He said noon?" I'm hurrying toward my bedroom to change. "Semiformal, correct?"

Freido grunts, not answering either question.

I dress in low heels, fitted slacks, and a button-down blouse, then comb my hair to a shine and layer in a few curls. Very classic. Very Hampton chic.

Not that Bastian will notice.

Not that I'm hoping he will.

I follow Freido across the pool deck and lawn toward the stone pavers leading up to the veranda. I immediately spy the tall dark-haired figure waiting beside a long, rectangular table. His grim expression hits home harder than a lead pipe.

Sandro. He's back.

Of course he is. His big announcement is *my* big announcement. Even if I've avoided thinking about it.

I draw near, and he glances at his watch. Like I'm late—except it's five minutes to noon.

He's going to make things difficult.

This is your life. Don't allow your marriage to begin this way. Befriend the arrogant jerk. It's pointless making an enemy out of your soon-to-be fiancé.

He pulls out a chair—it's a start.

I slip into it and murmur, "Thank you, Sandro."

Phone in hand, he settles into the seat across from me, then ignores me.

My brow furrows. The way his thumb glides across the screen—is he playing a game?

Just as well.

An assortment of meats, pastas, cheeses, and breads are arranged on the table along with a pitcher of lemonade. I sip my drink and study Sandro from beneath my lashes. Hair newly cut into a short military-style buzz. Freshly shaven face. Designer shirt, designer tie, designer watch, and, although I can't see them, designer shoes. He could work on Wall Street by day and be a hired mercenary at night.

His lips curve like he scored a point on his phone.

Only two places are set at the table. So I won't be facing his father's inquisition.

Disappointment mixes with relief.

"Is that what you typically wear?" Sandro doesn't look up from his game. "My godfather likes leg."

Isn't Don Lucchese eighty-something years old? I look to the left, and then to the right, then ask innocently, "Do you see him?"

He scowls. "You can kiss this arrangement and your father goodbye if you don't impress him."

It takes great willpower, but I remain silent.

I'm marrying Alessandro Beneventi.

And he *hates* me.

"Fucking hell." He tosses his phone on the table so he can shoot daggers at me without distraction. "I'm stuck with a prim thing like you? Even your sister would've made a better match, been more *entertaining.*"

His words hit a nerve. Another condescending jerk comparing me to my sister? How dare he. My self-control crumbles. "You're nothing like Renzo. He's considerate and caring."

I press my lips together.

"And a pain whore searching for his next fix."

"He's your brother."

"He's weak. You spend five minutes together and think you can fix him? Well, you can't. The things he's seen, the things he's done, his hurt runs so deep, there's no digging him out."

Shadows dull his blue eyes. Is he speaking about Renzo or himself?

"Weak attracts weak. I shouldn't be surprised you found each other."

I stiffen. "You don't know me very well."

His eyes skim over me. "Not much to know."

What. An. Asshole. "So Renzo's weak, and you are what? Important?" I snicker. "News flash: Sebastiano Beneventi is the only man worthy of everyone's fear."

Sandro flinches.

God, why am I exchanging barbs with him?

Disengage. Immediately.

Except, it's too late.

His fist slams on the table, upsetting two dishes and the pitcher of lemonade. "Speak to me like that again, and I'll make you suffer."

"As opposed to the great joy and happiness you'll bring to my life?"

He's on his feet and charging around the table before I can escape. Grabbing my chair, he spins me around, and then gets in my face.

"Renzo's gone. It's you and me. So listen the fuck up if you have any sense of self-preservation. My men located your sister in Kyoto."

"What?" I cry out.

His smile's pure evil. "I found her, now what to do with her?"

"Do with her? Nothing. I agreed—"

"We're not married yet. Hell, we're not even engaged, not until Don Lucchese meets you." He leans in a fraction of an inch, then hisses, "Fear me now?"

"Don't hurt her."

He withdraws and then, ever so calmly, finds his seat. "I won't be humiliated, disrespected, or disobeyed. Capisci?"

I nod. Until now, I never considered Sandro's feelings. How mortified he must have felt when Bastian showed us that video. How frustrated he must be at being ordered to wed first Sienna, and then me.

"You'll pretend to love me while we act like the perfect couple. I give the orders, you obey. I say jump, your feet better be in the air. I want you to sit on my lap, you hop on. I kiss you, you kiss me back and pretend I'm the man of your goddamn dreams. I want your undivided attention. Eyes on me, and only me, and at all times. Then, we'll see."

"And your father?"

Sandro gestures for a server to clean up his mess. "What about him?"

"What are his expectations?"

"Expectations." He rubs his fingers across his chin and contemplates my question. "He has rules, not expectations. Rule number one: embarrass him in front of Don Lucchese, and he'll kill you."

I shudder. "And after we wed?"

"After?" Sandro sneers. "You fade back into the woodwork, and I live my life."

He makes it sound horrible.

Except the woodwork—particularly Italian woodwork—is exactly where I'd love to hide.

Bastian

"LOOK AT THEM." Don Lucchese pulls his chair in close and throws an arm around my shoulders, grinning like a romantic fool. "Sandro è pazzo di lei."

We're seated around a table on the veranda and ready to feast on the elaborate meal Nonna has prepared. The party has gone off without incident. I'll make the formal announcement after we eat, then the old man can bless the union.

The happy couple sits a few feet away. Sandro runs kisses across the little deviant's lips as if he's crazy in love. Touching her—on the back, thigh, breast—like he can't wait to bed her. As if the coldhearted prick within him is on vacation. Little Alessia plays along, a persistent flush warming her cheeks. Her innocence is like a drug. Like the finest whiskey—though no one expects the mind-blowing kick beneath the initial sips until half a bottle in.

She's sexy and sophisticated in a refreshing way. Blond hair swept up into a knot with a few locks hanging free. Short black dress showing off long legs. A classy pearl necklace setting off her pretty face. Makeup subtle, allowing her natural beauty to shine through. Fuck-me high heels drawing attention back to her shapely legs. I couldn't have found a more perfect bride.

Her eyes dart my way, sensing my perusal, before shifting elsewhere.

Subtle glances. Just like Sandro's.

Confirming this is for show—that they're both full of shit.

Still, Don Lucchese eats it up.

The old man's pleased with everything I've proposed. Dante will oversee the Atlanta expansion on my behalf while I focus on New York. And bringing a puppet like Amato into the family definitely has a few side perks.

"I reran the numbers." I flash a smile. "With the new tax incentive legislation Governor Amato passed to lure new businesses to New York City, our expansion into Brooklyn presents a more profitable income stream than even Atlanta."

"New tax incentives?" Delighted, Don Lucchese thumps his fist on the table. Drinks spill as everyone jumps. "Brilliant move. Amato's certainly proving his worth."

The good governor, hearing his name, pauses his conversation. I've placed the shady figlio di puttana at the opposite end, far away from Don Lucchese. His role today is to look pretty while puckering up and kissing my ass. Putting his mouth to a better use than sharing my secrets. For the most part, I ignore him.

Interestingly enough, so does his daughter.

"Speaking of famiglia, where's my favorite godson?"

I anticipated this question and decided the best lies are often sprinkled with truth. "Away nursing a broken heart."

"And missing his brother's announcement?"

I meet his eyes. "Seems Renzo developed a fascination with Sandro's bride. Time away will help him get over it."

Madonna mia. I should take my own advice. But how can I erase the memory of Little Miss Not-So-Innocent coming so hard, she fucking fainted? With rocket-like speed and from one fat finger. So responsive. So eager. Her eyes would roll into the back of her head if she rode my cock. She'd pass out cold while her juices run wild all over my hard dick. My name her last gasp before blacking out from pleasure.

"I see," Don Lucchese says, studying me thoughtfully.

I hope the old buzzard needs cataract surgery, and that my poker face is in place. What I need is a party of a different sort, one where I can unleash this pent-up tension I've been experiencing ever since little Alessia spread her thighs on my desk.

"I'd like to offer Luca Ricci a cut from New York." I change the subject to something that surprises the old man.

"Why do that?"

"Politics." Luca Ricci is my strongest ally. Tossing him a bone will keep him well-fed and loyal. More importantly, it'll signal to the other capos why working for me, instead of against me, is a motherfucking profitable alliance.

He nods. "And offer Benny a small percent from the Atlanta casino. He took a hit from Conti's sports facilities shutting down. Two percent should quiet Benny down."

"One percent." Benny can choke on his measly percent. "I'll bump up Dante's cut with the difference."

No argument there.

Laughter rings out.

Our attention returns to the lovebirds.

Alessia, bouncing on my son's lap.

Sandro, feeding her motherfucking grapes.

My blood boils.

I wave to a server, who rushes over. "Tell Nonna we're ready for the main course."

Alessia

DEEP-SEATED satisfaction warms my spirits when Don Lucchese asks for a second serving of lamb, but the way Sebastiano Beneventi licks his lips and moans over each bite awakens every fiber of my being.

Lord, he's sexy when he eats. Head back and eyes closed as he chews. Devouring my dish with intense pleasure.

My effort's paid off.

Another time, another place, another engagement luncheon where I actually want to be a bride, and I'd bask in my success even more.

Sandro pinches my side, as if I need a reality check. "A little black dress," he scolds. "How predictable." He offers me a grape. "At least it's short like I asked."

I fake a laugh and turn my head. Resisting the urge to smash the offering into his despicable face.

His fingers squeeze my thigh.

"Stop touching me."

He shifts his hand higher.

"Message received," I hiss beneath my breath. "We're in love." I clamp my hand down on his. "You get off on torturing me." Not a question, but fact.

"I could do a lot worse."

I change tactics because our arguing isn't helping. "Can't we try to be friends?" I say it with sincerity. Proving my skill at lying is at an all-time high today.

He places a gentle kiss on my nose. "I don't do girl friend."

"Right." His expression changes, and I study him more closely. "You're serious."

No answer.

"Why not?"

He shifts beneath me, and I lose my perch, grabbing his shoulders to steady myself. "What I need in a woman is complete obedience," he softly replies. "Something beyond what you are capable of."

I've hit a nerve. What skeletons is he hiding? Knowing his brother —his father—there's likely closets full.

He leans forward for another kiss.

"Enough." I pitch sideways as Bastian's voice rings out. To his credit, Sandro wraps an arm around me and prevents my fall. "Bring Alessia over here. Don Lucchese wants a word."

"Don't. Fuck. This. Up," Sandro grinds out. Then, with a comical grin on his face, I'm lifted and set on my feet. He stands, snatches my hand, and pulls me along toward his father and godfather. He manages a final warning as we draw closer. "Don't address either unless spoken to."

My eyes skim over their empty plates before I focus on the two men standing a few feet from the table.

Don Lucchese moves first, and pulls me into a hug. I force myself to relax and swallow back my nervousness. "You're too pretty not to touch," the grandfatherly man proclaims. "Isn't that right, Bastian?"

I blush.

Bastian grunts.

Sandro remains mercifully oblivious. "Did you enjoy my fiancée's cooking, Godfather?"

Don Lucchese pulls back to look at me. "It was perfection. If any remained, I'd request you freeze the leftovers for me to take home."

"If you have a sweet tooth," I offer with a shy smile, "I'll bake a special treat for you instead."

The old man's eyes light up with delight.

I avoid eye contact with Bastian. But Sandro's smug grin says he's pleased with this exchange.

"Bastian, your boy ready to begin earning?"

"He's twenty-three. There's time."

"What? And go against the Beneventi way?" Don Lucchese leans toward me like he's about to share a secret. "When Bastian was eighteen, he arrived at my Tuscan vineyard with the twins. Pretended to like my wine while he conned me into approving the Beneventi holdings. Bold as brass, even at eighteen, and always three steps ahead of everyone else."

"I liked your wine well enough," Bastian quips.

"You drink whiskey like it's water. What would you know about good wine?" Don Lucchese chuckles. "Now women …"

I flinch.

Bastian speaks, saving me. "Once Sandro's engaged, I'll find appropriate work for him."

Sandro's response is swift. "I'd like to run New York."

"New York?" Don Lucchese exclaims.

"*Once* I'm engaged …"

Oh sweet hell. Bastian's temper flares, his anger barely contained. If I sense it, so does Don Lucchese. Sandro's doing exactly what he warned me not to do—embarrass his father.

"Godfather," I interrupt in a soft voice. "I learned to cook in Rome."

For a heartbeat, Don Lucchese looks startled by how I addressed him. But then he nods. "È vero?"

"Sì, è vero."

He grins. "You speak Italian."

"Yes." My throat tightens. "It was my life's dream to study in Italy."

His chest swells with pride, like I've offered him a surprise gift.

"If only our paths could have crossed. See, my son, Dante, is over there." He gestures toward the man seated next to his vacant chair, who looks like a model and holds his audience captive like a Hollywood movie star. I understand the handsome man's appeal. Yet I'm not drawn to him like … My eyes dart to a scowling Bastian, then away.

"Very handsome," Don Lucchese continues. "Very Italian. He'd have made you very happy."

My cheeks warm. *Happy, I bet.*

"Now Sandro will make her very *fucking* happy."

The air charges, like it does during a lightning strike. It happens so fast, and then it's gone. But I can't help wondering if the thought of me being very fucking happy with either man displeases Bastian.

"With your blessing," Bastian adds, with less bite and the slightest hint of sarcasm, "of course."

Don Lucchese smirks. The sly old man. Pissing everyone off is the game, isn't it?

"How old are you, cara?"

Bastian responds before I can. "She's almost a fucking teenager."

"I'm twenty," I clarify. "A few years younger than Renzo and Sandro."

"Do you like older men?"

He can't *know*. I haven't engaged my soon-to-be father-in-law at all during the party. Heck, I've done my best *not* to think about him. But if this isn't directed at me, then who?

Sandro chuckles.

Bastian curses. "Cristo."

I feel dizzy.

"Answer him," Sandro pushes.

My eyes flicker to Bastian. I feel the tug, the undercurrent beneath the surface that's ready to swallow me up. It's alive and well, and unfortunate.

Please, Lord, don't let me ruin this.

"I truly like you." I lightly touch Don Lucchese on the sleeve. "But aren't you a bit too old for me?"

Everyone stills. Oh no. Did I insult the old man?

Laughter erupts, and he thumps a hand on his knee. "I like your young fiancée, Sandro. She cooks like an Italian grandma but has a youthfulness about her." He steps toward Bastian and throws an arm around his shoulders. "It's time to make a toast. I'll give this union my full blessing."

Sandro forces a smile.

My eyes dart to his father.

Who should be pleased. He's gotten what he wants, right?

Yet something simmers with his blue eyes that says otherwise.

IT'S A QUIET EVENING. The luncheon ended a few hours ago, and guests departed well-fed and in good spirits. My father gave me a hug and then—without even an "Are you okay?"—left in a limousine.

A hand-picked few are spending a night on the town. I overheard the guards say the Beneventi men were taking the old man club-hopping to celebrate the engagement. A bachelor party—before the wedding date's even been set.

I've been relegated to the woodwork, a hint of how life will become.

A blessing, right? So why do I feel sullen? Why wish for the slightest acknowledgment, the slightest praise, from a man more ambitious than my father?

This is a gift. Make what you can of it.

Nonna's been too busy for me to ask if she'd approach Bastian, on my behalf, about college. I'll insist my father pay tuition. It's the least my father can do.

My phone vibrates, and I frown. It's nearly midnight. I race toward the island to answer it. "Sienna?"

"Thank God you picked up before I'm spotted."

"Renzo?" I gasp.

"Lessie, I'm so sorry how things went down." His voice is strained, panicked. "How are you doing?"

"I'm fine. Are you okay?" I demand, suddenly worried.

"No. I'm sober as fuck when I'd rather be high."

My eyebrows form a deep *V*. "Then rehab is good for you."

He snorts. "It's overpriced and overrated, smells like a hospital, and is run by an ex-Marine."

"So, it's paradise?"

He chuckles, and I relax. Honestly, I'm thrilled he called.

"When's the announcement?"

"It was today."

"Today?" He sounds disappointed.

"And Don Lucchese blessed the union."

"My godfather flew to Rhode Island?" Renzo's as surprised as everyone else, except Bastian.

"Yes."

"My father must be thrilled."

I smile, still pleased with myself. "He is."

"And Sandro? He being a dick?"

"With a capital *D*." I sigh. "Though he's backed off now that Don Lucchese's taken a liking to me." Yeah, it was a good day. I might yet turn this horrible situation into one I can navigate.

"Of course he liked you." In the background, he shuffles about, and then out of breath, he resumes our conversation. "And is everything else okay? Is my father behaving?"

I cough. Do. Not. Think. About. Bastian. *Misbehaving*. I quickly recover. "Define behaving."

"You, living unprotected beneath his roof—"

"Didn't Zoey tell you?" I interrupt. "I'm staying in the casita."

"The casita?" His reaction's similar to Zoey's. Why is this news surprising?

"Stay away from him, okay?"

"That's the plan." And, if tonight's any indication, a plan I'll have little trouble implementing.

"Shit," he curses. "They're coming ..."

"Who?" An uneasiness sweeps over me.

"Sergeant Dickwad and his men ... Quick, before I need to hang up. Get my passport from the bedside table and stuff a bag with my shit. As soon as I escape, I'll come for you."

"Wait ... no ..."

"We'll elope."

"Please. Don't go against your father's wishes. Stay in rehab. I'll be okay."

"You want to marry my asshole twin?"

"No," I blurt.

"Look. I got you into this mess ..."

"Don't worry about me. Focus on getting clean."

He whispers. "Always an angel, aren't you?"

No. Not always. But I don't ... can't ... explain it to him.

"Back the fuck up." I freeze at Renzo's shout. "Or I'll—"

The call disconnects.

My hand shakes.

It's wrong. It's disloyal. It's for his own good. But I pray Sergeant Dickwad can keep Renzo in rehab. If he intends to save me, he'll need to save himself first.

Bastian

"THE BALLS ON YOU, BASTIAN," Don Lucchese admonishes. "A golf course?"

We're at the first hole, half-drunk from last night's festivities and from our new money-making opportunities. I'm feeling like a fucking king, with Don Lucchese about to hand over the kingdom. Only Sandro and Alessia remain disengaged from the celebration.

I've paired them up. Governor Amato is partnered with Don Lucchese. And Dante with me.

"When I'm not thieving, murdering, or whoring, I like a round of golf." Out of the corner of my eye, I see Alessia stiffen. The whiskey-charged devil inside me reacts. "Or corrupting innocents."

Her club wavers in the air, my words hitting their mark. Arms raised, she's about to tee off, and I've ruined it.

I smirk. If I'm not careful, reminding her about my finger in her tight cunt will become my next guilty pleasure. Good thing I like experienced partners and don't do kinky little virgins.

"Keep your arm close to your body, or your drive will be weak." Sandro tosses his hands in the air. "Why'd I get partnered with a woman."

Dante responds. "She's your fiancée, asshole."

My lips draw tight. "Sandro, grab us some beers from my cart, will you?"

It's not a question. His eyes widen, as do everyone else's.

Don Lucchese snorts. "It's ten a.m."

"And four o'clock in Tuscany."

Still, Sandro hesitates.

Our eyes lock, before he stalks off to do my bidding. Fuck. I better throw him a big fat bone, or he'll ruin everything.

"Fore please," Alessia repeats, her words laced with anger. Surprised, our attention falls on her as she swings.

A deafening silence spreads over the group. Even her father—who runs his mouth more than a greedy politician at a fundraising event—shuts up long enough to witness her ball sailing through the air and then landing perfectly in line for her next drive.

Figo—fucking fantastic.

"Goddamn," Dante comments. "Did you see that?"

Don Lucchese claps his hand before hurrying toward Alessia. "Beautiful, honey. Where'd you learn to swing like that?"

"Renzo taught me how to position my body."

"I bet he did," Dante murmurs beside me.

I elbow him in the ribs and he stumbles sideways.

Alessia approaches, her eyes darting to me. Like she's searching for my approval.

"You're good."

Her lips curve.

My dick stirs.

"I'll order new clubs sized better for your height and body type."

She stares at me like I've offered her the world. So responsive. So naive to the man I am, and the man I'll never be. "Consider it a wedding present."

Her smile drops.

Sandro smacks a cold beer into my chest. "Is there anything else I can do for anyone?"

"I'll take a beer, baby."

Sandro spins on Alessia. "Don't you fucking 'baby' me. And it's too early—"

"I've a toast," I grind out, interrupting the scene.

The little shit stiffens.

"Pass Don Lucchese a beer."

"Bring me a six-pack instead, son." Don Lucchese gestures to Sandro.

"Isn't he in his eighties?" Governor Amato chimes in.

Everyone pauses to glare at his blatant disrespect. Sandro brushes Governor Amato hard in the shoulder as he returns to the cart to fulfill his godfather's request.

"Speak out of turn again, Governor, " I calmly say, "and I'll club you over the head and bury you beneath the tee."

Amato blanches, message received.

Don Lucchese nods.

As for me, I'm done with fucking about on the golf course. It's Renzo's game, anyway.

And now Alessia's.

Sandro returns, every move heavy with anger. I wait for bottles to be passed around, before raising mine in the air.

"To new streams of revenue."

Everyone drinks, even Alessia. The way she's conducting herself pleases me.

"To Atlanta, and its new boss, Dante Lucchese."

Dante taps my bottle with his as Sandro drills new holes for the golf course with his eyes.

It's time for the little shit to prove his worth.

"I'm turning over complete control of the Riverview Casino to my son, Alessandro Beneventi." I stalk over to my stunned son and thump him on the back. "Pack your shit. You're moving to New York."

Madonna mia. Those better not be tears.

"Thank you, Father."

I nod. He can thank me by not fucking up.

"Alessia," her father exclaims. "You're coming home."

She flinches.

His insincerity pisses me off. I'll never win Father-of-the-Year, but this stronzo takes selfishness to a different level.

"No." My decision's immediate.

Fortunately, everyone except the Amatos are so caught up in celebrating the news that they miss my final words.

"Alessia stays here."

20

Bastian

THE TASTE of blood on my lip invigorates me. I lean into my opponent and, with a quick uppercut, send him flying backward.

"Fuck, it's on," Freido says.

The man grunts. Any fresh blood who walks in here always believes they'll swagger out. Part of the fun is allowing them to believe so, until the urge for violence takes hold.

Everything I hoped for is coming to fruition. Sure, I'll miss Don Lucchese when he's gone. He's been more of a father to me than my own. A role model. A mentor. Not that I trust him—the day that happens is the day I might lose everything. But right now, I'm sitting pretty and smelling goddamn roses.

Two weeks have passed since his departure. Dante's settled in Atlanta, and Sandro in New York. Dante likes to report to me in person, and Sandro's a motherfucking ghost.

Permits are approved. General contractors and construction crews are in place. Ground will break shortly in both cities. My patience is paying off.

My opponent lunges, and then swings.

I shoot my arm out straight and smash his ugly mug.

"Another knockout," Freido exclaims.

I shrug. In one way or another, I've been fighting my entire life. It's either win or lose—go fucking big or go home. I work hard to win. And I'm in my prime right now.

My men rush forward and carry the man away.

I unwind the blood-soaked gauze around my hands and toss it in the trash before drinking from a water bottle.

Freido waits until I'm finished. "Dante asked me to tell you Conti's been running his mouth."

"Of course he is."

"He flew to St. Louis to meet with Roberto Ferrara."

I flex my jaw. Ferrara's smart. But a phone call will reinforce the need to remain so. "Anything else?"

Freido clears his throat.

My eyebrows dip. "What is it?"

"Renzo. He nearly escaped the facility."

Ma va'! "I thought I said he's to be guarded at all times?"

"He is, sir. But Renzo's ... um ... creative."

My fists clench, and I immediately regret knocking out my opponent so quickly.

"Send two of our men. Make sure they understand my expectations."

Freido nods.

God, I need a shower, a drink, and a good cock-sucking. I cross the grounds and head back to the house, thumbing through the contacts on my phone for a throat skilled enough to take me deep.

Movement at the corner of my eye catches my attention.

Alessia.

In the garden.

Holding a basket filled with fresh-picked vegetables like she's Little Red Riding Hood.

She stares.

I keep walking. Because if I don't, there's no telling what this big fucking wolf might do.

NONNA CLUCKS her tongue as the kitchen door slams shut behind the three women who just left. Hair mashed, faces flushed, short skirts wrinkled, and wearing satisfied expressions I envy.

Four o'clocks are torturous.

It's Sebastiano Beneventi's *switching* hour, more like him switching a flogger across the trio's bottoms and less like him switching up the body count.

He's totally shameless.

I should be horrified, not disheartened—and on so many levels.

It's been over three weeks since the announcement. Has Bastian rubbed elbows with me, inquired after my well-being, or even acknowledged in any way, shape, or form my existence? Niente—nothing. My important role as blushing bride faded with Don Lucchese and Sandro's departure. What's worse is I've tried to catch his attention—why else would I help Nonna prepare dinner every day and subject myself to his four-o'clock delights if not without the hope of a chance encounter?

I assure myself this is because of school, or that I'm lonely or that I must get Zoey off the Beneventi banned-for-life list if I want her to come over.

But the truth is I'm playing a dangerously twisted game. I've shelved shyness for boldness, positioning myself in his path with the hope he'll notice me. It's exhilarating, and stupid. Risky, and disturbing. Inexplicable behavior, period. But I can't help myself. I crave even the slightest glance.

Except he hasn't given me the time of day.

Too busy. Too preoccupied entertaining a trio of kinksters willingly submitting to his every command.

Nonna shakes her head. Acknowledgment of my disappoint-ment? Or warning me my obsession with her boss can only lead to trouble? Without elaborating, she returns to stirring the sauce on the stovetop.

Someone behind me clears his throat.

My heart skips a beat as I spin in his direction, and then it drops like a containership anchor.

Freido.

"Adesso ha tempo per te," he says. He has time for you.

A nervous excitement rumbles through me until every inch of me quakes. "He'll see *me* now?" I'm flushed, and panicked. That's the harsh truth about reality: it can feel like a slap in the face. I craved his attention, but now that the opportunity's presented itself ...

Nonna sneaks up on me, then thrusts her sauce spoon at me. "Non far bruciare la mia salsa."

I blink, slowly processing what she's saying.

Don't let my sauce burn.

He wants to speak to Nonna, not me.

Disappointment rolls through me. Sebastiano Beneventi isn't interested in foolish girls. Why would he be, when he has a trio of eager women to entertain him?

With a sigh, I return to Nonna's place at the stove to watch over the sauce. Knowing I still need to speak to him about school. The sooner I do so, the sooner I can occupy my time thinking about beautiful things rather than obsessing over my future father-in-law.

21

Bastian

DAYS BEFORE HE WAS MURDERED, my old man offered me advice. "Soften your enemies with kindness so they'll have something to compare your punishments to." It's laughable in retrospect, considering his type of kindness was a punishment. Want to attend business school? Great. Pay for it by making our fraudulent scratch ticket scheme profitable. Think you can fill my shoes as the next Beneventi capo? Prove it by shooting this cheating stronzo in the head.

A dishonest card player or not, the man was a family friend, a guy who gave me chocolates as a kid.

I flick ash from my cigar into the ashtray perched on the tub and, with the same hand, raise my whiskey glass high. *To the mean bastard, may the devil deliver your brand of kindness.*

My father would be pissing buckets if he could see me now.

Expensive whiskey. Cuban cigars. A bubble bath scented with my personal favorite blend of leather and spice. Money—and more to come. Life is fucking good. I've achieved more than he imagined he ever could.

"I'll talk to Roberto Ferrara and inquire about Emilio Conti's visit," Luca Ricci says over speakerphone.

"Ask if Ferrara's keen on partially financing our expansion into the Ohio Valley." I pop a bubble with the tip of my cigar. "And what percent might inspire him to work with us." Despite a tense history and years dealing with Renzo's mistake, tossing Ferrara a bone can't hurt. Four percent should do it—let's see what he comes at me with.

Luca chuckles. "You certainly know how to warm a man's heart."

"Heart, and bank account."

"But, on a serious note, you plan on shutting Conti up permanently?"

I shift, causing water to splash over the side of the tub. "Let him talk. Benny's more of a threat, but I've eyes on him."

"Don't we all," Luca adds.

A guard appears at the door.

"Hold on," I tell Luca before waving the man forward. "What is it?"

"Alessia would like to speak to you."

I take a drag of my cigar, then blow out a smoke ring. The kinky little voyeur gets off on watching me, though come to think of it, I haven't seen her in several days.

"She insists."

Does she now? "Show her upstairs." I return to the business at hand. "What's the word on Seattle?" The low-ranking capo in the Pacific Northwest died last month without an heir. Leaving the region ripe for takeover.

"There's a nephew," Luca says with disgust. "A piece of shit street gangster who's stepping up."

"Sounds personal."

Silence. Oh, fuck. It is. *Interesting.* I pop a bubble that formed on my nipple.

He changes the subject. "When's the wedding?"

My shrug sends a wave rippling across the surface.

"Are you in the pool?"

"Something like that." I stub out my cigar in the ashtray, spilling the whiskey I'm holding in the same hand. "No wedding date yet. Sandro's busy with New York. Besides, there's no rush."

"Says the man who never commits to any woman."

"Why commit to one when I can be entertained by three?"

A gasp echoes across the bathroom tile.

Little eavesdropper. Like she isn't aware of the kinky shit I enjoy. Like she isn't at all curious what a man like me could do to an eager kinkster like her.

"I'm expecting an invite to the wedding," Luca reminds me.

"Of course." I smirk. "And I'm expecting a thick envelope as a wedding gift."

He chuckles.

"Gotta go. Call me after you speak to Ferrara."

Water splashes everywhere as I stand and then tap the cell perched on the stool beside the tub, disconnecting the call.

Her muffled choke fills the air. Like someone stuffed a fat cock down her tight throat and she's struggling to handle it.

I turn. Her eyes bore holes into the Venetian tile. Her cheeks are so red, they could set the bathroom on fire.

"You wanted to *see* me?"

My cock stirs at her embarrassment.

"Come here."

She squeaks yet shuffles forward. So young. So submissive.

It'd take little effort to pull her into the tub with me, and have her ride my cock while I finish a fresh cigar.

Except I don't do virgins.

Especially Sandro's virgin.

She can get off on spying on me all she wants but fucking her six ways to Sunday with my tongue or finger, toys or cock isn't going to happen.

A lesson Alessia best learn quickly.

She hovers before me, eyes downcast.

I pick up the loofah, intent on scaring her away. Her trembling lip suggests it shouldn't take much.

"Wash my body with this sponge while you share what was so goddamn important that you interrupted my bath."

I give her five seconds, at best.

One.

"I didn't realize ..."

Two.

Three.

Slowly, ever so fucking slowly, she drags her eyes upward, from the water pooled at my feet to my thick thighs, pausing briefly at my rock-hard erection before darting up and across my wet abs, chest, and face.

Madonna mia. She eye-fucked me so hard, I forgot what number I was on.

And it's in this moment, as she plucks the loofah from my hand, that I realize I underestimated the eager little Lolita.

Alessia

HE'S TESTING ME.

By teasing me.

And although this realization infuriates me—so much so I do the opposite of what every warning bell insists I do ... flee ... and snatch the loofah from his hand—I'm still hyperfocused on his gorgeously ungodly body.

He's nicknamed the Bull for a reason.

I'm not one for cursing, but holy shit. His cock is massive. Porn-star worthy.

He could root me into place with that thing. Bounce me up and down like a rag doll while licking away my whiskey-drop tears. A big bull like him would destroy me.

Ruin me in every imaginable way, and in more ways than even I can imagine.

I swallow hard. How does a violent image like this excite me so much?

His brow furrows, because Lord knows what's crossed my face.

We stand here. Him gloriously naked and dripping water on the tile. Me clasping the only thing separating us—the loofah.

He's shameless.

Yet evidently, so am I.

His grunt interrupts the intense moment, and then, without a care for who's watching or the mess he's causing, he climbs back into the tub. It takes a few more seconds for him to settle and a few more for me to catch my breath.

"You can begin with my back," he informs me in a flat tone. As if anything about this exchange is normal.

For him, perhaps it is.

The trio from a few days ago are fresh in my mind. Not that I noticed. Not that I care.

I plunge the sponge deep into the tub, and water splashes everywhere.

A bubble bath. Seriously?

And this bath is scented ... with leather and cardamon. Very male. Very mafia-chic.

"You waiting for the water to get cold?"

I smack the sponge between his shoulder blades and he laughs. Deep and sexy, like everything else about him. Swallowing hard, I begin tracing circles across his upper back.

With a sigh, he relaxes.

This pleases him, and my anger fades.

Touching him like this is the second most intimate act in my life, though nowhere close to his finger-fuck. A shiver runs through me at the memory of his hand between my parted thighs.

I bite my lip, my rational side forming a list of the ways this is wrong. Dangerous mafioso boss and soon-to-be father-in-law are tied at number one. Except my irrational side has me leaning in to wash his back.

Faded white scars crisscross his tan skin. Most are thinly lined, but a few angrier scars are raised. Did someone branded him with an X? I draw the loofah over the letter, as though the soapy water combined with the slightest friction will erase his scars.

"Lower."

I dip the loofah lower. What caused these scars? A control freak like Bastian enjoys dominating others, whether it be for business or pleasure. He's kinky as hell but definitely not the kind of man who'd self-mutilate. Most likely, an enemy did this? A rival mafioso, who whipped him hard enough to break skin? The temptation to ask is on my lips, but his low hum of pleasure stops me.

I draw a bubbly trail along his spine. Feeling his muscles flex beneath my touch. Enjoying the dips and valleys that lie between. It's so incredibly wrong how much I'm enjoying this.

Taking care of him.

Pleasing him.

Like I'm stealing a moment, a guilty pleasure that will fade into a memory once I marry his son. But I don't stop ... I can't. I'll scrub his back, yet I'll never wash away our dirty secrets.

Time stills, and silence settles between us. My heart flutters with his every move, my breath catching on his every hum.

"What did you need to speak to me about?" he gruffly asks, the interruption reverberating around the room.

"School," I quietly reply. "I want your permission to finish my degree online."

"A degree. In what?"

My spine straightens. "Art history."

Without warning, he emerges from the bath.

I gasp. Even his perfectly shaped ass is muscled.

He turns and sinks back into the water.

My cheeks heat. He enjoys flaunting his masculinity, doesn't he?

But then if I had a cock that size when limp and a crazy art history major bathing me on a whim, I would too.

I'm tired of defending my major. No matter how beautiful and enlightening, twisted and depraved, or shy yet adventurous, art reflects true humanity. It validates the lightness and darkness, and all the shades of grey between. It reminds me I'm not the only person with a beautifully warped and dirty mindset.

"You study the sick fuck who cut off his ear, and then mailed it to his brother?"

The loofah escapes my grasp and tumbles into the water. Wait, he's interested? "Van Gogh?" I exclaim. "Yes. I studied him briefly. But I prefer the work of Italian artists, like Caravaggio and Botticelli."

"Leonardo di Vinci."

"Yes." I blink in surprise. Not because he named off arguably the most important artist in history but that he named a Renaissance artist, which is my area of expertise. "And Michelangelo."

He leans back, places his arms on the tub rim, and cocks a knee.

My throat goes dry. When the bathwater stills, I'll see his cock. Someone should sculpt this brazen beast. Part man, part bull.

Lord have mercy.

His lips curl, as if he's daring me to look.

Nope. Not while you're watching me so closely.

After a long minute, he switches up the game. "I'd like another cigar." He nods to the box on the stool beside the tub. A half-empty whiskey canister, his cell phone, and an ashtray containing a cigar stub are beside it. I quickly do his bidding, withdrawing a fresh cigar and leaning over to hand it to him.

"Stand at the foot of the tub, put it between your lips, and light it for me. The lighter is on the floor."

Speechless, I do as he asks, retrieving the lighter before facing him, the cigar pinched between my lips. Not a smoker, it takes me three tries to light it. I offer him the cigar, but he shakes his head. "First, I want to watch you smoke it."

Confused, I resume my position at the foot of the tub, and scissoring my fingers around the cigar, slide the tip between my lips.

"Good girl."

His praise rolls over me like a warm blanket.

"Art history, huh?"

I nod.

"My father took me to Rome when I was ten," he tells me. "I killed time inside a chapel while he surprised a few enemies. I always remember what a contradiction it was, me inside a church and him as close to hell as any man gets."

I inhale, then cough as cigar smoke burns my lungs.

"Look at me as you suck in your next hit."

Our eyes lock.

I draw in the smoke in a slow, controlled inhalation.

His nostrils flare as he softly curses, "Cazzo."

I softly smile, and he immediately reacts, shifting, bending his other leg, and bringing both knees out of the water.

I choke so hard my eyes water.

Now his lips are curling. "Give it here."

I approach the side of the tub and hand it to him, an explanation on my lips. Because we're connecting and I don't want to disappoint him. "I never smoked before."

"Not even pot?"

I shake my head.

"Haven't experienced a lot of things, have you?"

"No."

He offers me a lopsided grin, and my pulse kicks up in response. "Like the angel sculpture inside that Roman chapel. So innocent. So pure. So about to get fucked by Cupid's arrow."

My jaw drops.

"Do you know it? The sculpture's called *Ecstasy of Saint Teresa?*"

Know it? "She's inside the Santa Maria della Vittoria chapel," I exclaim. "I spent a lot of time there studying the Baroque masterpiece. She's in a state of religious rapture. The sculptor is infamous for his highly sensual depictions of everyday people becoming over-wrought by faith." I pause, then add, "And the arrow's pointed at her heart."

"Debatable." He soaks the loofah in the water before dragging it across his chest, from one nipple to the other. As if coating his chest with bubbles is the most natural thing in the world.

I fight back a groan, and then force my attention toward the unexpected twist in conversation. Sebastiano Beneventi is interested in Italian art? "Gian Bernini is the sculptor," I say, testing to see how much he actually knows.

"Gian Lorenzo Bernini."

"Wait ... Lorenzo?"

"I named the little shit after the artist."

In life, there are monumental moments where your world shifts unexpectedly. Mama's death. Daddy Dearest's abandonment. My engagement to Sandro. Sometimes, though, instead of knocking you off-balance, it deepens the connection. This is that moment. I can't believe it. Sebastiano Beneventi named his son after an Italian masterpiece. If Saint Teresa was enraptured by God, this man has me thunderstruck.

And his smirk says he knows it.

"And Sandro?" I clasp my hands, needing to know.

"When I was younger, I thought Venus naked on that clamshell was the hottest fucking thing I'd ever seen."

I exclaim, "*The Birth of Venus*."

"Painted by Alessandro Botticelli."

Oh my God. Both twins are named after Italian artists.

"I paid a lot of fucking money and bribed a few people to have their names legally changed after the paternity test came back positive. My old man was livid—thought it was a sign I'd be distracted by them. He had his mind set on taking them away because of it." He takes a long drag of his cigar, then blows rings into the air, as I quietly contemplate the rare glimpse of emotion in his expression.

It pains me that Renzo's childhood was so difficult and that Bastian's early days as a father were so harsh. At the same time, I'm thrilled with how he's confided in me. I get the feeling few people are allowed into his world, and fewer still privy to his private struggles.

Our eyes lock. And just like that, the game we're playing morphs into something deeper.

His brows dip into a deep *V*, and a chill sweeps through the air. He regrets opening up. He's seconds from shattering this fragile connection.

I blurt out something, anything, to lighten the mood. "Is he really buried near the ninth hole?"

I'm immediately horrified. Why ask such a morbid question?

His eyes grow wide, and then he bursts into laughter. It reverberates from his stomach, and comes out of him as a sexy rumble. "Did Renzo tell you that?" he asks between gasps.

I shake my head.

"I caught the little shit out there digging with a plastic shovel like he was searching for dinosaur bones." Another rumble escapes him as it suddenly dawns on me. It's easy to see how Sandro's serious personality comes from his father. But what's less obvious yet ten times more enlightening is his influence on Renzo's. Is this the reason I'm enraptured by Bastian? The heady combination of "do I dare?" and "I don't mind if I do?"

"Make a list of supplies for school."

"Okay," I quickly reply.

"Give it to Freido along with the registrar information."

I shake my head. "My father will pay my tuition—it's the least he can do."

"Like fuck he will."

I stare at him. Bubbles cling to his broad chest. Five-o'clock shadow dusts his jawline. Wet curls hang around his face. He's as naked as the day he was born, sex on legs, and names his twins after Italian artists.

"Eyes up here."

I gasp, caught red-handed.

"Mac or PC?"

My eyes widen. "Mac."

"You'll have one by tomorrow."

"Thank you," I murmur. "Um ..." Go on. Ask him. If financing college was this easy ...

"I'd like to invite a friend over."

"No unvetted visitors. You understand why."

"She's ... vetted."

His eyebrows knot. "Who?"

"Her father works for you. Her name's Zoey."

"The arsonist?"

I'm taken aback. But Sebastiano Beneventi is running this kingdom, so not much escapes his notice.

"Zoey Mangioni?"

"Yes."

He shakes his head no.

I frown. Can I have a little more Renzo without any Sandro, please? "It was an accident."

"Is that what she told you? You can't be that stupid."

Stupid? I stiffen. What. A. Jerk. "A vaping canister—"

"You'd like to hang out with a girl who has no gag reflex and who's deep throated every man on the estate?"

I'm horrified. "Every man?"

You?

Hurt, betrayal, anger collide. I'm not stupid, but I am naive. So freaking naive. I'm a toy he's decided to play with while the other toys are ... recovering. Pull me in. Twist my emotions. Seduce me with his body and his words. Fire me up. Then snuff me out like a used cigar.

I back away.

"Ma va'! You can invite her over, be my guest."

"Thank you," I practically growl.

"You can leave the estate if you take a guard. Go shopping or to dinner, and shit. No bars. No clubs. No street corners—especially if Zoey Mangioni is with you. Capisci?"

He's handing me my freedom. A friend. I should be thrilled.

"Answer me."

"I understand."

I hurry toward the door before my tears erupt and I completely humiliate myself.

"For the record," he shouts as I'm halfway down the hall, "only good girls blow me."

22

Alessia

IT TAKES three margaritas for me to ask Zoey the question that's plagued me all week. "Are you a good girl?"

We're sunbathing beside the pool, much like we've done every day, wearing new matching bikinis and margarita-fueled expressions.

Why not? It's four o'clock somewhere.

Except not at the Beneventi estate. My eyes may be deceiving me, but there's been no sign of his four o'clock snack. Either the trio has entered through the front door or aren't around. Fact is, I haven't seen them at all.

"Hell no." My friend emphatically answers. "How drunk are you?"

"Compared to you?" I wave my margarita in her direction. I rarely get drunk. Hangovers are too painful and a waste of time. But liquid courage was the only way I'd ask Zoey my question. "Only good girls blow me," Bastian had shouted. And Zoey's had alien sex, so who knows if her martian was good or bad, or even a girl. Still, Zoey answered with such an emphatic no ...Lord, why do I care who he hooks up with?

"Like on a scale from zero to ten," she continues. "If you say zero, I'll know you're plastered."

"And you've never blown the Bull?"

"What in the hell?" She jerks her head back. "Where's this

coming from? Did I blow the Bull?" Her voice raises. "Are you out of your mind?"

I tap my lips. "Shhh. The guards will hear."

"News flash, Alessia. They've seen the Bull. The man doesn't own bathing trunks. He swims naked."

My eyes widen. "You've seen his dick?"

"Everyone has."

Right. His brazen display in the bathroom was par for the course. He's barely glanced my way, and if I do catch him looking, a glare always follows. As if nothing transpired between us. He paid my tuition, permitted Zoey's visits, and allowed us to leave the estate to go shopping—then dismissed me.

"The answer's no." She takes a deep sip from her margarita glass. "I'm excellent at giving head and enjoy it. But the Bull is too much for even an expert like me."

I relax. Zoey has no filter. Like none, whatsoever. She overshares everything, and her boldness sometimes shocks me. Yet she's honest and unashamed of her sexuality. I couldn't have found a better friend to lean on.

"We should go clubbing."

I shake my head. "He won't allow it."

"Okay. Drinking. There's this sports bar downtown ..."

"No bars allowed."

"You're so damn obedient." She arches an eyebrow. "Are *you* a good girl?"

I wobble to my feet and stagger toward the pool. "I want to be. But I shouldn't be. I really, really shouldn't."

"What do you mean, you shouldn't?" she asks, but I dive into safer waters without answering her.

"HEY, SANDRO," Zoey hollers. "Looking fine in that suit."

I sink lower in my chaise as Sandro flashes her the finger and disappears into the main house.

He's home today for a big meeting. Mafiosi have been filtering into the mansion all day. Sandro arrived around nine o'clock without so much as a greeting. Offering me a taste of married life, though I'm struggling to decide if being ignored by him—and his father—deserves my bitterness or a celebration.

"Please don't antagonize him, or you'll be banned from the estate." After yesterday's animated discussion about Bastian's enormous bull, it's a wonder we're still permitted to hang out.

"He's such an asshole. Your first time shouldn't be with that selfish jerk." She glares at the direction Sandro disappeared in.

"Zoey, please. This isn't helping."

Hangovers should never be accompanied by loose tongues. Admitting I'm a virgin to Zoey is like handing her a blowtorch, and then telling her not to use it. She hasn't stopped and is now hyperfocused on "fixing" the problem.

"Gosh, me and big mouth. It's not like you have a *choice*."

I roll my eyes. "You're still doing it."

"I'll shut up now." Pause. "He sure is a shit fiancé."

It's true. I've had no interaction with Sandro.

"He looks relaxed. Probably has some poor woman tied up and waiting for him in New York."

"Zoey."

"Oh crap. Sorry." Pause. "Even if it's the truth."

I sigh. "He flipped you the bird. That's him being relaxed?"

Our eyes collide, and then we burst out laughing. How did I manage without her? We're wearing identical bikinis again. Red ones twice as skimpy as yesterday's. No one informed us a meeting was scheduled. But no one pays us any mind. Why would they when Bastian waits inside his office?

Several minutes pass.

Until Zoey slides right back into her topic of choice. "We'll sneak out and find someone suitable to stamp your V-Card."

Yep. Yesterday's margaritas are today's kiss of death. "'Stamp my V-Card?' What decade are we living in?"

Zoey falls somber. "It hurts the first time."

"So does childbirth, yet people continue having sex."

"It can't be Sandro. He'll cause you pain in ways you can't imagine."

But I can imagine it—though not with him. I silently curse the margaritas. "He hates me."

"He hates everyone. It's in his nature."

"Bastian isn't like that." I freeze. "I meant Renzo ..."

"You call Mr. Beneventi Bastian?"

I shrug, downplaying it. "Father-in-law. Mr. Beneventi ..."

"He lets you address him with a casual nickname only his closest friends use?"

Every fiber of my being stills.

"Holy shit, Alessia. Keep away from him. Sandro may hurt you, but Sebastiano Beneventi could kill you. Like, literally."

I understand her concern. But he offered me a glimpse at a different side of himself. A man who loves his sons. A man who'd defy his father to protect them. Family matters to him. And I'll be part of it.

Even if I'm on the periphery.

"I saw something when I was twelve that terrified me," she whisper-yells. Luckily, because of the mafioso visitors, the guards are spread out around the estate and aren't within earshot.

"Maybe it's best if you don't share ..."

"They hauled a man inside the grey shed off the driveway. It's where the lawn mower, snowblower, and landscaping tools are kept."

I hold up a hand. "Zoey, don't—"

"Remember how I lived here for a while? My parents were out of town one weekend, and I was sneaking back onto the estate. The guard at the main gate let me in, or I would have used the staff entrance. I was halfway across the front lawn toward the staffing quarters on the north end when I heard the Weedwacker start up."

"Stop. Don't."

"I didn't know it was the Weedwacker. If I did, I'd never have stolen a peek inside the shed." Her brows pull together as a shiver races up my spine. "Mr. Beneventi was covered in blood, and two fingers lay by his feet. The man was whimpering—saying things about Benny Manocchio, who is a big shot capo in the South."

I glance around nervously.

"I ran away when I realized what was happening. Sometimes I wonder if Mr. Beneventi saw me." She swallows. "But I'm still alive, so ..."

"Please," I whisper, my voice trembling. "Don't ever share this story with another person."

I knew this about him—I mean, he threatened my father, didn't he? Being here, on his estate and inside his casita, and living inside this bubble, it's easy to forget he's a ruthless and violent man. I'm lucky to be graced with a bit of freedom. To have earned his trust in some minute way. But I'm delusional to believe the man in the bubble bath wouldn't fire up the Weedwacker and dismember my body if I betray him.

Sebastiano Beneventi is the wrong man to lust over.

We both sit taller in our chaise lounges when mafiosi exit the kitchen door. The meeting must be over.

For a long while afterward, we doze in the hot sun. My head hurts. My heart hurts. And my obsession with Bastian might very well be what ends up hurting me the most.

23

Bastian

"WHY IS Zoey Mangioni hanging around with my fiancée?"

I glance up from my computer to glare at Sandro, but I can immediately tell he's not going to let this shit go. He likes to be in control, and at all times. An admirable quality, if he wasn't always strutting around with a stick up his ass.

"I gave permission for her to be here."

He looks dumbfounded. "Why?"

Well, isn't that the question of the century? I was dead set against Miss Deep-Throat's presence until Alessia gave me little-girl-who-lost-her-puppy eyes and I caved like some pussy-whipped stronzo. I might praise my partners and call them "good girls," but I've no interest in babies.

My partners have been groomed to perfection. They understand my peculiarities and the little things that turn me on. They satisfy my voracious appetites, and the ever-changing menu—like the harder scenes I'm into lately. One never seemed enough. Two felt like a competition for my attention. And three has even started to bore me. Still, why would Alessia believe I'd play with someone like Zoey Mangioni?

My long silence has Sandro seconds from erupting. "You're an uptight little shit," I grind out.

"That's not an answer."

I lean back in my chair, fold my arms, and stare at him. New York has taken some of the edge off him. His swagger's broader, his confidence growing. He's been trying to impress me his entire life. Unlike his brother, whose mission is to upend everything I've built.

"I can't stand that chick. I'd jerk off with sandpaper before I'd let her touch me."

I snort. "Again."

Sandro's eyebrows pitch in surprise. Didn't anticipate I'd be up in his business? "Zoey won't simply be a bad influence, she'll corrupt Alessia."

I clench my jaw. Could this be why I've allowed their friendship? *Ma va'!*

Alessia's the forbidden fruit, isn't she? One I could pluck and take a hard bite of, if she were anyone else but my son's fiancée. *If* she were my goddamn type.

I gave her to Sandro, with Don Lucchese's blessing, so what does any of it matter?

"She's your responsibility." Sandro flinches, which makes me push harder. "You can spend time with her. Show your fiancée off at important events like the Riverview Casino's groundbreaking party."

"The party was four weeks ago."

"Then host another goddamn party." I fucking hate the idea, but I press on anyway. "Take her to New York with you. You can get to know your bride better."

He pales.

And I relax, studying him closely. Perdio. There's someone else, isn't there? Whoever this woman is, she better have strong survival skills, because Sandro doesn't have a gentle bone in his body.

"If that's all." His words cut like a knife. "I'll inform Alessia to pack her shit."

He hates this. But he'll do as I ask anyway. Loyal and dependable.

Miserable.

"Sit down."

Within seconds, he's seated.

"Alessia stays here, and I'll worry about her being corrupted." My cock stirs. Fucking terrific. "You can keep your plaything."

He relaxes. Is it because he gets his way? Or because he actually likes this woman? No way. A proud shit like him? That's all this is about. Still ... "Make sure Tommaso accompanies you, or another dependable man."

His back straightens.

I cross my foot over a knee, and reach for the imaginary popcorn. The goddamn show's about to begin.

"I'm not a little fucking kid anymore," he exclaims, thumping the desk with his fist. "When are you going to acknowledge that? What do I have to do to prove myself? Have *I* failed you or made you look weak? Haven't *I* done exactly what you demand, no matter how much I despise you for it? I get it, trust me. So does Renzo. Becoming capo di tutti capi means the Beneventi famiglia will thrive." He spreads his arms for the dramatic conclusion. "Take a look around— we're already thriving. Yet it's never enough, is it?"

I clap my hands in applause.

His head jerks back like I punched him.

Once upon a time, I sat in the same seat across from my father. Like Sandro, my only mission was to earn his respect. I never did. Yet I earned Don Lucchese's respect, and in retrospect, that's all that truly matters.

"You're doing a bang-up job in Brooklyn."

He glares at me.

I touch the computer mouse, and the screen awakens to the spreadsheet I pulled up earlier. "Spending looks good. C&C Enterprises is on schedule with no delays."

"I know what you're doing," he grumbles.

"You should give the new commissioners a private tour once the drywall is up."

"I already contacted them."

I offer him an honest smile. "Good work."

He nods, pleased by my compliments.

I might be a shit father, but I love the little shits. "About Tommaso, do as I say. Benny's been running his mouth about payback for Atlanta. Don't leave yourself vulnerable, capisci?"

"Capisci."

My sons are soft and need toughening up. But they're mine. And I always, always protect what belongs to me.

I stand, as does he. "How about a late lunch before the drive back to New York?"

<hr>

BEING the punctual tight ass he is, Sandro departs at two o'clock sharp, and I hole myself up inside my office, while my men conclude whatever face-to-face business they need to discuss.

But my focus has been hijacked, and by two fucking words—corrupt her.

I curse beneath my breath and grab my phone. This is goddamn ridiculous.

My thumb glides through my contacts for a solution, yet none interest me. I've grouped women by threes based on hair color. I had a good hit of Molly when the idea first struck—to find the tastiest combination of bush; vanilla, chocolate, and strawberry. Believed it'd spice things up.

Except I don't eat pussy, ever.

Women don't color their bush, so finding a natural trio is harder than you'd think. Most women these days are bare, and by the time my playmates grow things out, I'm bored and moving on. Finding anyone with a neat bush for my bull to plow is like searching for an ebony unicorn.

A thought creeps in. *The little voyeur has tight blond curls. Cute as a motherfucking button.*

I toss the cell on my desk, disgusted. My head needs to be back in the game, and my needs addressed.

One of my parties will help. Change things up and recharge my bull.

But business before pleasure.

I open my computer to confirm Freido booked my flight to St. Louis for Wednesday. Ferrara's being a stubborn segaiolo. Ten percent? Cristo. The fucker holds a grudge like nobody else. Like it's my motherfucking fault his girlfriend seduced my son or she was stupid enough to get caught. No proof it was Renzo, thank fuck. But Ferrara and I both know he had his filthy mitts all over her.

At least he wrapped his dick and wasn't surprised by a doorbell that ended his rowdy teen years. Chip off the old block, if you discount the soft heart and hard drug use.

I rub a hand across my jaw. A huge scene where anything goes will take the edge off. Hell, I'll dust off the key and open the Red Room. How long has it been since I played in there?

Whistling, I head to the kitchen in search of Freido.

Only to find Dante Lucchese. Eating my gelato out of the carton like an animal. And he's so goddamn enthralled by something outside the window, he doesn't hear my approach.

I come up behind him and, before he can react, snatch the carton from his hand, knocking the spoon to the floor. My irritation grows and then hits the ceiling—only a few spoonfuls remain.

"It was in the freezer."

"My fucking freezer. My fucking food. My fucking gelato." I'm itching to slam a fist into his perfect nose and ruin his movie-star good looks. "A morto di figa like you shouldn't be eating ice cream if you aim to keep the housewives in Hollywood satisfied."

Instead of responding, he nods toward the window. "She's not so inhibited when no one's looking."

I shove by him, the carton joining the spoon on the floor, and look outside.

And there she is. Alessia, wearing two tiny triangles over her luscious breasts and a matching patch over her bush. She's dancing with Zoey—who's lost her bikini top. Alessia spins, and my throat tightens. Her tight ass is on full display.

Che cazzo? I see red. And not because she wearing tiny scraps of the fucking color.

"She's always buttoned up." Dante chuckles. "Bet Sandro has no clue what she's been hiding."

"Don Lucchese's son or not, you talk about my son's fiancée like that again, and I'll knock your teeth in."

"Whoa." Dante jumps back and puts his hands up. "No offense. I'm just surprised, is all."

"Be surprised on the car ride home." I signal toward the hallway so he'll leave through the main entrance. No fucking way is he going out the kitchen door.

He shoots me a puzzled look. "I'll send you a yearlong subscription for the best gelato in Italy. Okay?"

I grunt.

"Call you from Atlanta."

I wait for him to go before returning my attention to the action outside. Alessia's bent over a table, fiddling with what must be her phone, and presenting her heart-shaped ass to anyone looking.

And everyone's looking. My guards. A few men. Madonna mia, if I search hard enough, the motherfucking gardener's probably lurking around.

"Freido," I bellow.

Zoey sashays up behind her and slaps her bottom.

And what does Little Miss Innocent do? She fucking wiggles it. I should have listened to Sandro. Zoey is going to corrupt her.

Before you get the chance.

"You called, Sebastiano?"

I force myself away from the window.

Freido steps back like I'm coming for him.

But it's not *his* head I want.

"Go. Get." I point to the kitchen door. "*Her.*"

"What did Zoey do this time?"

My jaw tics as I stare at him. Is he shitting me, asking me questions now?

"If Alessia isn't in my office in the next few minutes, you're fired."

Complete and utter shock flashes across his face and lasts a few seconds before he hurries outside.

I wait until he's dragging Alessia by the elbow toward the house, and then return to my office to wait.

24

Alessia

"RUN!" Zoey's scream should have sent me flying rather than frozen like an animal caught in a bulldozer's headlights.

But Freido grabbed my elbow, and all I could do was watch Zoey dash off, wearing nothing but her bikini bottom.

"What's happening?" I gasp, struggling to free my arm.

He ignores me, and half carries, half drags me across the lawn, up the stone stairs, and across the veranda. We don't stop in the kitchen, and I'm forced down the hallway. Bastian's office door is open, and I catch a glimpse of his face before I'm shoved forward and, as the door slams behind me, locked inside with him.

I place a hand over my racing heart.

Bastian lifts off his desk and advances.

My eyes go wide. *He's furious.*

A finger curls around my bikini strap, and I jump as he snaps it like a rubber band.

"Is it ... my father?" I whisper. Zoey's warning rings out in my mind. *Don't let him drag you into the shed.*

"Not." He curls his finger beneath the material covering my right breast. "Your." He pulls, then releases. "Father." My top slips sideways and now barely covers my nipple.

"Tell me the truth." His low growl shakes the room. Or is it me, who is trembling and off-center? "Did you wear this fucking tiny-ass bikini to catch my attention?" His finger graces my skin, and my quiver turns into a shiver.

"No," I gasp. "I wasn't thinking about you at all."

"That right?" He cocks an eyebrow. "Then who were you hoping to attract? My men? My guards? The goddamn gardener?"

"What?" I stammer. "No."

"Well, you succeeded. Every man with eyes will be jerking off and working over their partners with you in mind. That what you set out to do, Little Miss Not-So-Innocent?"

His blue eyes pierce into me. Assessing my reaction, ready to pounce on a lie.

I'm fascinated with him, true. But more terrified than I've ever felt. All week long, I've been reminded of who he is and what he does. Men jumping to do his bidding. Guards positioned around the estate to keep trouble at bay. Zoey, with her stories. He hurts people.

"Know what?" he snarls.

I don't dare answer.

"It doesn't fucking matter. Let them look."

The air trapped inside my lungs escapes in a rush. Except his expression grows less angry and more sinister.

"Know what else?" His tone is raw and whiskey-laced.

The room spins, and I sway.

"No one can touch you but me." He presses a hand to my shoulder. "Get on your knees."

I drop so fast, my head spins.

Is this what he ordered the man in the shed to do before he chopped off his fingers? Is this how he'll execute me?

"Zoey and I thought it'd be fun to buy matching bathing suits," I explain in a rush. "No one informed me you were having meetings ..." I stop talking. Because ... oh, Lord ... he's unzipped his dress pants and is taking out his cock.

"Look at me."

Our eyes connect.

"You a bad girl or a good girl?"

My voice cracks. "Good ..."

"Louder."

I inhale deeply. "I'm a good girl."

"Do good girls flaunt their bodies at every Dick and Harry?"

Wait ... it's almost like he's jealous. And suddenly, the thought settles deep within my bones. "What if her actions weren't intentional?" I softly reply.

He shifts and my eyes drop. He's stroking his hard length with tightly controlled movements. This no longer feels like a punishment but reward.

"Beg me for it. Say, Bastian, please remind me who I belong to."

I raise my chin as a sense of calmness washes over me. "Please, I beg you. Remind me I belong to you."

He doesn't correct me. Right now, in this moment, he doesn't give two fucks I'm engaged to his son.

His eyes darken. "I'm going to mark you, and you better never fucking forget you're a Beneventi now. Capisci?"

I nod, eyes wide open. "Capisci."

With hard, aggressive strokes, he pumps his hand in earnest. Layering a bit of pain in with the pleasure.

My nipples harden, excitement rising.

He grits his teeth while his eyes devour every inch of me. A look of pure, unadulterated lust crosses his face as his attention lands on my lower abdomen, and then lower still. Without warning, he crouches, reaches forward and rips my bikini bottom off, exposing my sex.

"Goddamn it," he hisses. "Look at that perfect blond nest."

I glance down. Zoey suggested I wax the baby-fine hairs off. Or go Brazilian and leave a tiny buzz cut. Seeing the filthy gleam in Bastian's blue eyes, I'm glad I declined.

"Madonna mia, this won't take long." His movements become frantic. "Who are you?"

"A Beneventi." I lean back. *Yours.*

"After I mark this little gold nest, you don't wash it off. You're going to wear it all night long like a motherfucking Girl Scout patch."

Lord, he's filthy. And beautiful, in a dangerous take-no-prisoners way.

He shouts his release, letting loose a steady stream of hot come across my mons. Yet he still jerks harder, milking every last drop.

I can barely breathe, barely process what's happened.

I did this to him.

Me, and my little red bikini.

With a low curse, he tucks himself away, zips his pants and removes his shirt and then, with a blank expression that falls like an anvil into place and hides any connection and all emotion, tosses it at me.

I take the sleeve to clean myself off.

"What did I fucking tell you?"

My jaw drops.

"My come is going to dry overnight in your curls."

Confused, I stare at him.

"Tonight, I want me all over you. But every day that follows, you're my son's."

I flinch. His reminder's as frigid as ice water on the coldest day. This is a punishment. And I acted like he was gifting me with something special by claiming me as his.

My legs shake as I stand and slide into his shirt.

I enjoyed it.

I relished every filthy moment.

How could I be so foolish?

If *I* needed a reminder, this domineering man needs a wake-up call. He initiated this, and I submitted. But I'm done being a willing participant in his sick game. I'm Sandro's, not *his*. I strike out. "I should plan the wedding, then."

He strikes out ten times harder and lightning fast. I'm grabbed, spun around, and forced backward until he has me bent backward across his desk. Without a word, he withdraws his wallet, then a black credit card. Then with one hand, he pins me to his desk, and with the other, he slides the card lightly across my throat.

I blink back tears.

This is why he'll be the next mafia king. This is why I can never forget how terrifyingly dangerous he is. I might be Sandro's, but it's Bastian's power I'll live under.

He draws a line with the card across my trembling lips. "Next time you're at the pool, I better not find you in a tiny bikini." He steps back, leaving the card dangling in place. "Plan the motherfucking wedding," he orders. "Now run. Before I ruin you, and everything else."

I escape his office without looking back.

25

Bastian

"BENNY PAID ME A VISIT," Dante informs me over FaceTime. "Said he's reconsidered and wants in on a joint venture."

"That right?" I drum my pen on my desk. Benny's run his mouth a few times since the expansion. But nothing like the threats of his little puppet, Emilio Conti. Conti is like that one fly that won't go away, so small and so insignificant yet annoying as hell.

"We can add one of those trendy shopping plazas in the open lot behind the casino with the additional investment. Upscale stores with greenery and outdoor seating."

I frown. Why the fuck is Dante giving me a sales pitch on behalf of Bible Belt Benny? "You sign an agreement?"

"Without discussing it with you? Hell no."

Something's off. I can feel it in my bones. But I've been distracted and unfocused lately, so I chalk it up to that. "Offer Benny a half a percent."

"He won't like it."

I grind my teeth. "Add a clause that, if he kisses my ass for six months and shuts Conti the fuck up for the same length of time, his cut will jump to one percent."

"He proposed four."

Soft laughter filters in from the open window behind me. "Hold on," I snap, then click off the camera and spin my chair around, in time to catch Alessia crossing the grass in the direction of the casita.

Her blond hair is in a ponytail. Her pale blue dress reaches her throat and ankles. She wears the sweetest smile. But all I can fucking see is my come on her snatch.

Zoey, in a tube top, miniskirt, and high heels, sporting a Tenth-Avenue-street-corner style, scoops up a bag Alessia's dropped.

My eyes zero in on the store label—Providence Bridal.

Fuck me.

"Gotta go. Offer him whatever you think will benefit us."

"Wait," Dante exclaims. "There's more ..."

I had the foresight to close the camera, which I'm thankful for because the last thing I need is Dante witnessing me—*me*, the Beneventi capo and the next capo di tutti capi—salivating over virgin pussy that's been branded by my come. No matter how many times I jerk off, it's never enough. I'm wound up tight. Saturday night's entertainment can't get here fast enough.

"Offer him two, and go ahead with building the plaza. We'll talk tomorrow."

"But ..."

I spin toward the desk and disconnect the call. A few clicks later, and I have my black card account pulled up.

My jaw clenches.

She purchased a goddamn wedding gown.

Alessia

I STRAIGHTEN my skirt and fight off my nerves as I wait outside his office door. It's the second time in three days I've been summoned —if you count Freido's manhandling.

My mind races, searching for what this might be about. I'm careful how I dress, which isn't a hardship as my style's typically conservative. I spent his money, but he ordered me to get busy preparing my wedding, and they're expensive. I've occupied myself by selecting classes for the fall and even with baking Italian cookies I'll have mailed to Don Lucchese.

I've done everything he asked, and more.

But what I won't do—refuse to do—is submit to his whims.

"Enter."

I jump at his command. Pushing the door open, I force myself to step inside. He doesn't glance up, preoccupied with whatever's on his computer.

"Take a seat."

I swallow hard and obey.

He types on his keyboard, looking very much like a corporate CEO with his fine suit and serious expression.

"Did you do as I asked?" His tone's flat, disinterested.

I hesitate. During my last visit, he demanded I do several things. "Yes. Everything exactly, word for word."

His jaw tics.

But I won't deny myself the satisfaction of getting a rise from him.

He taps return on his keyboard a little too hard. Is he still angry with me? Zoey parades around in minimal clothing without reprimand.

But she's not a *Beneventi*.

"And the wedding?"

I frown. And? What are we discussing here?

"You set a date?"

Fear races through me. "No. Not yet."

"Sandro avoiding your calls?"

My eyebrows rise. How did he guess?

"I'll speak to him."

Silence falls. Is he expecting a "thank you"?

"Anything else?" he asks.

"No."

His eyes pierce into me.

What the heck—might as well tell him. "I purchased a dress."

"That right?" All the air seems to escape the room. "Let's see it."

I nearly fall off the chair.

"Show me." He stands and then stalks toward the door, fully expecting me to follow him.

And I do. Because I really don't have a choice, do I?

We walk side by side to the casita in silence. "My gown's hanging inside the closet in the bedroom," I say in a rush after we enter the living area. "Let me get it."

"Put it on."

I miss a step, and nearly tumble.

"*Dai.* Just do it."

I race into the bedroom, strip, and then step into the gown. The back hangs open, so he'll have to zip it up.

Or I face him the entire time.

Lord, why is he making me do this?

"Do I have to come in there?"

Tears spill as I hastily smooth the long skirt into place. I dressed up as a bride once when I was a little girl. I wore my sister's communion dress, my mother's white pumps several sizes too big for my small feet, and a sparkling tiara I borrowed from a doll. My mother was delighted. "One day, you'll stand before the man you'll marry and he'll weep when he sees how beautiful you are in your wedding dress."

Now look who's crying.

And Bastian isn't even the man I'm marrying. Yet he gets to see me first in my gown.

My mother's dreams were ruined by my father's ambition, with me stuck somewhere in the middle. I wipe the moisture from my eyes and straighten my shoulders. My happiness is in the hands of the man waiting in the great room.

Calming my nerves, I leave my bedroom.

He's sprawled on the sofa with a drink in his hand. His eyes rake over me, yet his expression gives nothing away.

Does he think I'm beautiful?

Or am I simply a distraction from his work?

He motions for me to turn.

I spin, then breathlessly wait for him to order me closer so he can zip up my dress.

For what feels like eternity, he stares at me. Until my palms are clammy and nerves shattered. No shocking comments? No filthy words as he orders me about? No teasing me or tempting me into reprehensible acts?

My eyes prick with unshed tears. The difference is that frustration fuels them instead of sadness.

What could he possibly be thinking?

"Nonna is returning to Italy."

I jerk back, surprised. Of all the things I imagined he might be thinking, this wasn't one.

"Her sister is ill, and she wants to be by her side."

"Oh no." I clasp my hands. "Poor Nonna. So that's what's been bothering her? She seemed sad lately."

He nods. "She refused at first. Didn't want to inconvenience me."

"And you said yes," I softly say.

He glares at me. "I'm an asshole, not a monster." With a flick of his wrist, he shoots back his drink, then stands.

I swallow hard.

"I'll need you in my kitchen, preparing my meals."

Words escape me. *Why me, rather than hiring a replacement?*

"You start Friday. I'll be away on business for a few days," he tosses over his shoulder as he stalks by. "Make the lamb dish."

Lord, he's bossy. And there should be a quota on surprises per day. The dress. The trip. The lamb.

But no dirty talk.

No tormenting me.

He hovers in the doorway and rakes his eyes over me one last time. Then, he not only hits the quota for surprises, he blows it off the chart.

"My son doesn't know it, but you're going to make him a very happy man."

26

Bastian

ENTERING ST. Louis, my car rolled past a rusting billboard with a quote painted across it in fading black letters: *A hard town for saints but an easy one for sinners.*

Fitting. St. Louis is a city that breeds devils, and none wear the horns sharper than Roberto Ferrara. Short temper, quick trigger, a bastard who built his empire on the floodplains of the Mississippi. Ferrara's the kind of man who bleeds people dry.

His house is a fortress on the edge of the city, stone and steel, with high gates and a view of the river.

We're in the basement, a sprawling den with a private bar, weight racks, and a pair of massage tables set side by side. Cigar smoke hangs thick in the air. Two women work our backs, earbuds jammed in tight because Ferrara made it clear: no listening, no repeating. Discretion is their life insurance policy.

I shift, then groan when the masseuse drives her elbow into a knot. Across from me, Ferrara smirks, like my pain entertains him.

"Four percent is more than Luca agreed to," I press, knowing it's a lie. The Beneventi don't shortchange allies, not when it suits us. But this is the game; he's a businessman like me and convinced he's smarter. His arrogance bigger than his bank roll.

He grunts as his masseuse digs into his thigh. "Four percent isn't worth my time."

The phone on the wall rings. He jerks his head, irritated. "I said no interruptions." He waves the women out and then grabs the receiver. "What?" His face reddens. "Arrested?"

I raise a brow.

He paces, growling into the phone. "Say that again." A pause. "She was caught boosting purses from a Target parking lot?" His laugh is humorless, bitter. "Handle it." He slams the receiver down and wheels on me, blaming me for his girlfriend's kleptomania with a hard stare.

"Keep your son away from St. Louis."

Cristo. This again? Goddamn Renzo. He better get his shit together or he'll be my ruin. "You're mistaken. He was in Rhode Island."

Ferrara leans in, voice like a blade. "She posted pics on social-fucking-media."

Yeah, pictures Renzo scrubbed, once he saw them.

"Is that why she's been arrested?"

Rage boils up inside him. And as much as I enjoy witnessing him unraveling—his girlfriend's a goddamn smokeshow—I'm here on business.

So, I soothe things over with a compliment. "She brings other women into bed? Lucky bastard. You up for that?"

His lips curl. "Fuck you."

We lock eyes, the silence heavier than gunfire, every second a standoff. Years of rivalry coil tight between us, two predators gauging who will strike first. We're almost equals, almost—but in the Life, there's no such thing as sharing power. One of us rules. The other bows his fucking head, or bleeds.

The two masseuses rush back inside.

"We're done here," he informs me, his misguided anger fucking things up.

Once Renzo's out of rehab, I'm having the little shit neutered. "Not quite yet. We haven't talked about your cars."

That gets him. "My cars?"

"How many cars *do* you own now?" He's been collecting cars for years. A real Jay Leno, only he prefers the latest gadgets.

One.

Two.

The vain asshole falls for it. "Twenty-one."

"No shit?" I sit on the table, then turn my head and cock an eyebrow.

His anger fades. "And four motorcycles. Three are Harleys."

"A few antiques but most the latest models?" He owns a 1966 Mustang convertible, two '70s Corvettes, and an '80s Rolls.

"The four older cars are fun to drive on a lark. Like my house, I enjoy modern conveniences." He pauses to nod at me. "Why? You looking to buy a new car?"

He didn't stroll but jumped exactly where I want him. "Maybe," I smoothly answer. "Or like everyone else, I'll wait until prices drop."

Open mouth, and the bait's immediately snatched.

"What makes you believe prices will fall?" He's curious, sensing —correctly—that I know something. "Prices could rise. Hell, every-thing's up."

I've his complete attention now.

"The New York Governor offered me some useful information. I'll share it, under one condition?"

He frowns. "Depends on the condition."

"The bullshit between us ends."

He's silent. But Ferrara wouldn't own twenty-one cars or have a garage large enough to accommodate them if he wasn't business-savvy. "Fine. This better blow my socks off."

I smile. "Friends in Washington have told him it's the perfect time to invest in American-made semiconductor chips. You know, the kind used in every fucking vehicle, truck, and God knows where else. You think we're corrupt assholes? Every congressman and senator is investing in chips on Wall Street before the big news is announced."

He spins on the table to face me.

Checkmate, asshole.

"A new bill is circulating. Trillions of taxpayer dollars will be invested into microchip production." I thump the massage table. "And listen closely, motherfucker ..." His eyes narrow, disliking the disrespect. Tit for fucking tat, you arrogant shit. "Guess where the three-billion-dollar plant will be built?"

His jaw drops. Yeah, smart but not nearly on my level.

"Ohio, motherfucker." I roll four fingers into the air. "Four percent, and we have a deal."

27

Alessia

LAUGHTER RUMBLES from deep within my belly and escapes my lips in a rhythm of uncontrollable bursts. I've shed enough tears to fill buckets over the past few years, so it feels great to let go.

"There's something wrong with the grip," Zoey informs our golf instructor.

I clutch my stomach as another wave hits me. My friend's golf ball lies lifeless in a divot, but her golf club—which, seconds ago, sailed through the air like a boomerang—rests on the grass a few yards away. Our golf instructor was nearly decapitated as the club sailed by. The poor man didn't see Zoey coming and likely believed the biggest threat to his well-being on the Beneventi estate was the man inside the house. The horrified look the instructor gave Zoey has me in stitches. One glance at Zoey—who's wearing a bright pink crop top that says, "I'll drink another Arnold Palmer," and matching pink high heels to play golf—and you'd know she was going to be a handful.

The poor guy is determined, though. Bastian hired him, so he must be the best around.

It's a gorgeous day, and I'm in good spirits. Not because I'm a natural—like Renzo said. Not because I love this game. And especially not because Bastian has returned from his trip; that has nothing to do with anything. I'm having fun, something that's been absent from my life for a while.

"Can you put tape on it so the club won't slide out of my hand?"

Zoey insists. A thick rubbery material is already at the end of each club. State-of-the-art material created for an expert grip. These clubs are the best on the market, or so our instructor has informed us.

The silly man insists on arguing with her. "Stop releasing the club after you swing."

Zoey chews her gum for a few seconds, then blows a bubble. "It's the grip."

"You're wearing gloves ..."

I shake my head. Zoey is a classic pot-stirrer. She enjoys busting balls and getting her way, mostly with gullible men. The more they engage, the sillier she acts. It's better than the social media video of a father running a lawn mower over his teenage son's video games as he shouts the excuses his son gave for not having a job. This golf lesson has viral video written all over it.

But I only lurk online. Any interaction might raise questions. Why rock the boat? I'm happier than I've been. My situation's improved. Upsetting Bastian will draw negative attention, when I'd rather please him.

Especially now.

He purchased these golf clubs and a laptop, as promised. Yet his generosity didn't stop there. A room off the kitchen and a few doors away from Bastian's office has been completely converted into a study for me.

The room's tricked out, with a new Mac desktop computer, iPad, printer, desk and chair set, and more notebooks than I could use even if I took classes into my golden years. An expensive book with color photographs of the Italian Renaissance movement is on the desk. But it's the painting on the wall that has me speechless. A beautiful oil painting replica of *The Birth of Venus*.

Not only does Bastian understand my passion for Italian art, he shares it.

One problem. Whenever I stare at the painting, I don't see Venus rising but Bastian—out of the bathtub. Muscles rippling. Bathwater cascading down his gorgeous body. His bull thick and daunting.

I can't be fooled by his generosity or my misguided lust.

I was ordered to plan a wedding.

To. His. *Son*.

Like a lamb to slaughter, he's keeping me well-fed.

The instructor clears his throat. "How about we give Mrs. Beneventi another turn?"

I lock eyes with Zoey, and stifle another laugh.

"Mrs. Beneventi?" She slaps a hand on her thigh. "Let's first make it through this game before Alessia marches down the aisle."

"I apologize, Alessia." He looks at my left hand and my bare ring finger. "I assumed, based on Mr. Beneventi's phone call—"

"Wait," Zoey screeches. "You spoke to Mr. Beneventi himself?"

"Early this morning."

"Sebastiano Beneventi?"

"Yes."

Warmth spreads through me. I'm on his mind?

"Can you believe it?" Zoey demands. "He arranged this lesson himself."

I haven't told her about my new study. I don't know why I've kept this from her. Is it because I'd rather not listen to her harsh warnings about him? Is it because I prefer to linger inside this dreamy bubble I've created, where he's drawn to me as much as I am to him?

Zoey narrows her eyes at me, sensing I haven't told her everything. "Why would he do that?"

I shrug. "Maybe he's compensating for Sandro's absence?"

"I don't think that's it at all."

My pulse races, yet I resist asking her what she means. Instead, I approach the green and set a golf ball in place.

"For dinner, I'm preparing the lamb ricotta dish. So maybe Bastian's simply reciprocating the favor?" I grin, excited to watch him savor every mouthful like he did at the engagement party.

Our instructor comes up behind me, then taps my right hip. "Swing from here."

"Got it."

His arms wrap around my body, and he straightens my arms. "Hold up. Let me get that club off the green."

He hurries away to retrieve Zoey's club.

"It's weird that you're cooking his dinners. And far too domestic—with his money, he could hire a Michelin-rated chef."

I sigh. "I love cooking ..." *For him.* Only because he appreciates my efforts. Only because it gives me something to do. No other reason. "Why do you think he personally hired a golf instructor?" I try to ask my question casually, but curiosity has the words rushing from my lips.

She stalks up beside me. "Fucking hell, but I believe you've caught his attention."

"Really?"

"Ugh, Alessia. You sound excited. Trust me, he's the last man you should want arranging your golf lessons. Everything comes at a price, understand?"

"He's my soon-to-be father-in-law."

"Let me ask you this—why aren't you in New York with Sandro?"

I make a face, the thought repulsive. "Sandro's busy building a new casino."

"And Sebastiano Beneventi isn't busy?" She snatches the club from my hands. "He wants you here."

Our conversation ends as our instructor returns. But her words keep replaying in my mind. He wants you here.

"Alessia," she snaps, raising the club and poking it in my direction. "Just keep away from him, okay?"

"I'll try." Part of me realizes this is the wisest choice. And the other part wishes for the courage to interrupt him in his office, perch my bare bottom on his desk, and completely, utterly submit to the wicked man.

A shiver races up my spine.

Zoey bends her legs and sticks her butt out, and I burst into laughter. My decision on how to handle Sebastiano Beneventi can wait.

The instructor hurries forward and attempts to reposition her. She sways her hips and makes it impossible. Shaking his head, he finally gives up and shuffles about a yard to her right.

Zoey grins, then shouts, "I'm gonna hit the ball now."

I take several steps back, and then several more.

"Golfers say fore before they swing," he immediately corrects her. "And keep a firm hold of the ..."

"Fore." Zoey swings, and the club goes flying sideways through the air, spiraling three times, then clipping the instructor's thigh and barely missing his groin before landing several feet to his right.

Cupping his privates in a belated attempt at protecting himself, he glares at Zoey.

Guards race toward us, and I eye them with suspicion. Are they coming for Zoey? Is Freido tossing her off the estate again?

Zoey blows a huge pink bubble, not concerned in the least.

And I lose it, laughing so hard, my classmates in Rome can hear me.

Bastian

"KNEEL." I unzip my pants and shove down my boxers. The three women before me understand the assignment, dropping to their knees, licking their plump lips, and waiting to choke on my big fat cock.

This is what I envisioned the entire ride home from St. Louis. Three of my favorite whores servicing me. A blond with a golden mouth. A brunette with her big fake tits, and a redheaded submissive with a tight ass and filthy mind. Typically, I'd bend them over the sofa, tan their asses, then find release on and in any part of them I like. But sometimes, nothing beats a good blow job.

I frown down at the blond. Not a hint of innocence. Not the slightest flush of excitement.

Not a little dirty-minded virgin, dripping wet for me.

I make them wait while I dip the homemade biscotti into a hot cup of coffee and take a bite. It's exactly how I like it, not too dry and not too sweet and with the slightest hints of almond.

Alessia's laughter draws my attention to my laptop, where my state-of-the-art security cameras track her progress on the golf course. She's naturally talented; it wasn't just a fluke. But her friend's a fucking nightmare. Yeah, I contacted the professional player directly and paid through the nose for the lesson. Now fucking Zoey is going to frighten the guy off.

While I was in St. Louis., I had Freido purchase the best golf clubs and gear and instructed him to convert the room near the kitchen into a study for her schoolwork. Fuck knows why I insisted she be inside the main house and not the casita. Not that the meek little baby will disrupt my work.

Not intentionally, anyway.

The brunette, growing impatient, clears her throat.

I wipe my hands on a napkin, then wrap fingers around my cock and stroke my bull hard. Over and over, waiting to feel inspired.

But the truth is, the scene bores me.

My tie is suddenly too tight. Lack of oxygen, that's what's screwing with my mind.

I've indulged in every kink imaginable, many times.

Except break in a virgin.

It must be the novelty of feeling her tight virgin throat gagging on my bull. Of being the first. Of teaching her exactly what I like. Of forcing her submission. She's uncharted territory. Virgin throat. Virgin pussy. Virgin ass.

Virgin *everything*.

My cock stirs.

The blond licks her plump lips. Cristo. Close your eyes, fuckhead.

I'm just about to do so—then shove inside her and keep shoving until I come—when movement on the security screen snatches my attention.

The golfer ... wrapping himself around Alessia like mother-fucking plastic wrap.

"Go," I thunder.

The three women scramble, grabbing their discarded clothing as they go. But they're not quick enough.

"Out."

They race from the room as I pick up my cell and tap out a message to Freido.

> Grab that clingy motherfucker and drag him
> to the front gate.

Seconds later, Freido responds.

> Who?

He's got his mitt on her arm now.

> The golf pro.

> On it.

I toss my cell on my desk, then pull up my boxers and tuck myself away. I watch and wait for several minutes, until the guards race toward the golfer, grab him, and drag him away.

I snatch up another biscotti and snap it into halves.

Saturday night is the party. If I can't take the edge off then, there's no telling what—or *who*—I'll break in two.

Bastian

HUMMING GREETS me as I enter the kitchen. Alessia is at the stove, stirring something inside a pot and oblivious to my arrival. Damp locks curl across the back of her neck. Her skin is tan from days by the pool, and a day spent golfing. Her body sways in unison with her stirring, and her ass gyrates while she cooks.

The little cocktease doesn't even realize her power.

Scowling, I pour myself red wine from a crystal decanter. Such a rule follower, isn't she, allowing the wine to breathe this way?

I drain the glass before taking a seat at the island and serving myself another.

The kitchen smells like a five-star restaurant. Did she prepare the lamb dish like I asked? My stomach growls, so I hope it's a yes. After eating burgers and fucking guacamole, a real meal will brighten my mood.

My mind turns to business while I wait for her to notice me. Progress in Atlanta is slower than anticipated. Especially compared to what Sandro's accomplished in New York. Permits have been approved, even those for the retail paperwork for the outdoor shopping plaza. A construction crew is waiting to break ground. Yet Dante hasn't set a date.

He tells me it's because of material issues. Which is bullshit—in the mafiosi world, no such thing exists. Construction is our typical revenue stream. The right men, the right pressure—monetary or physical—and things get done.

Every second we wait is money lost.

So what's behind the delay?

Something's up, I can feel it. Perhaps a surprise trip south is in order? Discover what's distracting Dante, if it's Hollywood-worthy pussy or something else.

"Oh," Alessia gasps. "I didn't hear you enter the kitchen."

"That was some racket you were making," I mutter.

She blushes.

I feel like the fucking Grinch. "Did you make lamb?"

Her smile is genuine. "It turned out better this time." She gestures to the dining room. "I set a plate for you."

"I'll eat in the kitchen."

"Okay. Hold on." She brushes by me into the adjacent room, then returns with my great-great-grandmother's china balanced in one hand and a tall burning taper in the other.

I snatch the candle from her before she burns my house down, and place it on the island while she arranges everything before me.

"I hope you don't mind," she murmurs. "I polished the silver."

Madonna mia. How long did that take her? The forks, spoons, knives, and serving utensils have been tarnished, and therefore unused, for decades.

Next, she sets salad on the island, but my attention falls on the antipasto platter she's arranged. A selection of meats, salami, prosciutto, spicy ham, cheeses, olives, artichokes, roasted red peppers, and deviled eggs.

The eggs are filled with a creamy yolk mixture.

I fucking love deviled eggs.

Our eyes meet.

She shrugs. "Freido said they're your favorite."

Fucking terrific. My most vicious bodyguard / personal assistant has been gossiping.

"Aside from the lamb, I prepared all your favorites as a thank-you for your generosity. I love my study. I also appreciate the professional golf lessons and hope to continue—"

"Not going to happen."

Her eyebrows rise in surprise.

I don't offer further explanation. Truth is, the idea of that stronzo's hands infuriates me.

"He was helpful."

"He's lucky he made it out of here alive."

She stares at me, confused.

"You going to argue with me or serve me?" Because any further discussion about that asshole and I'll hurl the wine decanter into the wall.

Her teeth drag across her bottom lip. "Serve you salad? And antipasto?"

"You heard me."

Drawing a disappointed breath, she hurries away. What did she expect, a romantic dinner?

She returns with salad prongs. Hand shaking, she dishes out a healthy portion of greens.

I wait until she's finished, then say, "Three tablespoons of dressing."

Her eyebrows pitch.

Yet, she does as asked, measuring out exactly three tablespoons of homemade balsamic vinaigrette—another favorite.

I take a bite and close my eyes. Is salad supposed to taste this good?

When I open them, she's arranged spicy ham, provolone chunks, marinated red peppers, and two deviled eggs on my small plate.

Still, I'm a dick. "You forgot the salami."

She stiffens. "I don't recall Nonna dishing out appetizers."

"She doesn't. You do."

I fight off a smile while she spears several slices like she's some warrior princess, with so much force, she has to pluck the salami off the prongs with her fingers.

With a sigh, she moves to the stove, and I focus on my food.

Believe it or not, but deviled eggs are a lost art. Old-fashioned, some might say, though never to my face. Ordering them out isn't an option—something so seemingly simple prepared incorrectly can cause salmonella poisoning for weeks. Nonna prepared them once, using mayonnaise without adding the spicy mustard kick.

I bite into one, and my taste buds go fucking wild. Yeah, they're as tasty as they look, with hints of mustard and ... is that pickle juice? I've devoured six before she returns.

She smiles, pleased I like her eggs.

"Keep still or I'll spill the platter," she informs me, then leans forward, her breast bumping my upper arm as she places the dish on the table.

My cock hardens at the brief contact, and my stomach rumbles. The lamb smells fucking wonderful, and I'm in sensory overload paradise.

She serves me two slices, and one more rub.

Suddenly, I'm considering eating something creamier than deviled eggs.

Madonna mia. I don't eat pussy. Ever. "Go."

She freezes against me. "What?"

"You heard me."

"But I haven't put out the asparagus ..." She inhales sharply. "This dinner was meant as a thank-you."

"You're welcome."

Disappointment fills her eyes. Little Miss Michelin Chef gets off on cooking for me, doesn't she? Conspiring with Freido, hours over a hot stove, polishing my great-grandmother's goddamn silverware. *She likes pleasing me.*

And damn if I don't fucking relish the idea.

"You can thank me on your wedding night," I mutter.

She looks thunderstruck. And then angry.

And then so positively furious, she storms out the kitchen door with the oven mitt clenched in her hand.

29

Alessia

MY CELL PHONE CHIMES, and I abruptly awake. It feels like I just fell asleep, my frustration with Bastian's callous indifference disrupting my peace. I don't know what I expected. What I do know is my efforts were underappreciated, and I won't be so invested in pleasing the coldhearted brute anymore.

Thank *him* on *my* wedding night?

As if.

I roll over and fumble with my cell phone. "Hello?" I finally manage in a husky, sleep-deprived voice.

"Lessie?"

I roll up to a seated position. It's nearly three o'clock. "Renzo?"

"Did you find my passport?"

Alarm bells go off in my mind. "Not yet."

"Get it." His tone is urgent. Oh no. No. No. No. "It's in the top drawer in the nightstand beside my bed."

I inhale sharply. "Please listen to me. You have to stay in rehab and get clean. Focus on getting better and nothing else."

"I'm coming for you, Angel."

"I'm fine, and don't need your help. Your brother lives in New York and is busy opening a new casino. Zoey is allowed back on the estate, and we've become fast friends. I registered for online classes to finish my degree. And I've been swimming, golfing, and cooking—I'm actually filling in for Nonna, who returned to Italy, and I will now be preparing dinner for your father." Renzo quietly listens—at least I hope he's listening. "Are you there?" I hastily ask.

"Sandro's in charge of the Riverview Casino?"

I hesitate. "Yes."

He grunts.

"I bought my wedding dress," I blurt out.

"Fucking hell," he grunts. "The date set?"

I shake my head, a useless gesture as Renzo can't actually see me. But it helps clear the cobwebs. If Renzo insists on leaving rehab, I'll need my wits about me to convince him to stay put. "Not yet. Your father insisted I focus on wedding preparations."

The truth is, I bought the dress out of spite. After all, Bastian played with me like I was his favorite toy, then ignored me. Why do I enjoy him ordering me about? Why do I obey his filthy whims, like falling asleep with his dried come on my pussy? Why do my darkest desires always revolve around him?

"And he's behaving?"

I blink. "Who?"

"My father."

It's my turn to grunt. "Behave? In many ways, he's a lot like you."

Silence greets me.

"You there?"

"You fucking my old man?" he demands.

"No."

"Be honest. He get in your pants? Because the way you answered me ..."

I swallow hard. Technically speaking, the answer's no. "Of course not."

"Keep it that way, okay?" he warns. "Or he'll ruin you just like he's ruined our lives."

His warning has merit. My life would be ruined if I had a different mindset. But I'm completely, utterly awake when I'm in

Sebastiano Beneventi's presence. Like I've risen from a deep sleep and entered a world where my curiosity's sparked and my mind's invigorated. This is more than a crush. Closer to being enraptured by him and my base desires. I feel secure in his home and on his estate. Protected from my father's indifference and a harsh world that swallows up shy people like me. And Bastian understands me on so many levels.

"He cares about you, Renzo."

"Holy hell. Are you … defending him?" His tone is filled with hurt. He's carrying so much pain inside, he'll crack without professional help.

I reply as gently as possible. "You'll see things differently once you're clean. Stay in rehab."

"Too late."

I squeeze the cell phone harder. "It's not too late. You can do this."

"Not that—I've escaped."

My thoughts spin. "Where are you?"

"Still in Maine, unfortunately. The woods around the facility are scary as shit at night."

Lord, what do I say? What do I do?

"Pack your bags," he informs me. "I'm coming for you, Angel. Later."

The call disconnects.

And I do what has to be done, and with Renzo's best interests in mind. I hurry toward the main house to alert Bastian.

THE INCESSANT KNOCKING STOPS the second I jerk my bedroom door open. "What the hell?" I growl at the guard standing there.

"Sir. She insisted."

I blink. Because, sure as fuck, Alessia is in the shadows beside him, eyes wide and hungrily devouring my dick. Did she expect I'd be wearing pajamas with bulls printed on them?

My eyes narrow. Desperation is written all over her. I know she watches me when she thinks no one is looking. A few tastes, and now the little kinkster loves my dominating manner, doesn't she? Who'd believe her attraction would escalate this far? It takes balls to show up at my bedroom door at this hour. Yet here she is, hovering in the hall-way, all flushed and meek. Nervous about disrupting my sleep? Or is she reconsidering her ploy to get into my bed?

My eyes rake over her.

She's dressed in nothing but a white crop top that stops under her gorgeous breasts and the tiniest pink shorts that show off her long legs. Her feet are bare, her toenails painted baby-girl pink.

Looking so ripe for the plucking I feel like punching the door.

"I have something important to tell you," she stammers.

"Of course you do." What I should do is send her running scared or remind her which Beneventi her attention should be focused on. But I drank several whiskeys earlier, and I'm not thinking clearly, so I do the opposite, snatching her elbow, dragging her inside, and slam-ming the door in the guard's stunned face. I'd laugh, if I weren't fucking keyed up, my overconsumption of booze a poor replacement for the hard fuckage I need.

Which is why Chiara Renselli will be at Saturday night's party. She likes it rough, submits so beautifully, and knows better than anyone what I like. It's been a few years since I entertained one woman, but Chiara's tears always excite my inner demons, and that's exactly the release I'm looking for.

I should be in bed and jerking off at the idea, not entertaining some curious little kinkster I've dragged inside my bedroom.

This is my fucking sanctuary. I've been with tons of women, but never invited them into my private space. I entertain them in other rooms, or in the Red Room when I feel the urge.

Frustrated, I glare down at Alessia, and discover a strange expression on her pretty face as she soaks up the decor.

Everything's my favorite color—black. The wallpaper and paint, brick fireplace, furniture, light fixtures, bedding, even the soft silk sheets. Only my king-sized bed frame and the oak floors are a natural wood color. And the massive painting over the fireplace is black and white.

I give her ten seconds to acclimate herself before pointing to my right. "On the bed."

She jumps and spins and then, like a deer caught in the headlights, simply stares at me.

Platinum-blond hair cascades around her shoulders. Not a stitch of makeup on her face. Breasts bouncing and nipples at attention beneath a practically transparent shirt.

She's fucking stunning.

This is the perfect time to send her running. Yet my mouth's already repeating my demand. "On. The. Bed. Now."

Her throat bobbles, but this time she obeys, climbing onto the mattress and sitting with her legs swinging over the edge.

One push, and I'd have her tumbling backward, and second push, and I could be inside her sweetness.

Fucking hell, *sweetness?* I grimace.

What the hell is she thinking seeking me out?

I charge over to the nightstand. Little Lolita needs a harsh dose of reality. Without a word, I retrieve my handcuffs from the drawer, then, before she can guess my intentions, hook an arm around her waist and drag her across the mattress to the headboard.

"What are you doing?" she cries out as I pin her down and cuff both wrists to the ornate wood.

"Securing the premises from little sluts who show up at my bedroom uninvited."

"What?" She tugs on the cuffs, testing them.

My dick instantly hardens.

"I woke you to tell you something important," she insists.

I straighten. "Right."

Her eyes widen. "You don't believe me?"

"Bingo." My eyes rake over the body stretched out on my mattress, and I immediately realize my mistake. Because I fucking love seeing her like this, tied up in my bed and at my mercy. "Admit it —you came to ride my bull."

Her chest rises like she's drawn in a deep breath.

What am I doing? Maybe it's the joint I smoked after the whiskey? Strong Colombian shit—the effects must still be lingering and clouding my judgment. I should let her go with a warning. Don't tempt me, or I might just snap.

Instead, I run a finger across her lower abdomen, right above the elastic waistline of her tiny fucking shorts.

She whimpers.

The sound penetrates like an electrical volt. My resolve falters. I want her crying and quivering in need.

And Little Miss Innocent's eager for me to do it, too.

Fuck it.

I draw a line on her skin to her waistband. "My little slut begging for another finger-fuck?" My hand dips beneath her shorts until my fingers reach her pretty nest.

Her hips jerk.

Greedy little baby's anxious for me to rub her clit. Let's see if she earned the right. "The truth, or you'll disappoint me, capisci? You love the dirty things I do to you?"

Her chest heaves. "Yes," she murmurs, her tone so low, I strain to hear her.

"Louder."

She wiggles, and my finger slides toward the target. "Yes," she breathes. "I love how you finger-fuck me and warm my skin with your come."

Even though I demanded it, her honesty—along with her dirty little mouth—stuns me.

"And I did as you asked," she adds.

"Which was?" I'm slow to process.

"I slept with your dried come on my pussy."

Holy. Fucking. Shit.

In a room of black, I see red. Within seconds, I crawl across her body and straddle her hips with my thighs. Fired up, I stare down at her.

Who'd believe a vulnerable baby like her could tempt me this much? Her exhales come in short bursts as her chest moves beneath me.

Do it.

Take what she's so sweetly offering.

Sweetly. Goddamn it. Next I'll be opening a candy store.

"Wait, Bastian," she pleads.

"You slept with my mark on you?"

Our eyes connect.

She nods.

"Say it again: I left your come on me all night."

"You asked for the truth," she murmurs.

Ma che cazzo. I'm six seconds shy of substituting my dick for my finger and shoving inside her tight pussy.

"But please listen to me," she pleads. "This is important."

"Go on." My tone's gruff, like a randy teen frustrated by his self-constraint. When was the last time I denied myself this way? When was the last time I so desperately desired to completely possess someone, from her tight little pussy to shy little soul to her deviant little brain?

This is why a beast like me never plays with innocent babies, no matter how curious or willing they are.

"Say it."

"It's Renzo."

Perdio—what the hell?

"He's no longer at the rehab facility."

The worry in her eyes registers first.

"The little shit escaped?" I snarl.

She nods, then swallows hard. "I hate betraying him this way, though it's for his own good. He was in the woods near the facility when he called. I immediately came to alert you."

I spring from the bed. Then, cell phone in hand, I pull up the head guard's contact information.

The call rings twice before he answers, completely frazzled. "Shit. Mr. Beneventi. You heard?"

I slam my fist into a wall. "I heard, but not from you. Why the fuck is that?"

"We discovered he was missing less than five minutes ago, sir. I was about to notify you."

"Search the woods, and get a dog to help track him."

"The woods," he shouts to whoever is nearby. The thump of running boots fills the line.

"If Renzo's not locked inside the facility in the next half hour, you're dead." I disconnect, toss the cell phone on the dresser, and pace the room.

Fuck.

I cross the room, back and forth, but it doesn't calm me down. "This little shit is going to ruin us," I mutter, sitting on the bed.

"You're a good father," Alessia murmurs from behind me.

Stai scherzando?

For a few seconds I hesitate. Her soft expression says she's not kidding, that she actually believes I am. Some tension eases as I reposition my body on the mattress so I'm facing her.

"I protected him," I admit. "Indulged him and gave him choices—something I never had as a kid."

"Renzo's a free spirit. You nurtured that in him."

I grunt, her assessment spot-on. "His ass should have been locked inside the dungeon the first time I discovered him with drugs. Figured it was a stage. Fucking growing pains."

I'm suddenly tired, so goddamn tired. "He tell you what happened? How I learned I was a father?"

She bites her lip, then nods. She cares about the little shit, doesn't she? And if Renzo's involved her in his business, it's likely reciprocated. Ma va'! I should have let Renzo have her. She'd be a calming influence on him.

"Know how old I was when I started caring for the twins?"

"Young," she murmurs.

"Eighteen. What the hell does an eighteen-year-old know about raising kids? And my father was no help. He's the reason I didn't trust anyone with them—not the nannies, not their teachers, not the parents of their friends. Alcohol and drugs were my vices—I never expected a good-humored kid like Renzo would take things this far, and repeatedly." I run my fingers through my hair. "Merda. If they don't track him down ..."

"They will," she softly reassures me. "No one dares defy you. They'll find him and help him."

Her soothing tone relaxes me, as does her sweet face. High cheekbones. Perfect little nose. Plump, pouty lips. All framed by a halo of blond hair. Her heated cheeks and the nervous flutter of her eyelashes add to the wholesome illusion. I bet no one thinks twice about what she is or isn't. She probably spent her life overshadowed by a greedy father and a wild-ass sister. Alessia just *is*, and I can't help but find her attractive.

"And, if you visit him in the facility," she continues, cheeks red from my regard, "and show him how concerned you are, maybe it'll encourage him to finish rehab."

It's a good idea. "Tomorrow. I'll take the helicopter." I exhale sharply, decision made, then before I reconsider my actions and stop myself, I stretch out beside her on the mattress and curl into her.

Her body's warm, and her hair smells like vanilla. She's soft in every way that counts, and exactly what I need in this moment.

I nuzzle her ear. "You did me a solid. I won't forget it."

It takes a few minutes before she relaxes against me.

And a few more for me to fall asleep.

30

Alessia

I WOKE up in his bed, my wrists free and Bastian gone. The guards tracked my uncomfortable walk of shame back to the casita, assuming something happened because I spent the night in their boss's bed. But what did happen is not what they think.

Bastian confided in me.

He trusts me.

A mafioso capo, who'll soon rule all the famiglie.

And he took my advice and went to check on Renzo in Maine.

It's early afternoon, and I'm inside the main house for the very same reason—to search for Freido to inquire about Renzo.

I locate Bastian's main man in the great room, as he's closing a secret door disguised as a tall bookcase. He locks it, then places a key inside a hollowed book, catching my interest.

My curiosity runs rampant. Keys to a hidden room? What could the room be used for, exactly? Torture? Sin? Pleasure?

I hesitate a few seconds more before clearing my throat.

Freido spins around.

I hide the fact I'm beyond intrigued and offer him my most innocent expression. "Did they find Renzo?" I ask.

He frowns. I can tell he's debating whether to answer. Probably afraid Bastian won't like his business being discussed with the likes of me.

He nods yes.

Thank heavens. "And Bastian arrived at the facility safely?" I blurt out. Lord, I sound like a concerned wife. The sexy man slept naked and curled around me without initiating any sexual contact, and now my brain's rewired.

Freido's head rears back in surprise. That I'm aware Bastian is in Maine or that there's only one way I'd know this—that Bastian confided in me?

"Where our capo goes is of no concern to you. If I were in your shoes, I'd make myself scarce whenever he's about." Freido stalks toward me. "Tomorrow, he arranged a private viewing at the Providence Art Museum, an afternoon at the Mandarin Hotel spa, dinner, and a night out with that hoodlum Zoey."

"He forbid me from going to bars and clubs."

"He'll allow you into Beneventi-run bars and clubs, but you'll take a guard with you."

I nod, pleased with the additional freedom.

"Pack a bag because you'll be staying overnight in Providence." He lowers his voice. "And if you're smart, you won't let Zoey raise hell, or we'll have a problem, understand?"

Understand? One night, I'm in Bastian's bed, and the next I'm at the swankiest hotel in Rhode Island? A night on the town—*with* Zoey?

Is this Bastian's way of thanking me?

"A car will pick you up at ten o'clock."

"Does Zoey know?" I ask, my excitement overshadowing any lingering puzzlement. Because the Providence Art Museum is hosting a traveling exhibit featuring several Italian artists. I'm thrilled about the private showing and about chatting with the curator.

How thoughtful. Proof Bastian understands my passions, and my vices.

"Zoey's already pressed her luck by asking for spending money," Freido grumbles, then hurries off, probably avoiding any more questions he likely can't answer. Is he surprised by Bastian's consideration, too? Is that why he warned me to make myself scarce whenever his boss is around?

My lips curve.

Because, after last night, I intend to do the exact opposite.

The painting across the hall draws my attention, and I study it with an entirely different mindset. Bastian sees himself as the king, doesn't he?

If so, then who is the woman at his feet?

I listen carefully until I'm certain I'm alone before positioning myself on the carpet in the same manner, legs curled beneath me and eyes raised, pretending I'm seated between Bastian's parted legs with my cheek pressed against Bastian's muscled thigh.

"My dirty little slut," he'd murmur, wrapping his fingers in my hair and tugging hard, forcing my head back and our eyes to lock.

His look is black like his bedroom, but his words are pure gold. "Look how you please me."

A shiver runs up my spine.

I've been searching for a father figure, haven't I? An experienced man who other men respect. An alpha male who'd protect me and tempt me, order me about and teach me how to sin. A person who'd understand the dueling facets of my nature, the shy girl and the inexperienced kinkster.

A sexy man who'd test my limits and force me into dirty, reprehensible acts.

Just like the woman in the painting who so beautifully submits to her king's will.

I close my eyes, and my imagination roams free.

When I open them, I'm focused on one thing—that key.

Rising from the floor, I shake the numbness from my legs and approach the bookshelf.

The book slides free with one tug, and I fold my hand around a key with a tiny red ribbon looped through the eyelet.

The lock isn't immediately obvious—you'd miss it if you weren't looking for it. Pushing the key inside, I turn it, and the bookcase swings open.

I'm greeted by a staircase leading downstairs. My heart thunders. Freido charged off. Bastian's in Maine. No one will know.

Do I dare?

Five steps and I'm standing inside. I leave the door slightly open behind me so it won't be obvious I'm snooping about. Slowly, I descend, curious, nervous, and dreading what I might find.

I reach the landing, enter the large red room, and stare around, aghast.

Bastian mentioned a dungeon, though this room can't possibly be what he was referring to.

This space is sin incarnate, with everything from a spanking bench to a Saint Andrew's Cross, from ropes and chains hanging from a beamed ceiling to a buffet of whips, floggers, and feathers displayed on a large table.

Bastian's bedroom is black, but in this room, everything is red.

I swallow hard. But nerves don't stop me from exploring. I begin with the bench, and position myself over the hump, face down with bottom up. Imagining the spanking I deserve for my disobedience. Would he use the whip? Would I enjoy it?

I approach the chains and pretend my arms are secured and my body suspended and constrained. So vulnerable. So at his mercy. Trust is the key to letting go, isn't it?

The table is next, and I take inventory of the items I've seen online and in the art movies I enjoy: clamps with a soft felt interior; small, medium, and large floggers; a sharp red leather whip; and a metal object that resembles a penis, with a thin tip, wide middle, and a notch to hold it in place when inserted.

It's big, but not even approaching the size of Bastian's bull.

A box of condoms and a bottle of lubricant are to the right.

I trace my finger across the closed seal on the condoms, pleased that the box isn't opened. The room is tidy, and I get the sense it's been unused for a while. He hasn't brought his rotating trio of women here anytime recently.

I don't know why this pleases me. Why jealousy factors into how I feel about him or who he entertains. This is far more complicated than a crush. It's not simply sexual attraction, either.

There's an irresistible, inescapable pull whenever he's present. A magnetic connection drawing me in, even if I'm occasionally repelled by his dominating manner. It's undeniable, and has magnified since I moved onto the estate.

And he feels it too.

He didn't throw me out of bed. The opposite, actually—he hand-cuffed me and made sure I'd stay put while he found comfort in my body.

We bonded.

We connected.

I glance around the red room once more before heading back upstairs.

Because I know, deep within my soul, this isn't the last time I'll visit this room. Bastian invited me into his life last night, and that's changed everything.

31

Alessia

"I'VE NEVER SEEN SO many small dicks in one place," Zoey exclaims.

The massage therapist, Tyrone—a really handsome man who's instinctively addressed all my trigger points—stops kneading my shoulders.

It takes a few seconds of awkward silence for my friend to realize she's insulted both men.

"No. Not you guys. I'm here to relax, not check out your dicks, though I'm sure Samuel here has nothing to be ashamed of given the size of his hands. I'm referring to the tiny dicks the Renaissance artists liked to paint."

Her massage therapist, Samuel-with-the-Mighty-Hands, chuckles. "Not sure if there was a compliment in there or not."

I'd roll my eyes except a cucumber-infused eye mask covers my lids. "This morning, we had a private tour of the Renaissance exhibit at the Providence Art Museum. People copulated to reproduce, not for pleasure—and that is how society preferred sex to be represented in art. Small appendages were the ideal."

"God bless the twenty-first century," Zoey exclaims. "I'd give you a dick worth staring at if I were an artist. The bigger the better."

The men laugh, along with me, which only encourages her.

"Dick art. It'll be all the rage."

Fate placed Zoey in my life, didn't it? Though opposites, we've quickly become best friends. How would I have navigated my new life without her wit and love of life?

The truth about me—and my *interests*—would shock even the unshakable Zoey. I've kept her clueless about the exchanges between Bastian and me. It'd blow her mind if she knew, in vivid detail, the way my father-in-law fingered me and marked me, and how hungry I am for more.

Bastian gets me—the art enthusiast, the sensualist, the curious kinkster.

It's a strange predicament because a predator like him is definitely not someone you open up to, and easy prey like me never reveals her desires, twisted and otherwise, to anyone.

Yet here I am, my mind still stimulated by the private museum tour, and my body energized by Tyrone-with-the-Magic-Touch's expert hands.

Zoey grunts and groans on the table next to mine as Samuel resumes work.

I'm tempted to ask her about Bastian's sex dungeon. If she knows it exists? If she's heard who he invites inside to play with? Yet I keep quiet, worried my interest in the room—and in Bastian—might shine through.

Several minutes pass. Then a frantic knock on the door interrupts the silence.

"For the love of God," a panicked woman exclaims from a few feet away. "Stop touching her."

My massage abruptly ends.

"What's happening?" Zoey exclaims.

"We apologize for the mix-up, Miss Amato," the woman continues, ignoring Zoey's question. "Kim and Kathy will be your therapists for the remainder of your treatment."

"No. We'd like Samuel and Tyrone to stay. Isn't that right, Alessia?"

"Yes." I remove the cucumber mask and, securing the thin sheet around my breasts, roll to sit.

Zoey's done the same, minus the sheet.

The woman's midtwenties and wearing the same signature Mandarin Hotel uniform Samuel and Tyrone have on. They seem as confused as we are, but the woman is dead serious. "Tyrone has another appointment." She waves them toward the door. "Enjoy the spa free, compliments of the Mandarin Hotel, while you wait."

"Samuel, wait," Zoey calls. "Come back. We'll pay extra …"

The woman pretends not to hear her and focuses on me. "Enjoy the rest of your stay, Miss Amato." She spins and follows the men from the massage room, the door closing behind her.

Zoey hops off the table and chases after them but returns less than a minute later. "Unbelievable," she exclaims, breasts swinging as she charges over to stand beside my table. "Think she was listening in on our big dick talk? I wasn't harassing Samuel, right? I mean, his hands are freaking enormous, so the natural assumption …"

I shake my head. "No. I don't believe that's it."

"Did you notice she kept addressing you as Miss Amato, like you were Hollywood royalty or something?"

I did notice, and also that she never once addressed Zoey. Why is that?

Zoey sighs. "Let's not let this buzzkill ruin our fun. How about we take advantage of the free spa amenities, use their world-famous shampoos and lotions, then go shopping?"

With the sheet secure, I hop off the table. "There's a new privately-run bookstore downtown. They've a small multilingual selection I'd love to check out." I read online about the opening, though I never expected I'd visit the shop. They don't accept online orders yet, though browsing the shelves is part of the fun. I was hoping to purchase novels in Italian, and now am giddy at having the chance to do so.

"A bookstore? Seriously? That's your idea of shopping?" Zoey sighs with exaggeration. "My thought is we spend some money. I mean, Freido did give me the black card."

"Freido did?" I ask, surprised. Yesterday, wasn't Freido griping about Zoey's demands for spending money? He actually trusts her with the black card?

"We can shop for drip outfits to hit the clubs in. After visiting the bookstore, if that will make you happy?"

"I don't know about going to clubs."

"Mr. Beneventi gave us permission ..."

"He did. But our guard will no doubt report everything back to him." *Do good girls flaunt their bodies at every Dick and Harry? Bastian was jealous when he discovered me in that red bikini. Would he react the same way? Do I dare tempt the beast?* "It's not a good idea."

"No one will care what the guard has to say. Everyone will be too busy getting off at the party at the estate ..."

My stomach drops. "What party?"

Her eyes grow wide, then her hand flies to cover her mouth.

"Getting off," I grind out as I piece together the news. "Like having sex?"

"Oh, shit. Me and my big mouth. Freido threatened that I better keep this a secret."

Everything I thought I believed comes spiraling down like a tornado ripping through my soul. Bastian didn't gift me with a near perfect day because he gets me. Or as a thank-you for my loyalty. Or because he cares in the slightest and wishes to make me happy.

Bastian arranged for me to be away from the estate for the night so he could host a party.

"You looked pissed."

Pissed. Hurt. Toyed with.

"It's in your best interests. Mr. Beneventi did you solid by arranging this weekend and sheltering you from his kinkfest. From what I've heard, you'd be shocked at what goes on at his parties."

"What. Goes. On. Exactly?" I croak out, enunciating each word.

Zoey hesitates.

"You're bare-ass naked right now, and I've barely blinked." I scowl. "Tell me."

"Okay. But if Freido finds out I've been gossiping ..."

"He won't."

Zoey takes the abandoned sheet from her table and wraps it around herself.

The longer she stalls, the worse I feel.

"Ever hear of the director Stanley Kubrick?"

"He directed *Eyes Wide Shut*." My heart flutters, and something stirs deep within me. Oh, Lord. To witness a gathering like that. A kinkster's playground fused with a sensualist's paradise? It's a wild fantasy, set in reality.

And I've been sent away like some innocent virgin while Bastian ... *partakes*.

My fists clench.

What did I expect? An invitation to my father-in-law's kinkfest? My first true taste of debauchery? A visit to his sex dungeon?

"Think masquerade, with men in suits," Zoey explains, oblivious to my inner turmoil, "and women in expensive gowns and lingerie. I hear Mr. Beneventi likes human furniture." She pauses, then explains. "Naked people, posing as tables and such. If they spill the drinks on the trays on their backs, he has them spanked. Or he has someone, man or woman, eat them out or offer a blow job, with the same rules in place."

"Let's go shopping," I snap.

"Right. Too much for your delicate ears. Off to the bookstore we go. Whoo-we! Still, you're marrying a Beneventi, and it's probably better that you're aware of all Mr. Beneventi's particularities ..."

"Gown shopping."

Zoey stares at me, slow to catch on. "For the clubs?"

I shake my head. "We'll need masks that'll conceal our identities."

If I weren't so angry, her expression would be comical. "Wait. You want to sneak into Mr. Beneventi's party?"

Mind set, I stalk toward the spa.

"That's exactly what I intend to do."

32

Alessia

ITALIAN OPERA MUSIC greets us as we exit the Uber.

Zoey grins from ear to ear.

My throat forms a knot as the beautifully twisted lyrics wash over me. *My kiss will dissolve the silence that makes you mine.*

"Opera, at a sex party?" Zoey exclaims.

"Not any opera—Puccini's "Nessun dorma" or "No Sleep." Am I surprised Bastian's taste extends to Italian opera? Not anymore. And, of course, he's playing the most twisted aria ever. "Pavarotti's singing about a princess who threatens to execute her entire kingdom if her suitor's name isn't discovered. Listen to the female chorus in the background. They're singing, 'Everyone will die.'"

Zoey laughs. "How bent yet appropriate."

I straighten my mask and smooth my gown across my hips, part intrigued and part annoyed. Bastian arranged my weekend away so he can play. But why? To shelter me? Protect his privacy? Or did decency prevail—because having a daughter-in-law present at his orgy is as twisted as the aria playing?

Yet that's the nature of our attraction, isn't it? Wicked and beauti-fully bent with boundaries broken and beyond repair. We crossed a line I don't care to step back over. Bastian just doesn't realize it yet.

Jealousy spurs me forward out of shyness's shadow. Lord knows what I'm entering.

"Your ass is everything in that gown," Zoey gushes from behind me as we enter through the front door. "The pale silver suits you, too."

The silk glides across my curves, luxurious against my skin. The steel grey shimmers when I move. Subtly sexy yet sophisticated. Unlike Zoey's short red dress with a plunging neckline, my gown covers me from collarbone to ankles. Three-inch silver-beaded heels and a tennis bracelet complete the look.

"How can your tits be so naturally perky?"

"It's the material." My entire body's hypersensitive, but my lack of undergarments elevates the thrill.

I can barely believe we're here.

The guards at the front gate were too busy eye-fucking us to pursue why the fake names Zoey offered them weren't on the list. They waved our Uber through as Zoey winked and laughed, "Suckers."

"That was easy."

She grinned. "I used names they're familiar with."

My fists clench even now that we're inside. The reminder I'm posing as one woman within Bastian's revolving three-packs keeps my jealousy alive and thriving.

"Vanilla, chocolate, or strawberry?" a butler hired for the evening asks. My fingers are numb, I clench them so tight.

Three baskets sit on the credenza on the right wall.

"Wigs," Zoey exclaims, dashing forward and plucking out a short red bob cut. "I considered going red. What do you think?" She fixes the wig over her hair and tucks her brunette locks beneath it. Readjusting her mask, she's totally unrecognizable.

It's a gift. A blessing we won't be discovered.

Still, I'm livid.

I snatch a long bleach blond wig and arrange it over my blond locks.

Zoey protests. "Aren't you tempted to select a different color? Why not try brunette? That wig's too close to your original hair color."

I offer her a shrug. "Blondes have more fun." Says the shy wallflower who has lost her mind. Because the tiniest, most reckless part of me hopes Bastian might recognize me. And then what?

She stares at me like I've tugged on an alien head. "Are you okay?"

"Yes."

"Because you're acting strange." She lowers her voice to a whisper. "Where did sweet Alessia go?"

I shift on my heels, and fake blond locks brush against my hips. "I'm still sweet, but tonight my name's Sugar."

She claps her hands. "And I'll be Spice."

From behind us, a man's whistle startles us.

We turn, and I immediately recognize Bastian's associate, a minor capo from the MidAtlantic, a few feet away. He gestures. Our eyes lock, and fear races through me. Lord, please don't recognize me.

"Come here, sweetheart."

"Shit," Zoey says beneath her breath. "He means you."

I grab Zoey's elbow, and we hurry away. But the man follows us down the hall. "Mark my words. Bastian will fucking wreck her before the night's over."

"Holy fuck, did you hear that?" Zoey hisses as we enter the great room.

"No."

"Let's go before Mr. Beneventi wrecks you."

A shudder racing through me, my eyes skim the room in search of the man who'll be my complete and utter destruction. What I find instead turns my stomach.

Zoey gasps. "It's freaking four o'clock everywhere you look."

Women have gathered in threes based on hair color. Some wear expensive gowns half-pulled down and hitched beneath an exposed breast. Others are barely dressed in sexy lingerie and high heels. A few sport G-strings and nothing else.

Most men wear expensive designer suits; dressy pants and jackets but no shirts, ties, or shoes.

My gaze falls on the human tables, the men and women on hands and knees, naked, frozen in position, with trays of champagne perched on their backs.

And people are fucking. Beneath my favorite painting and over by the bar, in groups or with partners.

My heart thunders.

Even Zoey's eyes resemble saucers. "And I believed Renzo was the wild Beneventi."

"Do you see him?"

"No. Unless he's escaped rehab …"

"Not Renzo," I correct. "Bastian." I search the room once more but don't find him. I'm relieved and unsettled. The bookcase door leading to the sex dungeon is closed. But still, he could be there … entertaining someone else …

I grunt with displeasure.

Zoey's unusually quiet, which draws my attention.

"Is something wrong?" I manage, in response to her eyeballing me through her mask.

"Is there something you're not telling me?" Her eyes narrow. "You called Mr. Beneventi by his nickname. *Again.*"

"Nothing to tell." That much is true, anyway. Whatever transpired between Bastian and me is a shattered illusion. I pluck two champagne flutes off the nearest human table and pass her a glass. "To living on the edge." I clink her glass with my own.

"Who are you?"

"Sugar, remember?"

She studies me a second longer, then taps my glass with hers. "To not falling off the edge."

Lord, if she only knew the truth. I've fallen, and off the most precarious peak.

We drink and look our fill. And there's a lot to see.

We've entered a decadent scene straight out of the movie *Eyes Wide Shut.* Highbrow kink, where you're invited to look past the outwardly sophisticated vibe and discover sinful pleasures just beyond. It's an art movie on the surface and pure porn at the core.

My throat hitches. Am I prepared for the situation I might find Bastian in?

Maybe this is for the best? Maybe a heavy dose of reality will end my obsession with him?

Women approach the human table and reach for the champagne glasses. "His biceps are enormous," a red-wig-bearing woman gushes.

The blonde's quick to respond. "Big biceps, massive dick."

They laugh. When things finally fall quiet, the brunette strikes. "I hear he ruts like a bull."

I squeeze my champagne flute.

Zoey nudges me. "They're talking about Mr. Beneventi."

"Define massive?" the redhead demands.

The other two make measurements in the air.

"Eight inches. And thick like a soda pop can." Another gorgeous brunette draws up beside me. It's not her comment but her tone that catches everyone's attention. Like she knows firsthand how magnificent Bastian's cock is.

She shrugs. "So I hear."

My anger flares. Because she's lying, though not about Bastian's cock size.

"Mind if I complete your trio?" she asks Zoey.

"Well, since you asked ..."

"Sugar," I introduce myself, interrupting my friend before she says yes.

Zoey sighs. "Spice."

The woman chuckles. "And everything nice, though not tonight?" She's stunning and edgy, with enormous breasts and a tight little waist, and a python tattoo running down her right arm. "I'm Chiara Renselli."

I flash a polite smile yet don't say a word, instead choosing to drink deeply while listening in on the conversation in front of us.

"He's started the selection early this time."

My stomach drops. What selection?

"We'll pass with no problem. Not with your pouty lips and her tight round ass."

"Go bull or go home."

They laugh. Like this is a game. And it is, to them.

But not me.

My future is intertwined with Bastian's. And what I really want, deep down inside, is to shape it into a form I don't dread but desire.

"First time, Sugar?" Chiara asks. Lord, my eyes must give me away.

I nod. "What selection?"

"He gets off on picking his partners publicly like a king does his subjects. Everyone calls it the selection." She smirks. "Except tonight, he's switched things up."

"How so?" Zoey asks.

"The selection's already been made."

Everything stills. The activity around us. The air. My heart. It's upsetting that Bastian loves being with three women at a time. It's devastating learning he's now chosen one—Chiara Renselli.

"Don't tell anyone, or you'll ruin the fun. But he called me and demanded I attend." She lowers her voice. "I christened the Red Room when he first had it built and can't wait for our scene later on."

"What Red Room?" Zoey screeches.

I say the first thing that comes mind to change the conversation. "I left something in the oven."

That derails the discussion, though the train wreck's already happened. She's exactly his type. Experienced and confident. Familiar with his kinks and, if she was personally invited back, clearly skilled at satisfying his needs.

I fight back tears.

She touches my arm. "You're young, I can tell. One day, you might catch Sebastiano's attention." Her expression hardens. "But not tonight."

"Let's go," Zoey snaps, clasping my elbow and practically dragging me away from the horrible woman.

We cross the hall and enter the movie room. It's usually locked, so I've never ventured inside before. I take in everything at once. Giant reclining chairs make up three rows. An enormous movie screen hangs from the high ceiling to the floor. A theater-style stage standing a few feet high is pushed in front of it, and on it's an oversized chair.

And that's where I find him.

Oh. My. God.

Bastian's sprawled across the chair, shirtless, maskless, barefoot, and dressed in black silk pajama pants. Thighs parted and one arm on the chair rest, he drinks straight from a whiskey bottle, and lazily watches the three women at his feet kiss.

He's so sexy I could cry.

"God help us but he's hot," Zoey mutters.

I don't reply. How can I without giving myself away?

He raises the bottle again, and I catch his scowl. That smug woman is right. I feel his disinterest, his disengagement from the scene playing out at his feet. Irrational or not, I feel betrayed. Like I have some claim on him. Like he's mine. "Next."

Everyone jumps at his sharp command. The three women flee, and a new group assumes their position.

In a selection I'll never be included in.

One day you might catch Sebastiano's attention.

I gasp. Wait. She called him Sebastiano.

I stare at him for a long time, my thoughts in turmoil.

He glances my way, once, then twice.

That means something, doesn't it? Surely, if she were someone special, she'd call him Bastian ...

"Are you nuts?"

I freeze and face Zoey. "No."

"Oh freaking hell. Sebastiano is still looking over here."

"He is?" I breathlessly respond, then immediately glance in his direction.

He curls his fingers, signaling me.

"He's gesturing for us to come over," Zoey cries out, panicking. "What do we do?"

I hesitate. Part of me wants to test him. Pretend I'm sugar sweet and see what happens. But what if he does select me? What if I'm invited to play?

The bravado that accompanied me from my shopping spree to his party vanishes. I'm playing a dangerous game with serious consequences. Losing my innocence this way will shatter his trust in me. I can't bleed on his big bull without him noticing, then disappear. He's going to know it's me. I mean, how many virgins did he invite to his party? Zero, no doubt.

Bastian stands.

If I understand one thing about him, it's this—he takes what he wants when he wants it. And right now, that's me.

I grab Zoey's hand.

"Run."

<hr>

Bastian

"NEXT."

I wave off the women at my feet and fall back into my seat as the trio scrambles from the dais. Large tits, small tits, round asses, tight asses—a feast at my disposal. Yet my bull isn't hungry.

Is it that I'm jaded? Bored? After all, I've participated in every imaginable scene, most multiple times. Sex is half-physical, half-psychological. On paper, tonight was a smorgasbord of everything I like—or used to like.

The three women at my feet are an exact redial of the others. What's the count now? Eight? Ten?

Fuck. Chiara doesn't even spark my interest like she used to. A hard scene with an experienced submissive doesn't stir my blood like it used to.

Even the whiskey doesn't mellow my frustration.

The blond at my feet boldly stares up at me.

Wrong vibe. Wrong eye color.

Little Miss Innocent's probably tucked away in her fancy hotel room bed. Dreaming of rainbows and lollipops, and Italian gelato.

I bring the bottle to my lips and drink deeply. My own fucking fairy tale is coming true. I should be rejoicing, not feeling empty inside.

Everything's set. My becoming capo di tutti capi is a dream my old man never envisioned. Still, I don't wish for Don Lucchese's death. In fact, I dread the day the news arrives. He's been a better father to me than my own.

I flex my knuckles, remembering the day I realized I'll never be the man my father wanted me to be. That I was stronger and wiser than he'd ever be.

His friend cornered me in the barn and placed a knife to my throat.

I waited for the fuckhead to shove me to my knees and withdraw his cock before removing my Swiss Army Knife from my pocket and driving it into his kidney.

Dick out and writhing on the barn floor, I returned to my father's office to inform him what had transpired.

I'll never forget his reaction. He shoved his face into mine and snarled, "You allowed him to touch you without a fight? No one touches a Beneventi without permission."

"It was tactical. I did what was necessary until I could position my knife," I calmly explained. "Then, not only did I fight, I killed him."

"The other capos will demand an explanation."

I shrugged. Not my fucking problem.

"Did he touch you or not?"

"Yes. But ..."

"You're a disgrace. Unworthy of my name. Word gets out and I'll be a laughingstock."

"Dead men can't talk," I replied.

He never loved me like I love my sons. They may be little shits, but they're my blood, my family. Touch them or hurt them, and there's no place on earth you can hide.

"Fear makes you weak," Don Lucchese wisely informed me, explaining my father's business style without directly addressing him by name. "Respect makes you powerful."

A lesson I learned well, and from a man more father to me than my own. A man deserving my unwavering respect.

The brunette nudges my thigh with her cheek. "We're here for your pleasure, Sebastiano." She licks her plump lips. "Use us."

Nothing.

I make a go at finishing the bottle. As I do so, a flash of silver draws my attention.

A gorgeous woman in a blond wig and grey gown hovers by the door. Her dress is conservative, hugging her curves without exposing too much skin. Her beautiful breasts aren't on display like most guests. But it's her stare that captures my complete attention.

With such intensity. Such *need*.

My dick rears to life.

Madonna mia.

The woman in the red dress next to her demands her attention.

Cockblocked—that's what this is. *No fucking way.* She glances my way, and I curl my fingers, beckoning her over.

The redhead becomes animated, and cockblocks me again.

In my own fucking mansion.

At my own goddamn party.

I snap.

I'm on my feet and moving.

But so are they ... disappearing lightning fast from the movie room.

I chase after them like an inexperienced teen pursuing his first love. Yet my excitement's undeniable, and as I follow them down the hallway toward the kitchen, all the deliciously filthy things I plan on doing to Miss Hungry Eyes spur me on.

I enter the kitchen at a full sprint, but the door is open.

Exiting, I summon the guard outside. "They head around to the front?" I demand, though I've already reached the steps. When I catch her, I'm going to pin her on the front lawn, then fuck her six ways to Sunday.

"That way, sir." He points toward the casita.

I descend, taking two steps at a time, intent on hunting her down. Like an animal pursuing his prey. It's not until I spy the blond and her friend disappearing inside the casita that the whiskey fog clears. Seconds later, the lights come on and confirm it.

No fucking way.

A few feet further, I stumble upon sparkly grey heel and a long blond wig in the grass.

I'm going to kill Zoey for putting Miss Innocent up to this.

My pulse races. Because I'm tempted, so goddamn tempted to do it. Take what she's offering, consequences be damned.

End the spying.

End the teasing.

Teach her everything I like, and everything the little kinkster isn't even aware she needs.

I kick the wig and send it sailing. "One. More. Time. And I'll do it, no matter the consequences."

33

Alessia

FOR THREE DAYS, I avoided the main house by pretending I was ill. Fear mixed with outrage keeps me casita-bound. Zoey and I barely escaped the party, and I've been walking on eggshells in anticipation of Bastian calling me into his office and demanding an explanation.

And the angry side of me—the side fueled by Chiara Renselli's late-afternoon departure two days ago—seeks my own explanations. Why her? Why not ... me?

But no one cares what I do.

I'm invisible. Forgotten. Failing, in every way, shape, and form, in getting a private audience with Bastian, whether I want one or not.

This sunny afternoon, I'm inside his kitchen and baking pies. Baking is arguably more scientific than cooking. Every pie is different. Every one my own creation. A therapeutic task that keeps my mind off things I shouldn't want. The secret to a perfect pie is the crust. I've carefully researched the best ingredients to ensure the crust is flaky and tender, and narrowed it down to one.

My favorite ingredient—vodka.

Busying myself, I forget my troubles. But on the fifth pie, I run out of liquor.

I bite my lip. Do I dare?

I pass Bastian's office. His door is closed, yet I hear him talking inside. Heart racing, I keep moving until I reach the bar in the great room. Luckily a bottle of expensive vodka is inside the bar fridge. I'll chill a second bottle from the shelf behind the bar while finishing the dough I've already begun.

Bottles curled into my chest, I trek back down the hallway, only to stop in surprise.

His office door is partially open.

I hesitate, and ignore the warning bells blaring in my head. *Keep walking. Don't be foolish. What if he confronts you about the other night?*

Temptation guides my actions, and I steal a peek inside.

He's *there*. Alone. Typing away on his laptop with an intense expression.

Lord knows, he's easy on the eyes. His suit jacket's hung over the back of his chair. Sleeves rolled up to expose big firm forearms. Tie loose and shirt unbuttoned. He's tan. He's sexy, even while working.

The chill against my chest reminds me of our first encounter. Him, plucking an ice cube from the bucket and popping it into his mouth. Me, not knowing where to look or what to do, yet so insanely attracted to him.

The things he could teach me.

The things I yearn to experience with him.

Bastian grunts, rolls back in his seat, and glares at his laptop. Heavy is the mafioso crown he wears.

He's sexy without even trying to be. Pure, unadulterated male ...

"What the hell are you doing?"

Sandro's growl makes me jump and nearly drop the bottles. He stares at me, then at the open door. Eyes narrowing, he grabs my elbow and steers me down the hallway.

He waits until we reach the kitchen before going off on me. "Why are you spying on my father?"

My cheeks warm. "I wasn't ..."

He gets in my face. "You were. I caught you, so don't deny it."

"I wanted to ... ask his permission," I stutter, "... to use the vodka from the bar." I hug the bottles to my chest, as if they'll protect me from further attack.

"What did you hear?"

"Nothing. He was working at his desk."

He runs his fingers through his hair. If his temper weren't so ugly, he'd be attractive. "Even my father believes your innocent act, isn't that right?"

No. But it doesn't make a difference, does it? I stiffen. "Maybe he's more perceptive than you?"

Sandro slams a fist into the wall behind my head. "Or maybe you've mastered the art of manipulation."

"Let me go."

"Too late for that." Yet he drops his arm and steps back. "You couldn't leave things as they were," he grinds out through clenched teeth. "Why'd you do it?"

"I told you. I'm baking pies and needed vodka—"

"Not that. Why'd you push him into demanding we set a date?"

"A date for what?" I mimic the condemnation in his tone.

His laugh is downright sinister. "Our goddamn wedding date."

I rear back. "What?"

"The plan was to delay things indefinitely. But he's snapped, and it's all he can talk about."

My face pales. "No."

"Yes." He locks eyes with me. "The question is why?"

I'm stunned, and suddenly furious. "There is no why." I thrust the vodka bottles into Sandro's chest with such force, he steps back. "Bastian does as he pleases, whenever he pleases. I'm only a means to an end." I push by him and make for the door. "And for the record, setting a wedding date to marry an asshole like you is the last thing I want."

"Christ. Wait," Sandro hollers after me. "Since when do you call him Bastian?"

34

Alessia

Sandro: November 2nd.

AFTER READING ALOUD my asshole fiancé's text, I want to hurl my phone into the pool. That's all he has to say? With a sigh, I place my cell on a poolside table, pick up my margarita, and approach the pool.

"That sucks," Zoey replies. "Almost as much as he sucks."

I kick at the water and send a wave across the calm surface. My life is like that, rolling in one direction, then another, at the mercy of larger forces in nature. A swim might cool me off, though it's doubtful. Rage has lit a fire within me, and with no outlet, I rebel in little ways.

By drinking.

By refusing to prepare his dinner.

By wearing whatever style of bathing suit I feel like—and today, I'm in a white crochet one-piece that covers my body like a cobweb woven together by a drunk spider. The peekaboo gaps reveal nearly everything, though the weave is tighter over my nipples and private area. I purchased it based on how soft it felt against my skin before realizing whoever designed the flimsy yarn suit wasn't thinking swimming or sunbathing.

I was thinking stiff middle finger statement piece when I put it on.

Like Bastian would even notice. Even care.

I sigh and kick the water once more.

"Sandro's not that bad." Zoey joins me by the pool. "And setting a date was inevitable, right? I mean, you've been resigned to this marriage, even happy. Sandro will marry and then abandon you, leaving you to do whatever you want so long as it doesn't reflect poorly on the Beneventi name. I thought you accepted how things are? What changed?"

I'm tempted, so tempted to confide in her. "Maybe my interest lies elsewhere?"

Her eyes light up. "It's a guard, isn't it? Which one?" She looks toward our ever-present audience discreetly stationed closer to the main house. The men pay us no mind, no doubt under strict orders to leave us alone. Zoey glances around like the man I'm referring to is hiding nearby in the bushes. When, in fact, he's not hiding at all—he's simply washed his hands of me.

"He'll kill anyone who so much as glances at us."

"What happened to our golf instructor is all on you, Alessia. Mr. Beneventi isn't part of *my* cheering section."

I snort.

Through the grapevine, Zoey discovered Bastian had ordered the golf pro off the estate because our instructor was repositioning my body. For a wistful moment, it seemed Bastian might be jealous. Now, I believe otherwise. "Must protect Sandro's innocent bride from being corrupted, right?"

"You would have thought the poor guy was helping you with his cock stroke and not your golf stroke. And you'd expect a devil who hosts orgies to understand the difference."

I grind my teeth. Because, let's face it, the party was a disaster.

"You can run."

"What?"

She exhales sharply. "If you hate marrying into the Beneventi family, I'll help you escape."

I glance toward the guards. "Not so loud."

Zoey tosses back her margarita like a tequila shot.

"Escape how?" I whisper.

"Leave the country. I've a contact in Mexico who sells fake IDs and passports. You'll ask Sebastiano about wedding shopping in New York City. We'll rent a car, drive to El Paso, and cross the border there. Hell, I still even have my red wig. Instead of Sugar and Spice, we'll be Thelma and Louise."

I close my eyes. Envisioning the scene, and then Bastian's rage if I disappeared. Why does breaking his trust bother me this much? I shake my head. "My father works for the Beneventi famiglia. Sandro keeps tabs on my sister. And Thelma and Louise drove their car off a cliff."

"Oh crap. They did, didn't they?"

My chest tightens. "There's no avoiding marrying that asshole."

Zoey is quiet for half a heartbeat. "Sandro'd be thrilled if you moved to Rome to finish school, and left him to pillage and plunder unsuspecting women. He can't control you the way he likes, so he'll ignore you. If you're careful and discreet, you can have a revolving door of lovers." She pauses, then frowns. "Scratch that. Mr. Beneventi will freak."

"You think so?"

"Totally. Respect means everything. He chopped off some guy's fingers for skimming from the payroll. After he's capo di tutti capi, he'll be twice as vicious, mark my words."

I thought about him the same way, didn't I? Fear and violence distorting my perception. True, he radiates undeniable power and, like Sandro, thrives on control. True, the consequences of betraying him are severe. Bodies may or may not be buried on his golf course. But he's intelligent, with good business sense, and an excellent strategist. He loves his sons, even if both are a handful. There's a possessive side to him that draws me in. When his focus is on me, I never want it to stray. In fact, I crave it ... and everything that comes along with it.

Stockholm syndrome. My reality's become distorted, twisting in his favor.

"Ever skinny-dip?" Zoey abruptly asks. Her bikini top hits the pool deck before I can respond.

"The guards."

"It's not like they haven't seen everything before."

Zoey tucks the empty margarita glass beneath her chin, then wiggles her hips. Everything that follows happens in slow motion: The glass breaks free and tumbles toward our feet. She screeches, then pivots, reaching for it, but the bikini around her knees restricts her progress and throws her off-balance. Her arms flail as she swan dives toward me, and then the next thing I know, we're both in the pool.

I surface, gasping and treading water.

Her head breaks the surface next to me. "Holy shit."

We burst into laughter.

It takes us both several minutes to notice the stringy white cloud floating around us.

"Um, Alessia. Your bathing suit is disintegrating."

I sink into the water to assess the damage, then readjust and reassemble the messy clumps over important areas until I'm out of air.

Resurfacing, I give up hope. Zoey's no longer in the pool and can toss me a towel. Then I'll change into a more reasonable bathing suit, and the afternoon can resume.

Zoey waves at me.

"Aren't you proud?" I raise my voice. "I'm basically skinny-dipping."

She gestures toward the main house.

"The guards can't see me."

"Get. Out. Of. The. Pool." Her voice is low but her tone sharp. So foreign from her typically loud hilariousness.

"I can't. Not until you toss me a towel."

I tread water, waiting and watching, while she tugs on her bottoms and a T-shirt. Where is she going? She suddenly looks up, and her lips form an O. Then her movements become downright frantic.

"Is it the guards?" I call out.

She shakes her head. "Worse. Much worse. Sorry, Alessia. I gotta go before ... he kills me." She sprints toward the casita, then around the back, and takes off in the direction of the golf course.

I blink and paddle quicker in a half circle.

There's a loud splash behind me, then a wave of water.

Good Lord. No.

I dive forward and swim in the opposite direction, toward the large built-in bench. I'm almost there when fingers grasp my ankle and I'm yanked backward.

I kick free but only for a second. Hands grip my hips, and I'm lifted and tossed forward, the shallow water over the bench breaking my fall.

His chest slams into my back, and one of his thighs slides between my legs, which dangle off the bench.

I turn slightly.

Water clings to jet-black lashes framing furious blue eyes. "My men are jerking off in the motherfucking bushes."

"What?" I gasp.

"What did I tell you?"

I struggle against him. But when his palm presses against my stomach, I still. "Is this about my bathing suit?"

"I warned you. Men are stationed all over the estate."

Lord, it is. "No one saw me."

"I saw you," he hisses.

He steps back, yet his hands remain. Water sluices across his muscled chest, and my eyes follow the droplets as they drizzle over his gorgeous body before hitting the pool ... Wait ... he's wearing suit pants?

I glance up.

And he's staring down at the clump in his hand. His eyes close. "Madonna mia."

It hits me all at once. Nothing remains of my bathing suit but white clumps of yarn. And he's not unaffected by me or my nakedness ... In fact, he's struggling ...

I'm terrified yet yearn to see how far he'll take this.

"Tentami ancora una volta," he mutters.

Tempt me one more time.

Then his eyes flash open.

"On. The. Bench."

He tosses aside the yarn in disgust and shoves me down so my chest touches the tile.

"Start counting," he orders, then—*whack*—his palm connects with my butt cheek.

I gasp.

He curses, then strips away the little bit of yarn remaining. "I don't hear you. Count."

"One," I say on a rush as his hand descends once more.

"Two," he corrects.

"Two," I repeat, then hesitantly add, "three." Oh dear Lord. He's spanking me. And it stings.

And I rise onto my toes, eager for more.

"Madonna mia," he repeats, before the devil within him takes over. He spanks me quickly and efficiently, like a man possessed, and I lose count.

My bottom's on fire. Being at his savage mercy has me ready to combust.

"You enjoy being a little fucking Lolita?" he demands. Whack. "Tell me."

I nod. Your little Lolita.

He reaches around me to touch a breast. First palming it, then cupping it like he's testing its weight.

I squeal as he pinches a nipple.

It stings for a half second, then a shiver races up my spine.

"Fuck," he groans.

Without warning, I'm lifted and rearranged on the bench, facing him. "Know what happens to little cockteases who prance around naked?" His eyes penetrate deep. "They get good and fucked."

I blink. Is that what happened with Chiara Renselli? Did he fuck her so good, she couldn't walk until the next afternoon?

"No one will touch me. I'm Sandro's fiancée."

He pinches my nipple.

No one but him—is that his message? While he entertains multiple women ... and now one ...

"Did you fuck her?" I demand.

His expression's almost comical. A combination of annoyed, surprised, and curious. "Who?"

I swallow hard. "Chiara Renselli."

The hand on my breast stills as he considers me. "No. Didn't touch her."

"Not even in the Red Room?"

Now I have surprised him. "You've been snooping."

I shrug.

Something in his manner changes ... softens. "No one has been in the Red Room for quite a while. As for Chiara, I introduced her as a distraction to a friend who kept pestering me about the beautiful blond in the grey dress."

Lord. I can't tell if he's angry or not.

"An uninvited guest, who came close to being utterly and completely destroyed."

My throat hitches.

"Except, she'd like that, wouldn't she?"

There are moments in life when everything turns Technicolor. Yellows and oranges, pinks and reds, purples and blues, crashing into the palest sunlight. If only you could capture and bottle it up for harsher times, for when reality paints everything black.

Whatever I'm about to say gets lost when he sinks to his knees.

With the slightest push, I fall back with a splash. Anchoring my legs over his shoulders and parting my thighs, he angles me up until my pussy's mere inches from his face. My ass burns beneath hands that hold me, but I'm too focused on the wicked gleam in his eyes to care.

"What are you ... oh?"

He licks me with a long drag of his tongue.

"But you don't ... do this."

His tongue flickers over my clit, and I jerk in surprise.

"Say it."

"You don't eat pussy."

"You want me to fucking stop?"

I shake my head vigorously.

"That's what I thought." He smirks, and my heart stops. But when he lowers his head and plunges his tongue deep inside my slick channel, I die a thousand deaths. His hands bounce my bottom in unison with his thrusts. Every so often, his eyes lift and lock with mine as I greedily watch him pleasuring me.

Ink-black locks curling around his face.

Knowing eyes gauging my eager response.

I'm tempted to fork fingers through his hair and force him closer ... "Deeper," I groan.

He rolls me up as he stands, then sets me to kneel on the bench.

"Part your thighs, you demanding little slut."

I do.

He turns, lies back, and places his head between my legs.

"Ride my face."

Oh sweet heaven.

He doesn't wait, tugging my hips down and my pussy onto his waiting mouth.

"Ahh," I cry out, shocked and excited. For a man who dislikes oral sex, he's completely committed.

I lift then lower my body.

He tongue-fucks me like he can't get enough of me. "Madonna mia, that's it," he grunts. I'm close, so close. "Squirt all over my face, little rock star."

I moan, loving his dirty talk. But then I offer him my own filthy words. "Your tongue belongs in my tiny pussy. Make. Me. Yours."

And he does. So completely, so thoroughly, I'm suddenly flying across the tallest peak, seconds from shattering.

He grunts. "Madonna mia. I'm harder than fucking steel." His hand spanks my ass, his confession hitting deep. I did this to him. Despite everything, he wants me.

Punish me. Fuck me. Chain me to his bed. He can have it all, and more.

I come so hard, my body shakes.

"I meant it," I blubber. "I don't want to be a virgin anymore."

He goes rigid beneath me. "What?"

"You can have all my firsts, Bastian."

He withdraws so quickly, it stuns me. Wide-eyed, I watch him dive and then swim across the pool.

He lifts himself out.

Why, oh why haven't I learned my lesson. I offer him everything, and he rejects me. No more. My body might want it, but my heart can't take it.

My eyes close as my knees go weak and I collapse on the bench.

A towel falls over my head.

"Wrap yourself up." His commands are razor sharp. I unravel myself, then stare up at him. "Then go inside the casita and lock the goddamn door. Capisci?"

I blink up at him.

The man I fled three nights ago.

He charges off, leaving me with one mind-blowing thought. Who's running now?

35

Bastian

I SPEAR a piece of spicy beef with my chopstick and bring it to my mouth. Takeout, again.

And I've grown weary of it.

You can have all my firsts.

I chew, then wash the Chinese food down with whiskey. Tasting neither, because I can't get the taste of sweet temptation from my lips.

Numerous reasons I shouldn't take what I want replay in my mind. What would Don Lucchese think if I'm fucking Sandro's fiancée? How would my son react? Or his lovestruck twin?

Dante will have something snide to say, for sure.

The other capos might misinterpret my actions as weakness—like I'm some randy boy who can't control his appetites or a gullible fuckhead who's led around by his cock.

Governor Amato could balk.

And then there's the fucking wedding—I won't go back on my promise to the old man. He's smitten with her, too. Come hell or high water, Alessia will walk down the aisle.

You said one more time, one last chance, and she failed.

The lights in the kitchen turn on.

"Holy shit, sir," Freido says. "Didn't realize anyone was in the dark."

I grunt and spear another beef medallion.

"Chinese tonight?"

Observant fuck.

I wait for him to comment about the three other take-out dinners this week. At least, Little Miss I'll-Give-You-Everything had enough self-preservation to listen earlier, and lock herself inside the casita. Because when a man like me crosses the motherfucking line, a corruptible baby like her better lock herself away.

Especially considering I'm struggling to cross back over. "How long have we been friends?"

Freido draws up a counter stool. "Acquaintances, since our early twenties. Friends, a bit later."

I grunt. Honest and loyal—as well as my most ruthless enforcer.

"What's my greatest weakness?"

His eyebrows rise. "Sir?"

"Tell it to me straight, no bullshit." I wait for confirmation that my sons are my weakness. That love—no matter the shape or form—is my Achilles heel.

He hesitates.

"Love. Say it. The twins?"

His head shakes. "We Italians value family over everything else. If anything, the twins make you stronger. You lead with purpose, and with the famigilia's future in mind."

"I love the little shits."

He grins. "So do I."

I push the fried rice container toward him. "Eat."

"Your weakness is that ..." He answers my question as he dishes himself a plate. "... you make yourself miserable by overthinking things."

That catches my attention. "How so?"

"Before any major decisions, I've seen you holed up in your office, weighing the pros and cons and everything between. Yet if you actually ask yourself, did your decision change from when you sat down to when you concluded, I bet it never wavered. That you already decided."

I chew and consider his reply. "Things get messy when you don't consider different angles."

"Things get messy even when you do."

"True." I snort. "I like being in control."

"Yes. You do."

"And one step ahead."

"You always are." He pauses. "But you've been wound up for months."

I sip my whiskey from a paper cup. "The sex, drugs, and rock 'n' roll aren't helping." The party was meant to mellow me. Except the little gate-crasher ruined things ... and if I'm honest, she upended my life the first time in my office. An inexperienced woman with a curiosity for darker play—I didn't see it coming. But earlier in the pool, with her pussy juice all over my mouth, my cock was hard with need. I could play with her. Teach her. Ruin her six ways to Sunday and back. Jus Primae Noctis—right of the first night.

An old Italian custom.

My right.

Freido points a chopstick at me. "You take care of yourself in every way but one, Bastian—never here." He thumps his heart.

Love, for a woman, he means.

Like I have time for that.

I toss my chopsticks on the paper plate. "We need a plumber."

He stares at me for a few moments longer, and then grunts. "Do we? No one said ..."

"And an electrician."

His brow furrows. "Okay."

"Tonight."

He stands.

I nod to his half-eaten plate. "Finish your food before you have the men cut the power and water to the casita and make the calls."

Never, in the fifteen years I've known the man, has he looked this flabbergasted.

"Then tell Alessia to pack her shit. She's moving into the main house tonight."

36

—

Alessia

MY HEAD FALLS back against the shower tile with a moan as I climax to Harry Styles singing "Watermelon Sugar," and to the memory of Sebastiano Beneventi licking me like he believes every word of the song.

The music abruptly stops, and the bathroom goes black.

My hand drops from between my thighs. Not only is the bathroom's electricity out, but the spray from the state-of-the-art shower has stopped running. Have I popped a fuse? I smirk. Sex can be so earth-shattering, can't it?

Exiting the shower, I fumble around for a towel. Finding it, I secure it around my body before I head into the living area to investigate.

A man looms outside the glass doors ... Freido. That was quick.

"I'm not dressed," I holler.

He enters anyway. "Start packing."

"Packing?" I bite my lip. "Where am I going?" Oh no. Bastian's sending me to New York, isn't he? Same song. Same dance. We overstepped boundaries, and now he regrets it. Why deny the attraction? Why push me toward his son when he could officially claim me for himself?

Disappointment numbs me. Famiglie first, and always. He announced I'd be marrying Sandro, and that's that. His promise is nonnegotiable. No going back on it, or the other famiglie might think he's indecisive. And untrustworthy—because what father proudly announces his son's engagement, then steals his bride away? I'm Bastian's pawn and occasional plaything, nothing more.

"I was directed to help you."

I grimace. "Can I at least get dressed?"

"Be quick."

Between my phone and the moonlight filtering in, I find yoga pants and a tight sports bra. At least I'll be comfortable on the miserable ride to New York City. To finish the outfit, I pull on ankle socks and sneakers. Then I drag two suitcases out of the closet. There won't be enough room—Zoey and I spent *a lot* of time online shopping, with her nudging me to spend *his* money. *"Mr. Beneventi said to purchase whatever the fuck you want, right?"* My wardrobe isn't nearly as conservative as it used to be, though compared to Zoey, I dress like a nun.

I've changed, too, right? Less shy, more familiar with those around me. More free, and less concerned about keeping family out of trouble. I've grown bolder, too, drawn to him like a moth to a raging flame, aware of the danger yet still consumed by the fiery depths.

And now Bastian's shipping me off to his son.

"I'm decent," I inform Freido.

"Better be," he mutters in such a low voice, I wonder if I'm imagining things.

"The dresser first, I guess."

He opens the suitcases and begins packing clothing from the drawers. I run a comb through my damp hair before knots can form, then cull through the walk-in closet. "Can you ask him to send someone to bring whatever's left behind?"

He grunts. "Sure thing."

"I'm going to miss this casita." My voice cracks. Sandro setting a wedding date hurt, but this is hell. "Does he plan on saying goodbye?"

"Why would he do that?" Freido asks, confused.

I flinch. Right. Why would he?

"I prepared his dinners. That, at the very least, is a reason." *At the very least*—I keep quiet about the details of my complicated relationship with his boss.

"And you polished the ancestral silver—he boasted about it for days."

I exit the closet to stare at Freido. "He did?"

"Bastian likes traditions. When he decides how something should be done, that's it, and a routine is set. Which, I suppose, is why it takes time for him to make up his mind."

It makes sense, knowing Bastian as I do.

"If you establish a place within his life and are loyal, you'll always be part of the Beneventi famiglia."

Is Freido offering me advice? I draw in a breath. "We're not discussing silverware anymore, are we?"

"No."

I frown. "Then why ship me off to New York?"

Freido pauses in packing. "Who said anything about New York?"

My heart does a dance. "I'm not being sent to Sandro?"

Freido scowls, his face phantomlike, half moonlight and half shadows. "That's where he should be sending you."

"Then where *am* I moving?"

"The casita has an electrical and plumbing issue."

"Both at once?"

His expression pinches. "Yeah. An electrician and a plumber will be called."

"How bizarre, right? Did someone sabotage the estate?"

"Not the estate. The casita." He snorts. "Which is why you're moving into the main house."

"I am?" Excitement bubbles out of me.

"Immediately, per his directive."

"And into Sandro's suite?"

Freido releases a long, drawn-out sigh. "The guest suite in his wing."

I clap my hands, eager to get moving. I close each suitcase, mindless that they're half-full, and then I hurry toward the glass doors.

Before the electricity and plumbing can come on, and I'm informed this was all a twisted joke.

Bastian

MY CONCENTRATION IS SHIT TODAY, Freido's words from last night running on repeat. "She's settled in like she belongs here." His smug face said it all, didn't it?

I drag my fingers across my jaw.

You made a decision, now deal with it.

Glancing at my watch, I turn to the business at hand, and Face-Time Don Lucchese. I'm greeted by heavy coughing, then finally his face appears on camera. "You're late," he grumbles.

"How many cigarettes you smoke today?" I make light of his deteriorating condition. Pale face, glossy eyes, and thin, so goddamn thin. Yet even if I asked, the old man wouldn't respond. Discussing health issues is admitting weakness, something no wise mafioso will do.

"Cuban cigars. A gift from Luca Ricci."

"That right?" I casually reply. I spoke to my friend a few days ago. Luca never mentioned sending our capo di tutti capi fucking cigars. I make a mental note of it, then set the uneasy feeling aside. "Trying to kill you, is he?"

"Aren't you all?"

I chuckle. "The Twelve Famiglie aren't such greedy fucks, or you'd be six feet under. War means our joint ventures fall apart. It'll hurt our pockets worse than the stock market crash."

"You've always been the smartest of the lot, Bastian."

"You taught me well."

The old man blinks, my kind remark hitting home. Fuck, I'll be happy if he lives past one hundred.

"Construction's begun on the Riverview Casino."

He claps his hands. "Right on schedule, eh? Sandro has your passion for moneymaking. Aren't you glad you gave the boy a chance?"

"It was the right decision for everyone," I respond carefully. Sandro always does the right thing—that being whatever the fuck I demand. His desire to please me supersedes everything else. Yeah, I'm proud he's stepped up, and I'm an asshole for not praising his accomplishments. But he's wound so tight, one day he'll snap, tell me to fuck off, and then begin making decisions independent from mine. It's what I did to my incompetent father. It's what Renzo's fought to do for years, marching to his own drum until I marched his ass straight to rehab—not that it's done any good yet. Hard to say what's worse: a sulky, despondent Sandro or an off-the-motherfucking-rails Renzo.

One day, they'll recognize tough love is still *love*.

"Any word on Atlanta?" the old man asks.

I duck my chin so he doesn't see my frown. "No date yet."

Don Lucchese grunts. "What the hell is holding him up?"

"Dante's not with you in Italy?" My men on-site down south informed me Dante was in Italy. An impromptu trip I know nothing about but assume was a family affair. Now, I'm thinking otherwise.

Why is Dante Lucchese in Italy?

Don Lucchese covers for him. "I bet it's a surprise."

Nothing could be further from the truth. Like me, Dante has control issues. Surprises in any shape or form are not his thing. I took him under my wing. Shaped him into a capable man worthy of being my right hand when I take over the Twelve Famiglie. So what bullshit is this?

"Will this do?" Don Lucchese stares wide-eyed and open-mouthed at the camera and pretends he's surprised.

"The ladies should think twice about visiting you." He cackles while from my lap I text my contacts in Rome about Dante. "How's wine season going?"

"Goddamn global warming is killing me. Land's dry, even for grapes." He pauses. "We should be investing in salt water conversion equipment. Plenty of ocean water, right?"

"Desalination equipment."

He grunts. "Whatever the hell you want to call it."

The Middle East is ahead of every other world region in water distillation processes. It's expensive, and a poor monetary investment. Doesn't mean I won't toss money toward a good cause. "I'll look into it."

"And how's our Michelin chef?"

"Nonna Rosa's in Italy."

"Alessia." He chuckles. "The sweet girl shackled to a kitchen chair yet while she cooks for you?"

Perceptive bastard. No wonder he's retained power for years. Thoughts of shackling Little Miss Give-You-All-My-Firsts—to a kitchen chair, kitchen island, my bed, office desk, fucking Red Room spanking bench—have become my obsession. She's the pretty unicorn my jaded heart never expected to desire. With my history, the little virgin won't hold my interest for long. I can play with her, even fuck her. Claim my fatherly rights until I work her out of my system.

"She made the lamb dish," I smoothly reply, giving nothing away.

"I've booked my flight to Rhode Island for the wedding."

"Send me the details so I can send my man to pick you up at the airport." My hand balls into a fist. I wish I never confirmed the date with him. But he fucking loves Alessia, and kept asking about it.

"Thank her for the weekly packages of cookies."

I frown. What. The. Fuck? She's baking for the old man? "Sure thing." And it's not like the cookies swam to Italy. Goddamn Freido's involved, for sure. Ma che cazzo. She's probably feeding my most violent men cookies from her palm like some docile beasts.

I simmer while Don Lucchese has a second coughing fit. I'm

about to demand if he's okay when suddenly my office door swings open.

Gun in hand, I rise from my seat. Then relax when Alessia appears in the doorway.

I flick a glance at the old man. "I have to go." She's pale, swaying on her feet, one hand clenching the other. "Save some cigars for tomorrow, will you?"

"Ask Alessia to make me some biscotti, and I will."

I nod, and disconnect, just as she murmurs my name. "Bastian."

Then, like a rag doll, she faints and hits the floor.

Shouting like a madman, I haul ass toward her. "Call a mother-fucking ambulance."

Footsteps thud as my men race to do my bidding.

I drop to my knees.

It's then I see blood.

38

Alessia

I BLINK TWICE as I wake. Once to lift the fog, and a second time to process what I'm seeing—which is Bastian seated in his chair and sucking my finger.

Because I cut it with a vegetable knife.

Because I panicked at the sight of blood.

Because I burst into his office in search of his help, then promptly fainted.

And now he has my finger in his mouth and is soothing my wound with his saliva.

Holy hell. It's close to being the most erotic experience of my life—though we've had a few.

I'm sprawled across his desk. Papers scattered everywhere, like he brushed them aside.

Lord, what must he be thinking?

Slowly, he pulls his lips off my finger. Then does the unthinkable—and bites the tip.

I'm instantly wide awake.

Blood coats his bottom lip—my blood.

My attention shifts to the wound on my finger, the small cut caused by the vegetable knife.

"It's a surface wound," he says. "No need for stitches."

I'm completely, utterly mortified. I could have run my finger under water and achieved the same effect. A Band-Aid and an aspirin and I would've been good. Instead, I ran to him like a woman on the verge of dying.

I sit up, then dangle my legs off the desk as I face him. "Sorry I interrupted your call. It's just that ..."

"You faint at the sight of blood."

"Yes."

"You always this way?"

He drags his tongue across his lower lip and licks the blood away. If I was asleep before, I'm hyperaware now. Lord, he's tasted my blood. And I love the idea he's had part of me no one else has had.

"I accompanied my mother to several doctors' appointments. Every time they drew blood, I fainted." I blush. My poor mama always reassured me that my fainting spells helped distract her from her health issues.

"You'll be mafiosi. Blood comes with the territory. We have to prepare you better."

Says the man who cuts off his enemies' fingers.

"You'll adjust." He pins me with a firm look. "We all do."

"Nothing frightens you."

"Loss of control does."

I search his expression, my own filled with surprise that he opened up. Again.

"Your asshole father learned his lesson. But you, little Alessia, are programmed differently when it comes to power play."

A shiver races up my spine. "How so?"

He brings my middle finger to his lips.

My nervous system fills with adrenaline because I now know what he's about to do.

He nips my finger, and my pulse kicks up, then he soothes the tip with his mouth, and I relax. My body isn't confused, but my mind is dumbstruck.

His grin is devastating.

"You get off on my power."

"I do?"

"You're a submissive with a masochistic side." His blue eyes darken. Lord, he loves the idea, doesn't he? "Pain intensifies pleasure, and vice versa, if done the proper way."

The proper way. I stare at him. Proper way, like bite then suck my finger? Proper way, like bend me over the desk and spank me? Or proper way like *"Welcome to my Red Room Dungeon?"*

"Will you show me?" I plead.

He stares at me with such intensity, I nearly fall off the desk. Considering it? Or toying with me?

I breathlessly wait for his rejection.

But he shocks me by producing a Band-Aid from Lord knows where and then gently covering my cut.

"What were you chopping?" he asks.

"Cucumbers. I was going to pickle them."

"Not red meat or deboning a chicken?" He snorts. "Or fucking cookies for Don Lucchese?"

My eyes flicker to the *V* marring his forehead. "Oh, you heard about that?"

"Freido mail the care packages for you?"

I bite my lip. He'll find out anyway, yet I don't rat Freido out.

"Loyal little thing, aren't you?"

"It benefits all of us if Don Lucchese is happy."

His lips twitch. "Wise, too. You certainly succeeded. He's asking for biscotti now. Double the batch and save one. Capisci?"

Save some for *him*, he means. "Capisci."

"Good. Now I've work to finish."

I slip off the desk and hold up my bandaged finger. "Thank you for helping me."

He grunts.

I pause. "Would you mind if Freido helped me roll pasta? I cut my pointer finger, and am right-handed—"

"He's busy running errands." His tone's so sharp, I jump. "What time?"

"Three o'clock."

"Have everything ready."

I blink. "Wait, *you're* helping me make fresh pasta?"

He shrugs.

I don't know how to respond. How many people get a taste of Sebastiano Beneventi's sweet side? It's a gift, a hard-won victory, because he clearly trusts me. I should be delighted. Except I yearn for more. Because he's right, isn't he?

What thrills the masochist within me is his dark side.

THREE O'CLOCK COMES AND GOES, without Bastian's help in the kitchen. Odd, because even if he's toying with me, he wouldn't break a promise or, God forbid, interfere with dinner preparations.

At three fifteen, men flood the house.

At three twenty, I'm stunned when one whimpering man is dragged outside.

By three thirty, all hell's broken loose.

"What's happening?" I ask Freido as he charges by.

He shakes his head in warning.

Alarmed, I abandon the pasta dough and wash my hands in the sink, then go to search for Bastian.

Guards block my entry into his office.

My heart sinks.

"Let her pass," he commands. "I need to interview her, anyway."

He gestures for me to sit, and I do so immediately. "Is it my father? Has he ... done something?"

"Leave us," he barks.

His men close the door behind them.

Bastian slams a fist on his desk, and I stiffen in fear. Yet I still manage to speak. "Tell me, so I can help you."

"Can you contact Renzo?"

My lips part. "I can try." I rip my cell phone from my pocket, then dial the nurse's stolen cell phone number. The message I receive is the number's no longer in service.

"He hasn't contacted you?"

I shake my head. "Not since the night he escaped. I broke his trust by telling you ..."

"His friend—a man in my goddamn employ—sent him his passport about a week ago."

I start. "Are you going to kill him?"

"He's too useful. Renzo may still contact him."

Wait. "Renzo escaped rehab?"

Bastian nods.

"And he has his passport?"

"Thanks to that loyal pezzo di merda."

I swallow hard. "Renzo's in Rome."

Bastian pins me with unyielding eyes. "That so?"

"We've spoken twice. The first time, he called from within the facility. He was concerned about my welfare. He mentioned eloping in Rome."

"Eloping." If Bastian was furious seconds ago, he's borderline psychotic now.

"His plan was that we'd marry."

"You love him?"

My lips part.

"Answer me."

"No. We're friends. I don't love him that way. Besides, Renzo is deeply in love with another woman."

"Perdio." He shakes his head. "That little shit never learns his lesson."

"What can I do to help?"

"We wait while my men hunt the little shit down." He shoots a text off before rolling back in his seat. Tense and tired.

Suddenly, I'm standing. Without giving too much thought to my actions, I round the desk, then sink to my knees.

"Alessia," he hisses, staring down at me like I'm his last supper.

I don't know where I find the courage, but I do. "Is there nothing I can do to help?"

I place a hand on his knee, prepared to swivel his chair more toward me.

"Not right now."

Horrified, I scramble to my feet and race for the door.

"Alessia." It's a command, and I stop.

"I'll be out of the country for a few days."

"Okay," I murmur. "If Renzo contacts me, I'll immediately let you know." I turn to leave.

"That's not what I was about to ask."

Something in his tone, the rough, whiskey-like gravel that sends shivers across my skin, causes my pulse to race.

"When I return, you better fucking be prepared for me to show you what we both need."

39

Alessia

"RENZO BETTER PRAY Mr. Beneventi doesn't find him."

I pause in laying a delicate sponge cake for the tiramisu we're making into a baking pan and narrow my eyes at Zoey. "Renzo needs help."

"Not the kind Mr. Beneventi dishes out."

"He loves his sons."

Zoey cocks her head and inspects me like *I'm* the woman who dresses up for alien sex. And what she finds upsets her. "Why are you defending him?" Her tone's ripe with suspicion.

"Why can you only see him as the grim reaper?"

"What is going on between you and Sebastiano Beneventi?"

She delivers her question with such unrestrained loathing that I flinch. The sponge loaf crumbles in my hand. "Nothing ..."

"Incredible." She tosses up her hands, and coffee grinds go flying. "I knew something was up when the casita suddenly had mysterious electrical problems."

And plumbing—but I don't correct her.

She tugs my elbow and directs me to the kitchen window. "What do you see?" she demands.

"Guards. Lawn. Pool."

"Lights. The cleaning people are vacuuming the casita."

"So?" I say defensively. Like I had a hand in deciding where I live.

"The electricity's on, Alessia." She lowers her voice. "And you're in Mr. Beneventi's guest room."

"Then they fixed the electricity."

Her hands find her hips. "Tell me the truth. You flip the electrical circuit?"

"What?" I laugh, because who would resort to such a thing? "Of course not."

You didn't turn off the main water valve, either. Is that back on, as well?

"Don't fall for him, okay? You'll be in so far over your head, first you'll drown, and then he'll cut you up and use you as fish bait."

I glare at her. "You make him sound like a monster."

"He *is* a monster."

Bastian deserves the title with all the despicable things he does. He's like the whiskey he's always drinking: smooth, complex, and potent. And, if I'm not careful, my greatest addiction.

"No freakin' way. Are you in love with Sebastiano Beneventi?"

"It's not love."

"What is it, then?"

I stare at the floor.

"Holy shit. You're fucking the Bull." She grabs my shoulders and shakes me. "Have you lost your mind along with your virginity?"

"No. I haven't." I flounder. "I'm not ... I'm still ..."

She leads me over to a counter stool and pushes me down. "Talk."

"There's not much to say."

"Bullshit. Or is it that you don't trust me?" She pauses, suddenly insecure. Lies will do that to a friendship, though technically I only omitted sharing the truth.

"I trust you," I rush to say. "But he trusts me, so I can't tell you anything. I won't discuss certain things behind his back."

"So loyal."

I sigh. "I'm a Beneventi. Either be loyal or dead, right?"

That registers, briefly.

She slides into the seat next to me. "Yes or no, then."

“Fine.”

“Did you see his bull?” she demands.

I blush. “Yes.” I don’t elaborate.

“Is he as thick as a goddamn soda can?”

I guess my expression answers her question because her eyes go wide. “Did you touch it?”

“No.” How I wanted to. But that doesn’t count.

“What?” Her hands are back in the air. “Did he jerk off while you watched?”

“Yes.”

“That filthy, dirty man.” Pause. “Did you like it?”

“I loved it.” My hand flies to cover my mouth. Too late. Zoey’s already losing her shit.

“Unbelievable. You could barely make eye contact with that beast, and now you’ve watched him come? Next you’ll be telling me he went down on you, when everyone from Rhode Island to California to … Rome … wherever … knows he never puts his mouth on a woman …”

I can’t help it. My lips curl.

She starts dancing around the room like we won a state championship. “Oh no, he didn’t. Oh no, he didn’t.”

“Please keep your voice down.”

“Did he pull any kinky shit?”

This conversation’s gone too far and needs to end. “I’m not in love, capisci?”

She shakes her head. “Capisci? You sound like him, even.”

“Let’s clean up and see if we can salvage the tiramisu.” I slip off the stool, but she’s not done.

“You’re playing with fire, Alessia. A man with his appetites can break an intelligent yet inexperienced woman like you.”

And I’m done. “What if I want to be broken?”

Her jaw hits the floor. “Wow. Okay. Didn’t see that coming. Anything else I should know?”

I’m tempted, so tempted to bring up the Red Room. For days, it’s all I think about. Me, bent across the spanking bench. Him, flogging my ass pink. Us, together and acting out our fantasies. "No," I lie. "That's all."

"Just be careful." She drops her voice, then softly adds, "Above all else, guard your heart. Because that's the first thing a man like Sebastiano Beneventi will break."

40

Alessia

I WAKE up to the sweet smell of marijuana.

With a start, I roll up to sit. I'm in Bastian's bed. I fell asleep with his spicy cologne on my pillow and his wicked promise in my head.

A man sits in the shadows in a chair by the fireplace.

Watching me.

"Bastian?" I call out.

His silence sends goose bumps across my skin. Nervous, I glance toward the door. Freido's sprawled over the doorjamb. "Oh my God," I cry. For three nights, he's stood guard outside, each night offering me a stern look as I enter Bastian's space, allowing me inside despite his disapproval. Now, he's paying the price for protecting me.

I scramble from the bed and fall to the floor beside him. Still breathing, just incapacitated.

By the man in the chair.

A man who is *not* Bastian.

A man I've little hope of escaping, if whatever he's done to Freido is any indication.

Moonlight bleeds into the room. The man's wearing a suit, his ankle bent over a knee as he smokes a joint. I don't get a full look at his face, but I don't have to—what I see is enough.

Panicked, I rise and stare at Sandro.

Oh, shit. Shit. Shit. Shit.

"You're in his bed." His words are slurred, his voice nearly unrecognizable.

What can I possibly say to that? "What did you do to Freido?"

My ears strain to hear his response. "Sedative."

"Why?"

"Payback."

He takes a long drag, and my eyebrows lift in alarm. Shadows creep back into the room and cast us into darkness. Will the darkness protect me, or help the monster across the room?

"I've been through hell and back to get here, only to discover you're banging my father."

"I'm not." I roll my bottom lip between my teeth. "I'm sleeping here, that's all."

"Why?" he tosses my earlier question back in my face. Lord, he's completely unhinged, isn't he?

I open my mouth, but no explanation comes out. How can I explain my actions? This unstoppable craving for a man nearly twice my age and years ahead in experience. My father-in-law. *His* father.

"We won't be getting married now, will we?" I expect an angry Sandro, so his disappointment throws me off.

"He might ... insist."

"Doubtful."

"You think he'll call off the wedding?" Dread switches to hope, and suddenly this unexpected exchange with my stoned fiancé doesn't feel like an imminent disaster.

He shifts in the chair and, elbows on knees, curls his head into his hands. "Know what she said after I broke my promise?"

"Who?" My throat hitches. *Wait ...*

"She's going to ride every dick in Hollywood like it's her last fuck on earth, while I rot in hell. And believe me, Angel, she meant it."

"Renzo?" I gasp.

"Who'd you think I was—Sandro?"

"Well, yes."

"The suit is what got me inside, along with my twin's trademark glower. Everyone fell for it, even that asshole on the floor." He pauses. "Even you."

I rush across the room, and choke on the thick plume of pot surrounding him like a halo. "You're not in Rome."

"By way of California—had to break a few hearts before I got here ..."

"We thought—"

"We?" He raises his head from his hands. "You, and my father?"

"Well, yes ..."

"I told you I'd come for you. That we'd elope." He gestures at the bed. "But you're on his side now. I knew the first time he met you this would happen. He couldn't keep his hands off you, could he?"

My heart races wildly in my chest, thrilled by his question and the implications within it. But Renzo is hurting, and the burst of joy quickly fades. I drop to my knees and touch his hand. "I'll always be on your side, Renzo."

"That why you ratted me out? How Sergeant Dickwad and his goons hunted me down in the woods?"

"Yes," I murmur. "That's exactly why. You need help, Renzo."

"What if I'm not ready to give up my lifestyle yet?"

I stare up at him in shock, and then any emotion I've ever felt toward any Beneventi rolls up out of me, and I burst into tears.

"Holy fuck," he cries, alarmed. "Don't. I don't deserve your—or anyone's—tears."

"If that were true," I gasp, "I wouldn't be crying."

What demons lurk within him? What drives him to self-medicate? What makes him believe he can balance on the edge and not fall off? The Beneventis' enemies won't kill him. He'll do that by himself.

"I'll contact your California girl ..." I grasp at anything to get through to him. "... and explain our situation."

"Please, don't," his voice rumbles. "My father will kill me, then you if he hears about my visit. I promised him ...fuck..."

I sniffle. "You make an impression, don't you?"

"Europe's out then?"

New tears form. "He wouldn't like that."

Renzo shakes his head. "No he wouldn't."

"I won't hide that you were here. Or that you're heading to Europe."

"I know." My hand falls from his as he stands and then looks down at me. "You're too good for him, Angel."

My lips purse. No one, not even his sons, see beyond Bastian gruff exterior. And the realization bothers me.

"Last chance to escape?" He raises an eyebrow.

"I'm sorry," I murmur. "I can't. But you'll keep in touch, right? Let me know you're okay?"

"Sure thing." He walks past me to leave.

"Wait."

He pauses.

"And call him, too. He loves you."

His expression brightens.

And then he's gone.

41

Bastian

THREE GORGEOUS FLIGHT attendants offer me exceptional service on the plane ride to Rhode Island. I accept a whiskey and a soft feather pillow, and—hell knows why—nothing else. Am I wound up? Like a goddamn engine coil in need of fresh lube. We've taken this ride before; this trio is already in the mile-high club. Yet it's abundantly clear I'm not the slightest bit tempted.

I'm hell-bent on getting home.

Italy was a bust. The reason for Dante's trip to his homeland is unresolved, though he "surprised" his old man with a visit while I was in Rome.

Renzo fucking outplayed me. He was in my home while I was on a wild-goose chase in Italy. The little shit is drawing from a playbook that a broken condom and my excellent sperm count created. Pretending to be Sandro? So fucking brilliant, poor Freido fell for it— literally, too. Like the Beneventi men before him, Renzo took his revenge. I'd be thumping my chest with pride if the little shit hadn't tried to lure Alessia away.

She says he's headed to Europe.

I'm done playing nice, and I quietly have my best men searching for him.

Any of the eleven other capos discover my son's a pain-loving addict, and I'm done. How can a father who can't control his son lead the famiglie into the next chapter? How can Dante be at his side, when his loyalty is suspect?

I wave for the blond to refill my glass.

A bleach blond with bangs, big fake tits, and no pain threshold. Maybe she would look more appetizing tied to my spanking bench?

Why take her home when you've an eager little plaything at home? Madonna mia—the shine within her eyes when I promised a visit to the Red Room.

She had the perfect opportunity to escape.

Yet remained, waiting for me.

And all I want to do is get home, and reward her while I punish her.

Alessia

I ENTER THE KITCHEN. It's late, and well after dinner. I'm curious to discover if Bastian ate the plate of food I left to be reheated. Lasagna with the homemade sauce he loves so much.

He arrived home less than an hour ago. But I'm suffering from an extreme bout of shyness, so I haven't welcomed him home.

Or reminded him—in case he forgot—about the Red Room.

My heart thumps like it's projecting me forward. Don't be shy. Do it. Do it. Do it.

I bite my lip and open the refrigerator, the foil-wrapped tray remains untouched.

He changed his mind.

With a disappointed sigh, I trek across the kitchen I spent hours reorganizing and tidying.

A flash of red catches my eye.
A ribbon, attached to a key, on the island countertop.
And it wasn't there earlier.
I pick it up, and curl the blatant invitation in my palm.
My heart beats in rapid cadence with my thoughts.
Don't be shy. Do it! Do it!

Bastian

SHE JUMPS like a nervous filly when I turn on the light in the Red Room, the key tumbling onto the cement floor with a clang as I make my presence known. She freezes, her breath coming fast and deep, a shy flush warming her face.

So fucking innocent. A better man would send her away.

I'm not that man.

"Sit." I point to the leather spanking bench.

With a bowed head, she scampers to do my bidding and settles onto the flat section. She's terrified, yet here by her own will.

A man can only take so much before he reaches a breaking point. I've been exceedingly patient with the little kinkster, yet she keeps pressing my buttons. Tonight, she's going to learn the hard way why a lamb like her should never offer herself to a bull like me.

Several seconds pass before she draws the courage to look up.

My dick's so hard, it's almost painful.

"For your sake, do everything I ask tonight. I'm in a mood. Capisci?"

She quickly nods. So beautiful. So submissive.

"Strip slowly, without looking away. Then position yourself belly-down on the bench with your ass raised."

Her nostrils flare as we lock eyes. Madonna mia, she likes this, and we haven't even begun. Does she have the slightest clue as to the lengths to which I'm about to ruin her?

Lust pulses through my veins. Still, I resist shackling her with chains and taking what she so sweetly offered. I watch and wait, getting off on the nervousness I've caused, and how she ever so slowly fumbles with the buttons on her dress.

The material slides down her beautiful body.

Ma dai. What the fuck is she wearing?

She's gone from conservative babysitter to straight out of a porn flick. Her breasts practically explode from a red silk push-up bra. Her curls are barely concealed beneath the tiniest motherfucking thong in the same color. And a black garter belt—the old-fashioned kind with two snaps that hold up the stockings—frames her pussy beautifully. Sheer black stockings with lacey tops accentuate her creamy thighs. I look my fill, all the filthy ways I plan on playing with her racing through my mind.

"Take off your bra," I hoarsely mutter.

Her lips curve ever so slightly.

Fuck, she's asking for it.

More confident, she frees her breasts, sending them bouncing. I've never seen such full and perky globes, reminding me how young she is.

But as she climbs onto the bench, positioning herself over the hump and raising her juicy ass, I realize I don't fucking care if she's the youngest, and most inexperienced, woman I've been with.

A small moan escapes her. Resignation? Acceptance of the fact she's powerless and I'm in full control? Or maybe—knowing how the little Lolita's been begging for my touch—she's excited?

I study the scene before me, my dick thickening with blood.

"You a naughty little submissive?" I grind out, my eagerness getting the better of me.

"I think so," she whispers.

"One last chance. You understand what I'm about to do to you?" Though I ask the question, if she says no, it's debatable whether I'll let the little cocktease go.

"My body's innocent," she murmurs, "but my mind isn't."

"Is that right?"

"Yes," she breathes. "I like art films."

My eyebrows lift. "Art films?"

"Girl porn."

She's fucking perfect. Sweet yet filthy to the core. I remember how she responded to being spanked—loved it, didn't she? I cross the room to the table and pick up the leather flogger. Marring her smooth skin with the soft lashes is now foremost on my mind.

Her eyes track my movement until I position myself behind her. "I'm going to leave marks all over that pretty ass. You'll feel the burn for days."

"And if it hurts?"

"Oh, it's going to hurt." I'm rock hard at the thought. "Give me a word," I grind out, "and if it's too much, use it."

"Pasta."

I frown. So young. So at my mercy. "Just remember..." I raise my arm, ready to unleash. "You begged for this." I snap the leather, and it strikes her right cheek.

Her body tenses, then relaxes.

I bring the flogger down again, making a perfect crisscross. I might have lost interest in this type of play for a while, but I haven't lost my touch.

"I wish I could see your expression," she informs me, then in a breathy voice, she tempts me further. "Go on. Do your worst."

Her words are like tossing candy to a teen who's forbidden to eat sweets. "Worst, huh?"

I return to the table, then stand beside her on the bench. "Lift onto your elbows," I command.

She rises off the smooth leather as I open the first clamp. "Know what these are?"

"Nipple clamps."

"Let's see how far I can push you."

She rolls her lower lip between her teeth, then winces as I fasten the clamps.

"It's going to hurt like a bitch when I remove them."

Her eyes widen.

"Regretfully, I'm not going to fuck you, and watch you come in pleasure and pain." I scowl and resume my position. Fighting the sudden urge to do exactly what I said I wouldn't do.

Take her mouth, my thoughts whisper. *Flood her throat with your seed, call it a day, and hope it's enough.*

I snap the flogger and don't hold back, strike after strike, decorating her ass with fine red lines. A time or two, the little flogger-loving minx lifts to meet my strokes.

By the time I'm done, her ass is tender and pink, her stockings shredded, and my blood pounding.

"Flip over, spin around, and arch your spine over the hump."

I almost lose it when she repositions her body, clamped breasts swaying in the air, head rolled back, and eyes shining brightly.

"You enjoyed that," I state.

"I loved it. Your grunts, and my surrender."

White noise fills the room, yet all I see is red.

I unbutton my pants. "Lay your head back and breathe through your nose."

Her lips part in a gasp as she catches sight of my raging bull.

"Open."

She hesitates.

"Do it. I feed every inch into your virgin throat, and you're going to struggle. Better prepare yourself because, at this angle, I'm going in deep."

Her body hums with energy.

My lips twist. Yeah, she's as bent as I am.

She opens her mouth wide and sticks out her tongue.

If I weren't so fucking randy and ready to unleash, it'd be comical.

I step forward, lift her head in my hands, and position her exactly how I need her, then shove in.

She gags.

I allow a few seconds for her to adjust to breathing through the nose. "Feels fucking amazing," I groan, and she stops struggling, her panic settling. "You like my cock in your mouth?"

Her head shakes.

"Ready for more?"

Another slight tremble.

I soften my hold on her yet don't release her. "Go on. Swallow my bull."

She rocks her head, and I hiss. Madonna mia, this feels good. I arch forward, pushing deeper.

And she takes it like a goddamn pro.

It's when she opens her mouth, snaps her head back even further, and takes me home, I realize I'm royally fucked.

I grunt as we move together. Every suck, every thrust, growing more and more aggressive until I don't know which way is up. I start babbling, which increases our frenzy.

"I can't get enough of the way you feel."

She moans.

"These lips, this mouth, that tight goddamn throat is mine."

My body tenses with pleasure.

"You're going to drink every last drop, capisci?"

Fuck knows if she even understands what I'm saying.

My hands reach for the clamps as I withdraw almost entirely.

She screams as the tips of her breasts swell with blood, but I cut off her cry as I shove so deep, I see fucking stars. My balls tighten, and I come like a man possessed, my seed jetting a stream that never seems to end.

"Fuck, Alessia. Fuck."

The room spins, and everything stills.

Eyes closed, I stagger back.

She cough, and then says my name. "Bastian."

I open my eyes. She's staring at me, eyelashes and cheeks coated with tears.

"Are you okay?"

I rake my eyes over her. The tender flesh around her nipples, the marks my fingers made on her neck, her swollen lips and damp cheeks.

"Bastian?"

I've lost my motherfucking mind, haven't I?

"Wow," she says. "That was hot."

I stare at her.

"Was I ... okay?"

"Yeah." I can't manage more than that.

"How long do you think it'll take me to recover? Because ... I'd like to do other things."

Fuck me.

Fuck it all.

I don't know what I want anymore.

"Now what?" she asks.

Hell if I know. My stomach rumbles, saving me from answering. Or at least, answering in a way she's expecting.

"Now, you make me dinner."

43

Alessia

I'M at the stove and reheating the lasagna when he finally speaks.

"Did I hurt you?"

I face him. He's studying the whiskey I served in a liquor glass that must be a century old.

"No."

"Look. This doesn't change anything." He rubs the back of his neck. "You insisted we play, so we played. You wanted a kinky thrill, and I gave you one. And ..." He locks eyes with me. "... you loved it."

My heart sinks. *Doesn't change anything?*

"I won't touch you again."

He called out my name when he climaxed. Not Little Miss Deep-Throat. Not Little Come-Dumpster—*Alessia*. It was as personal for him as it was for me.

And now that I've submitted, he's done with me. "How long before the plumbing and electrical problems in the casita are fixed?"

His scowl is fierce. "Doesn't matter. You're staying put."

Lord, he's worse than Sandro.

I stare at the arrogant man in disbelief.

He clenches his drink. "Don Lucchese asked, and I told him the wedding date. His health is declining—who knows how long he has before I'm elected capo di tutti capi. Nothing's changed. You're marrying Sandro." He slams the glass onto the island. "I won't be tempted by a curious virgin who craves a rough touch."

His words feel like a slap. I trusted him, and now he's thrown everything between us in my face?

I hold up my hand. "Pasta."

He scowls. "What?"

"My safe word is pasta. I'm asking you to stop." I draw in a breath. "Do I have your permission to get dressed?"

No more reheating his dinner naked. Presenting his marks on my breasts and ass for his viewing pleasure—marks he's been feasting on like a man proud of his work.

"After we eat."

The spatula springs from my grasp. I bend to retrieve it, feeling his eyes rake over me once more. I rinse it off, ignoring him, then plate the lasagna before bringing his dish to the island.

I drop it before him with a thud.

"No salad?"

I charge toward the refrigerator and remove prepackaged lettuce, then from a lower cabinet, I retrieve the large salad bowl. The vinegar and olive oil under my arm, I return to the island and mix together a simple salad. All the while avoiding looking at the coldhearted monster.

It's not until I'm shaking salt and pepper that I glance up.

His blue eyes radiate hunger as he stares at my breasts.

I shove the salad bowl at him, ending his undeserving perusal. He looks at the salad bowl, the plate of lasagna, and then at me. "You're not eating?"

Lord. His callousness wounds me. But his concern is a dagger to the heart.

"Sure thing, Mr. Beneventi," I say in my most obedient voice.

His lips draw tight. Doesn't like me calling him Mr. Beneventi? Or does my mock obedience grate on his nerves?

I serve myself a small wedge and then, back facing him, eat it by the stove while tears coat my eyelashes. This lasagna was a labor of love. And now it tastes like cardboard.

He grunts behind me, and we eat in uncomfortable silence.

"Fine," he finally mutters. "We fuck about until you're wed."

Like he had no part in this. Like I bent him to my will rather than the other way around.

"No one will know," he relentlessly continues.

"I'll know," I seethe.

What was I thinking? I offered him all my firsts and played with fire. And he evidently won't be satisfied until he's watching me burn.

"Say yes." He uses that voice, the gravel-filled seductive one that draws me in, before tossing gasoline on top. "And I'll roll you back, stuff my face in your pussy, and lick away the pain I've caused."

Promising me orgasms, when I want ... need ... so much more.

I spin, and lock eyes on him. "I never had a father's love or protection, which is why I'm attracted to powerful men."

His eyebrows knit. He doesn't understand I mean him and only him.

"I yearn for stability, to be taken care of, to give up control completely to the right man. I'm not ashamed I like it rough. Or enjoyed your spankings. Or got turned on by allowing you complete control."

He looks ready to pounce, and I rush to finish. "Everyone has weaknesses."

"Enough," he growls. "Clearly I'm overthinking—"

"Ambition," I cut him off, "is your weakness. Same as my father."

The hairs on my arms stand in warning.

I don't hesitate, and bolt toward the door, with the island running interference between us.

"I'm nothing like that asshole." He dives across the surface, sending plates flying, but his reach is shallow. Recovering quickly, he rolls off the counter and onto his feet, then is within reach in seconds. His hands find my hips. I'm spun around and shoved into a pantry door.

"You're right," I manage.

"About?" Hands on both sides of me, he cages me with his big body. I want more than anything to sink into the heat coming off him.

But he's reduced me to toast that's quickly crumbling into tiny burnt pieces. Something you toss onto the lawn for the birds to eat.

"Honoring promises," I remind him. "Like the promise I made your son by agreeing to marry him."

He's livid, and I'm suddenly afraid. He can toss my engagement in my face yet hates that I do the same?

My body shakes with outrage. "'Little Alessia better do her duty, or else.'"

His fist rises, and I jump when he punches the pantry door. "Enough."

Not yet.

"No."

"No?" he repeats, astonished. Probably doesn't hear that word enough.

"The apple can't fall far from the tree, right?" I cock my head and glare at him. "Sandro can show me what I need."

He jerks back like I've scalded him. I hope I did—I hope my declaration burns deep. But I'm not foolish, and seizing the opportunity, I hastily duck beneath his arm and flee.

A litany of curses follows me down the hallway.

44

I'M NOT A NICE MAN. I take what I want. Empires. Lives. Everything between.

Except *her*.

Because family always comes first. I gave her to Sandro, and that's that—I won't touch her again.

I drum my pencil on my desk and watch her and Zoey's antics on my security camera. Zoey plays golf like a lost stripper who believes the magic way back to the men's club is by swinging the golf club one hundred times without it connecting with the ball. Theirs is an odd friendship, but if she keeps Alessia entertained, what the fuck do I care?

Phone in hand, I check on business. Stock market's up. The famiglia's having a good day. Everything's quiet. No bullshit to handle except for a request from Don Lucchese—who expects to FaceTime Alessia in less than an hour.

The old bastard wants to grill her about the fucking wedding. He's got a hard-on for Alessia, and probably imagines himself as the lucky groom.

I toss my phone onto my desk.

It's been days since my cock was buried in her throat. Days of eating takeout and disengaging from all contact with her. *Deciding my next move? Or avoiding making one?*

I grind my teeth.

Indecisiveness will ruin a man in my position. And Freido's right, I'm overthinking things. He can bring her back to the house. He's also smitten with her and has become her little pet.

Except I don't text him or toss him that bone. My fist crashing into his ever-so-smug face sounds like a better idea. A reminder to back the hell up.

Alessia's not to be played with. Not touched. Not flirted with or charmed or anything that could ruin years of hard work.

Still, she's my little burden.

She can cook and serve me dinner. Polish the silverware and wait on me. Jump when I say so. Obey.

If Zoey stops monopolizing all her time ...

Decision made, I stand.

My pretty little burden will understand exactly who's the boss by the time we return from the golf course.

MY CART IS a few yards away when they scatter like ducks.

I watch in disbelief as Zoey ushers Alessia into their cart and they race off in the opposite direction. Alessia's expensive designer clubs lie forgotten at the last hole.

I'm a predator. Run, and I'll hunt you down. I hit the gas, thinking the next time Sandro offers advice, I'll listen. Zoey's a bad influence, and drives like a four-year-old. Up ahead, she swerves around a bird and nearly ends a groundhog family, who scramble for safety, alive another day to chew up my fucking golf course. Twice, the cart gets air, then lands hard, tossing them both around like rag dolls.

She's going to kill them.

"Stop the motherfucking cart," I bellow.

Alessia swings her head around.

If anything, they pick up speed.

This is what I've been reduced to? A twenty-five-mile-per-hour cart race? That fucking golf pro sold me on the latest and fastest carts. I'm adding that to the list of Mr. Happy-Hands' crimes, which one day he'll pay dearly for.

On the southern end of my estate is a hill, and on the opposite side a pond fed by a natural spring. It's been years since I stocked it. When the twins were preteens, we'd spend hours out here. Sandro was dead serious and focused on catching the most fish, with Renzo, the thorn in his side, gleefully mixing gummy worms into his brother's bait bucket whenever Sandro wasn't looking. Fish didn't care. I told the boys one night, as we baked our catch over a campfire, that gummy worms made the fish taste sweeter. Sandro was skeptical, but Renzo bought it, hook, line, and sinker.

There've been moments when no one but we Beneventis existed. Do the little shits remember the good times? It's been a long time since we spent time together outside of business.

My doing. Ask them, I'm a shit father.

But love doesn't prepare anyone for the real world. My sons wouldn't survive if I didn't roughen them up. Sacrifices are part of the norm. They resent me for the demands I've made. *Soon, when they become princes in my new kingdom, I'll restock the pond again. Soothe Sandro's wedding blues and lure Renzo back by setting my own bait.*

Alessia's cart disappears over the hill, and seconds later, they're screaming.

I fling myself from my cart and up the hill.

"We're sinking," Zoey bellows, "and going to drown."

I hit the hilltop at a full run, and don't stop until I'm knee-deep in pond water and their cart a few feet away.

Zoey's halfway across the pond, swimming like a gold medalist.

But Alessia waits for me, seated in the half-submerged vehicle that's bottomed out in the mud.

I wade through the water and then scoop her up. "You okay?" I demand, carrying her back to my cart.

"I pleaded for her to stop."

I grunt. "That wasn't what I asked."

"I'm fine." She pauses. "You terrify her, that's all."

"Right now, she should be."

Alessia doesn't utter a word during the walk back or after I deposit her on the seat. She looks younger than twenty, with her windblown hair and pink cheeks. A wide-eyed innocent by all appearances, without the slightest glimpse of the little freak inside.

My head begins to pound, and I hit the gas harder than necessary.

She falls back in the seat with a cry.

We're halfway across the estate when I spy three carts up ahead and racing toward us. I curse beneath my breath. It's like I'm witnessing some boardwalk carnival game. "Stai scherzando? They look ridiculous."

Her giggle fills the air.

I soften, briefly. Yet I've rules that must be spelled out, and no time for sugarcoating them.

"Your job is to cook and serve me, capisci?"

She stiffens. "Serve you ... *how?*"

"Not my fucking cock. *Me.*"

Her chin rises in challenge. When exactly did Alessia morph into this beautifully bold woman? Or delude herself into believing she can defy me?

"Look at them." I wave toward the twenty-five-mile-per-hour speedfest. "Always on call, always ready to do my bidding. Your role is to be like my men."

"You spank them, too?" A fierce scowl transforms her pretty face. "Mark them with your come?"

Madonna mia. "Just do as I say."

"You shove your bull down their throats and make them swallow every delicious drop?"

I slam on the brake but throw an arm out so she doesn't go flying. I've no time for this bullshit. "That was a mistake."

She gasps, like I gut-punched her.

"Here are the rules. Cook. Serve. Polish whatever you like. No flaunting your body in see-through bathing suits. No sleeping in my bed when I'm not home. No tempting me like some eager Lolita."

This is my decision. Like my sons have, she'll learn. Sacrifices, right? I brush lint off my suit pants and ignore the water stains that've ruined them. With my demands firmly stated, I move on to Don Lucchese's call, and what I'd like her to say about her upcoming nuptials.

"Let's talk wedding plans," I grind out.

She jumps out of the cart.

Fucking incredible. I'm on the green and charging after her, part livid from her disobedience, part turned on by the chase. I'm within arm's reach as she makes a beeline for my men. Freido, leading the charge, sees her, too. Even at a distance, I notice how quickly his thunderous expression's redirected my way.

My most loyal man is certifiably pussy whipped.

If I tackle her, pin her lush body to the green, and press my erection against the curve of her sweet ass, my men will think the same of me.

I stop, pull my phone out, and shoot him a text.

> Her ass better be in front of my computer by one o'clock, or I'll kick yours all the way back to Italy.

45

Alessia

"MAKE YOURSELF COMFORTABLE," Freido commands, pointing to an enormous leather viewing chair. He whisked me off the golf course, then into the house, and ushered me inside the theater room, while another man brought in Bastian's laptop.

"My clothes are wet."

"You'll survive."

I frown. Over the weeks—and to my surprise—he's become my reluctant advisor to all things Beneventi. Doesn't mean he overshares Beneventi secrets or is disloyal to Bastian. Doesn't mean he isn't sometimes a no-holds-barred brute. He's accepted I'm part of the family now and probably realizes I'm engaged to a jerk yet held hostage by an even bigger one. "What is this about?" I ask.

I settle into a chair. It's ironic we're doing whatever this is inside a theater when my own drama is playing out elsewhere.

"He hates waiting." Freido passes me the laptop. "And he's early."

My eyebrows arch as I stare at Don Lucchese's face on the screen.

"Do yourself a favor and make the old man happy."

"Bastian approved this?"

"Yeah. Don Lucchese asked for you." He grimaces. "Brace yourself, and don't be fooled. This call is about the wedding."

"Hot topic of the day," I mutter.

"Ready?"

"I've nothing to share but the date."

"Not true. You're a blushing bride who's marrying her dream man."

"More like nightmare." I roll my eyes. "You're demanding the impossible."

"With Don Lucchese on your side, you won't only survive our world but thrive in it."

Right. Zoey says the wise old man murdered his way into power, then changed the rules. Money keeps the peace, with Bastian being the smartest earner. Bastian has Don Lucchese's respect and will assume his position one day. And in a small way—whether the arrogant jerk deserves it or not, and I'm inching toward the latter—I can help him.

You'll be like one of my men.

It's not like I've a choice, do I?

I plaster a broad smile on my face.

"Relax. You've got this." Freido unmutes the sound and turns on the video.

The mafioso man lights up when he sees me. "There's my girl."

"Buonasera, Don Lucchese. Come stai?" I greet him.

"In vita."

Alive.

He switches to English. "Your cookies keep the old ticker going, I'm certain of it."

"Then I'll bake more batches." Given his friendly demeanor, it's difficult to reconcile he's a mass murderer.

"Especially the biscotti. After the wedding, you'll come and stay at my villa, and bake for me. Nothing better than Italian ingredients."

"Thank you for the invitation, Don Lucchese."

Bastian steps inside the theater room. I blink. He's changed into dark jeans and a tight, fitted T-shirt. I pretend I don't see his approach and continue my conversation. "And what will Sandro be doing?"

"He can go pick grapes."

I laugh.

So does Don Lucchese.

Bastian scowls beside me, where he's settled onto an armrest. Lord, he's barefoot, and a poster child for the expression: "*Big feet, big cock.*"

"And Bastian, how's he treating you?"

I roll my bottom lip, three sets of eyes hyperfocused on my response. Will the old man sense a lie? I settle on an honest reply. "As to be expected."

The old man grins like a proud grandpa. "Demanding, right?"

I sigh. "He *insists* I prepare his meals."

"Smart man. Always has been."

My tension evaporates. Don Lucchese loves Bastian, doesn't he? And oddly enough, that makes me happy.

Why be happy for him? Why not, once and for all, squash any and all emotions I feel for him?

Oh sweet Lord. No. No. No. Do I love him?

"Bastian tell you I've booked my flight?"

I nod, unable to form words, and still processing the disaster wreaking havoc on my sanity. Love him? How did this happen? Why him, of all people? Is it Stockholm syndrome? Unfulfilled lust? Delusion? *Don't cry. Don't react. And whatever you do, don't look at Bastian.*

"How about I fly you to Rome so you can purchase a lovely wedding dress?" the old man croons.

I catch Freido's stern look. *Just make Don Lucchese happy.* "Bastian gave me money, and I bought the most beautiful dress. It's classic and feminine, with sheer sleeves, a princess neckline, white silk bodice, V-waist, and a full tulle skirt. The saleswoman said it was designed after Sophia Loren's dress in the movie *The Black Orchid*, except the veil I ordered won't have flower accents."

I pause to catch my breath.

All three men are dead quiet.

And foolish, foolish me, a glutton for punishment, glances Bastian's way.

Our eyes lock.

His hungry.

Mine growing more and more alarmed. It isn't a look you offer your men. Or one you give your chef. And it's completely, utterly not a look a father-in-law casts on his daughter-in-law. He makes me want to cry, or throw something at him.

He set the rules. If I'm required to follow them, so must he.

"Sandro's going to love it."

I drag my attention back to Don Lucchese and then, in an Academy Award–winning performance, give the blushing bride role everything I've got, spurred on by Bastian's furious expression.

46

Bastian

THE HAPPY LITTLE bride's enthusiasm was unexpected. Was it an act? Or is she genuinely excited about marrying Sandro? Che cazzo? I head abroad for a few days, and this fucking happens?

Freido's wicked smirk's no help. And he's been grinning like a madman ever since the phone call. All goddamn afternoon I've put up with his bullshit. If it weren't for the business at hand, I'd order him from my office.

I jab a finger at him. Daring him. "Something amusing you?"

He fucking chuckles.

Fortunately, my phone chimes and diverts our attention.

Except, if Alessia's change of heart inspires me to punch some-thing, the news coming from the Atlanta casino site sends my fist into the nearest wall.

"Atlanta's burned to the ground," I'm informed.

Freido gestures, and I place the call on speaker.

Men on-site are frantically shouting. "Touched with gasoline. No way to put the fires out." My man raises his voice so he can be heard. "Nothing remains, everything's ashes. Construction outbuilding. Construction equipment. Timber and pallets of materials. And we lost five men. Probably shot before they died in the blaze. The guards who escaped said gunfire alerted them."

"A messy job," Freido remarks.

Exactly right. Everyone would be dead if I'd sabotaged the casino site. Dead men can't talk. "They leave evidence behind?"

"We caught three of them, Mr. Beneventi. And you're not going to like this."

My expansion's ash before construction even began." I rub fingers across my jaw. "Go on. You know who's behind this?"

If he says Dante, I'm going to lose my shit. I brought him into my home. Treated him like an younger brother. Shaped him to be ruthless in the boardroom and resilient in dealing with the other Ten. Then he abandons the gold mine I handed him? Coincidence or intentional?

"It was Benny Manocchio, sir."

I relax slightly. Stupid stronzo, sloppy job, of course Bible Belt Benny did it. "You positive?"

"Joey, a local kid who runs errands for us, is a wannabe cowboy who hangs out in Nashville. Poor kid was delivering food when everything went up in flames. He recognized a guy. Get this, the man's been a bartender at Manocchio's country music joint for years. Joey actually knows the dude."

If I wasn't pissed off, I'd roll my eyes.

"I met the kid before," Freido informs me. "He's solid."

I exhale sharply to clear my head. Think like Benny. What's his next step? He scours Georgia to clean up his shit show? Sends every available man to search for our three captives?

"Get them out of there and head for Tennessee. Then have our men spread the news I'm coming to Atlanta to assess the damage."

"Understood."

Freido's quick to catch on. "I'll book a flight to Atlanta under your name." Phone already to his ear, he charges out of the room.

"Cover your tracks, capisci?"

"Understood, boss. Not a trace."

"Text me the safe house location once you secure one."

I disconnect, and then drum my fingers on my desk. It takes a few minutes to reach a decision, then I pull the stock portfolios for every famiglia up online—portfolios I manage. A few clicks, and we all take a hit, starting two days from now and lasting for a week. Initiated—by all appearances—by losses in Atlanta and snowballing into other investments. One big motherfucking hiccup, which I'll correct next week—and even double our profits—by heavily investing in made-in-the-US microchips. News will break on Monday about the government subsidizing the Ohio plant, and stocks will rocket. A few clicks, and everything will be golden again, except for Atlanta.

And Benny's decomposing corpse.

The stupid fuck assumes he's safe. A hit hasn't carried out on a capo in two decades. A testament to Don Lucchese's bureaucratic bullshit. Even though it'll look like an accident, no one will doubt it was me.

My fingers dance across the keyboard before I close my laptop.

If I plan things right, by the time the famiglie discover they're broke due to Benny's foolishness, not only will hits be issued, but there'll be a bounty on his head.

I stand. In the morning, I'll explain to Don Lucchese how things are going down and ask his permission to terminate Benny.

A half hour later, Freido brings the car around while I shove weapons—some marked, others not—into a duffel bag. Once ready, I toss the duffel over a shoulder and head out.

Alessia waits in the foyer.

"Not now." I stalk by her.

"What's happening?" she persists.

"A wedding." If she's so goddamn pleased about it, let her plan it. "The venue better be booked by the time I return."

THE AMBUSH PLAYS OUT like a spaghetti western.

Benny marches into his Nashville music bar and heads straight for the Blake Shelton look-alike bartender, eager to question Blakey Blake further about his two companions. Benny believes I'm losing my shit at the Atlanta site, instead of listening to sad country songs, eating shitty Italian food, and waiting for him to show.

For our bird's-eye view above, we watch Benny pull Blakey into an office, doing exactly what I hoped he'd do.

Inside and outside, my men are pricking necks right now, injecting Benny's boys with so many horse tranquilizers, Kentucky is crying. I won't kill them and make more enemies. When it's all over, they'll understand I spared their lives—or the ghost of Sebastiano Beneventi did. While Benny's men go nighty-night, most of mine will ride off into the sunset, cowboy hats pulled low.

We wait until the music bar is empty before turning this western into a horror movie.

Blakey Blake dies first; a quick bullet to the temple was his deal for helping us. We take his wallet, and toss a gun registered to a Nashville man outside the back door into the alley.

Wide-eyed and hog-tied to the floor, Benny panics. Maybe he's smarter than I give him credit for? I prowl forward, days of untamed tension spurring me on. The beating I already treated him to does nothing to ease it.

He rolls back and forth, squealing through the cloth shoved into his mouth.

I signal for Freido to remove it. Let's hear what he has to say.

He spits blood, then spreads his venom. "They won't let you get away with murdering me."

I kick him in the kidney. "You worried about me, you stupid *figlio di puttana?*"

"You think you're smarter than us." His eyes gloss over as he struggles to stay conscious. "You deserve what's coming."

Freido and I make eye contact.

And what would that be?

Is it Dante? Would he recklessly ally himself with the likes of Benny? I mean, why isn't he here? What's so goddamn important in Italy that he sneaks off and abandons his responsibilities? It's out of character. He's level-headed, cunning even.

And untouchable.

I'll take power with him by my side. Then, and only then, will I address my concerns.

Still, if Benny's offering information …

I kick him in the nose. Blood splatters as it breaks. "Don Lucchese's son—did you make a deal with him?"

He laughs like a lunatic.

I gesture to Freido, who hands me the chain saw. I start with a finger.

Benny's laughter turns to whimpers, yet he still persists. "The Beneventis will never lead the Twelve."

A second bloody finger joins the first on the floor beside him.

"Dante Lucchese. He in on this?"

"Just kill me."

"I chop you up and spread your body throughout your territory, or you die in almost one piece," I snap. "Yes or no?"

"No … not directly, anyway."

I nod, then lean down. "You're right for once in your miserable life," I murmur in his ear. "I won't lead the Twelve, because only ten capos will be alive. You'll be dead and your famiglia powerless, while mine fucking thrives."

Freido hauls him into the air and carries him outside to be deposited inside Blakey Blake's truck bed. Our cleaners get busy wiping down the room and will do the same with the truck.

As for me, I'm headed to Atlanta. In the morning, I'll make a statement to the police in my pocket, then an announcement to the press. Anyone with news relating to the fire is to come forward. And for local workers without a job, I'm offering stipends until we rebuild. I'll even use Benny's money, given this is his doing.

Sure, there'll be rumors—there always are.

I'm my father's son, after all.

I scratch the back of my neck, tired, spent, and ready to return home. Craving a little softness to break up the darkness.

I'M HOME BY MIDAFTERNOON, hands clean yet soul wrapped in blood. Earlier, I ordered a partial lockdown. Nothing obvious, but extra security will be placed on the Beneventi businesses, the estate, and my family. Renzo's safer lost than as an easy target inside a rehab facility. If he can break out, others can get in. And fucking believe me, my son can evade capture like nobody's business.

Everyone is secure. Threats to the family, par for the course.

Still, I linger inside the empty foyer.

Empty—with no Alessia in sight.

If I were a different man, I might regret my harsh actions.

Basta—*enough*. I need a drink.

Freido appears before I make it to my office. I stop short—his expression's frantic.

"She's gone."

Porca miseria. Alessia decided to run now?

"Find her."

He shakes his head. "Stephano drove her to New York City."

"Who the fuck is Stephano?" I snap.

"The kid with the big ears. Charlie's boy."

I grind my teeth. "Contact our men in New York and send them to Tribeca."

"She's not going to Tribeca, Bastian."

"Then where is she going?"

"To Soho."

Soho? "To Sandro's place?" I demand. Relief washes over me, yet it's temporary. And, although I know the answer, although I've dug this hole to lie in, I ask the question anyway. "Why the fuck would she go there?"

47

Alessia

"YOU'VE GOT to be kidding me."

Sandro rakes his eyes over me in disbelief. Showing up at his swank Manhattan apartment unannounced has started off miraculously well.

"Am I interrupting?" I ask because his hair is rumpled and his chin is darkened by a five-o'clock shadow. He's a hot mess.

More Renzo than the perfectly groomed man I've grown to despise. Still, I'm here for a reason. "Can I come in?"

Sandro curses beneath his breath as he spots Stephano lurking in the private elevator. Bastian's man insisted he accompany me. A stroke of luck, considering how difficult entering Sandro's Fort Knox would have been without him.

He shoves me aside and then, in a blink, clamps his fingers around my elbow and drags me inside. I look over my shoulder for help, but the elevator is closing, with Stephano hunched over inside.

"That's who he sends to protect you?" Sandro flexes his knuckles. Wait … did he hit the poor kid? "You should have called."

My lips part. Unbelievable. "You never answer."

"My bad." He stalks away, and I've no choice but to follow.

His apartment is incredible. Walls and walls of windows with panoramic views of the city. Real wood floors. State-of-the-art kitchen to the right, floor-to-ceiling fireplace to the left. His furnishings are expensive, and mostly white.

Took a page from his father's design scheme yet flipped the color. I scowl. *Black, like Bastian's heart.*

"I'd tell you to take a seat." Sandro falls into an oversized chair. "But then you'll assume I'm interested in anything you have to say."

I sit in a chair opposite him. "Like I *want* to be here."

He waves his hand, and officially ties for number one on my "Most Despicable Beneventi" list. Yet he seems tired, exhausted actually, with dark bags under his eyes.

"Everything okay with the casino?" It's a guess. Sandro will do whatever Bastian demands; haven't I learned this lesson well? Making the Brooklyn casino profitable and working relentlessly to do so is taking its toll.

His eyes narrow. "What've you heard?"

"What do you mean?"

Several seconds pass with me under intense scrutiny until he arrives at some conclusion. "You don't know?"

"Know what?" I frown.

"I should have sunk a bullet into that kid's gut instead of my fist." He flexes his knuckles, confirming my suspicions. He did hit Stephano. Something's wrong, seriously wrong.

"Oh my God." My words escape in a rush. "Is Bastian okay?"

"Bastian? He's Mr. Beneventi to you." His body stiffens with outrage. "What woman addresses her father-in-law by a nickname only his closest friends have permission to use?"

"Never mind that," I snap. "Is he okay?" I lean forward in my seat, then back, and then rock back and forth like the motion will help alleviate my worry.

Sandro treats me to another lengthy stare. "We're on a partial lockdown."

"What does that mean? Like a school lockdown?"

"All Beneventi businesses and personnel are under heightened security." He points toward the elevator. "And you come waltzing in with security a blindfolded child could overpower."

"Like you care." But my comment doesn't match my concern. A lockdown? Why? When?

"I don't." He sits higher in his chair, then mutters, "But he sure as fuck does."

"What did you say?"

"Not important. Not yet, anyway." He sighs. "The alert went out before daybreak."

"Maybe it doesn't apply to me?"

Sandro stares at me. "You joking right now?"

"Fine. I'm a Beneventi." I swallow hard. It's always been Bastian Beneventi in my mind. Not Renzo. Not Sandro. Never anyone else, as much as I tried to redirect my thoughts. "Don't punish Stephano. I would have driven alone if he hadn't insisted."

"Mine won't be the only bullet he gets." Sandro flexes his fingers. "Shit's gone down, and a capo is dead."

"Oh no."

"No loss. He deserved it."

I draw back, not expecting that.

"Burned our site in Atlanta to the ground."

Oh. My. God. "Bastian murdered him?"

"No."

I exhale in relief.

"He handed him a dozen roses—what the hell do you think?"

The room spins. Bastian's mafioso, and a control freak. He loves inflicting pain, on different levels and for different outcomes, enjoyable if he intends it to be, less so if he doesn't. When did my fear change to trust? When did misguided lust twist into love?

"Better not throw up on my white rug."

"Can I have a glass of water?" I squeak.

Sandro surprises me and, seconds later, removes the cap, then hands me a cold Fiji water. By the time he sits, I've finished half the bottle.

"Don't hurt my guard."

He rolls his eyes. "Why are you here, Alessia?"

"Where are we getting married?"

Sandro chokes on his water. "Where?"

"New York City? Rhode Island? A large or small venue? Any favorite places? Any suggestions?"

"What brought this on?" His alarm is palpable.

Fear doesn't drive me into action, though it should. Bastian *killed* a man. It's the harsh tone within Bastian's order to plan my wedding —dismissing me, dismissing us—that pushes me forward. "We need to book a venue, immediately."

Sandro's water bottle hits the floor.

"Goddamn it," he curses, jumping to his feet and getting a towel to wipe up his mess.

"I feel the same way. A venue seems so final." I pause, then grind out, "We need to book a venue immediately. Per his orders."

Sandro stalks to the kitchen, dumps the kitchen towel in the sink, and washes his hands. "What exactly did my godfather say?"

I roll back in the chair and stare at the ceiling. "Not him. Bastian."

"Bastian," he softly repeats.

"His words were, 'By the time I return, a venue better be booked.'"

Silence fills the apartment. And then Sandro begins laughing.

I'm on my feet in an instant. "What's so funny, dickwad?" Lord, I've resorted to cursing, even.

He laughs harder.

"You hate me, remember? And we're getting married."

"Are we?" He laughs so hard, tears form.

I raise my voice, panic and confusion and heartbreak setting in. "I can't go home until a venue is booked."

"And where is *home*, exactly?" His smirk fills the space between us.

"What?"

"You said you can't go home."

"Back to the estate, I meant."

He scoops up his cell phone from the kitchen counter.

"Sandro," I growl. "I swear, if you start playing games ..."

"Only the best game, one I've a lot riding on." Shooting me an odd look, he types away. Seconds later, he has me thunderstruck. "You hungry?"

I blink.

"Roscioli just opened, and we can order in."

"Are you being nice?"

Two hours later, I'm feeling better. Excellent Italian food helps. Sandro's frighteningly polite company does, as well. And when his phone chimes and a message confirming our wedding venue comes through, I can at last savor the flavors in the dish before me.

"Done," Sandro comments.

"Done," I reply. "Though Tavern on the Green is unexpected."

He grins. "Nothing but the best for my *wife*."

"Stop."

"Stop calling you *wife*?"

Lord, does he have to ruin our moment?

The elevator pings once more. We turn toward it as the doors open and Stephano appears.

"Not yet," Sandro tells him.

The doors close, and the elevator descends.

"I should be going."

"Not yet. Soon."

I roll my eyes. "The poor guy's anxious. He understands there's a lockdown."

"A day late and a dollar short."

I return to my meal, as does Sandro.

I'm full by the time another text comes in. Unease spreads over me at the downright gleeful look in his eyes. "What is it?"

"Showtime."

"What?"

He retreats toward the kitchen and uncovers the uneaten food before packing it into a tall bag. "You can take the leftovers with you." So polite. So kind.

"Are you drunk?" I look from the empty bottle to him.

"Nope. But finish your glass, because you're going to wish you were."

The elevator chimes.

The doors open.

And a raging bull charges into the room, yelling up a storm. "You have a death wish, disappearing during a lockdown? Do you have any goddamn clue what could happen to you?" Bastian rakes his gaze over the enormous space until his eyes settle on me. Then he makes a direct beeline for me.

I jump from my seat.

His hands find my arms, his body halting inches from my own.

"Take it easy on her." Sandro comes to my defense. "She didn't know about the lockdown."

Bastian is like a wild animal struggling for control. I'm terrified—yet slightly, ever so slightly thrilled he cares enough about my welfare to lose his mind.

"You had to push my buttons," he growls.

Wait. I pushed *his* buttons? My chin goes up. "You mean ... tempt you?" I wave toward Sandro. "Even he's a better choice to seduce."

"Oh, shit," Sandro utters. "Alessia. Stop."

"Why?" I cry. I'm hurt, so hurt. Broken, and fragmenting into pieces all over Sandro's white carpet. "The wedding venue is booked, as he demanded ... Ahhh!" My world spins as I'm hauled off my feet and over his shoulder.

A litany of curses accompanies us as Bastian carries me into the waiting elevator. But not before shouting orders at Sandro. "Tommaso better be with you at all times. Capisci?"

"Jesus Christ. I'll never prove myself capable, will I?" I don't need to see Sandro to know he's devastated.

"Just do as I say," Bastian snaps back, then punches the down button like he can't get us home quick enough.

<hr>

I SLEEP on the private jet ride to Rhode Island, waking up only once, with Bastian watching me from the seat opposite.

He hasn't uttered a word since Soho.

Neither have I—because I'm nervous, confused, and slightly aroused. He literally hunted me down, then tossed me over his shoulder like an invading barbarian. Like his sole focus is on possessing me, which is crazy. Why insist I plan my wedding? I'm kinky, but I've limits. No way will I be passed between him and his son.

I arrive at the estate without the clarity I need.

His man escorts me to the guest room while Bastian disappears into his office.

I wait, and wait. Overwhelmed by a barrage of questions. Will he come? Does he want me? Why bother with me at all? What's he thinking?

Indecision overrides my growing urgency.

Until suddenly, a ray of clarity kicks down the doors of confusion. What about you, Alessia? What do you want?

And the answer is the same as it's always been.

Him.

48

Bastian

A MAN CAN BE TEMPTED ONLY for so long.

And I'm done denying myself.

The little tease freezes, sensing my presence. She's inside my bedroom, offering herself up for the taking. That's exactly what I have in mind for the little seductress. To take, and keep taking, until my hunger quiets.

"I ... um ... didn't see you there." Her beautiful blue eyes suggest otherwise, that her appearance inside my room is intentional. Innocent, yet so fucking naughty. "I was just—"

"Go put on your wedding dress."

Her eyebrows shoot up.

I stare at her hard, daring her to ask why.

Her throat bobs, but then she hurries off toward the guest room. I pace my room, waiting for all the reasons I shouldn't do what I'm going to do to race through my mind. Instead, a calmness washes over me. Whether I've acknowledged it or not, everything leading up to this moment was meant to be.

Alessia returns, her wedding dress still on the fucking hanger.

"I said *on.*"

"Okay," she replies, breathless.

"Nothing underneath, capisci?"

She hums with excitement as she strips. My baby's as twisted as I am.

My cock swells at the sight of her. Long legs, tight ass, cute snatch, big fucking breasts, hesitant smile, and eyes eager with anticipation—I'll never grow bored of the view.

She slides the gown up her body. "Will you zip me in?"

I pull the zipper into place.

She turns. "What now?"

The little bride leaves me speechless. She'd be a vision walking down the aisle. An innocent package with a naughty prize inside, waiting to be unlocked. Every dick would rise at the chance to pluck the ripe peach from the golden nest.

My temple throbs as she smiles softly.

And I'm suddenly fucking overwhelmed by the urgency to taint her pure white wedding dress with her virgin blood and my seed.

Her eyes flash as she senses the change in me. And knowing she's stirred the beast, she bolts.

She makes it to the oversized chair by the fireplace. Believing the chair between us will protect her.

It won't.

She dodges right, I shift left.

I pivot right, when she ducks left.

Swallowing hard, she freezes, and I'm hurdling the chair.

She cries out as I grab her waist and hoist her high, then spin, toss her face-first over the chair back, and flip her dress over her head. Her bare ass will be my first reward.

"Don't fucking move."

She wiggles.

I smack her cheek, then palm my handprint, the heat invigorating.

"Tell me what happens to naughty little teases?"

"Naughty little teases deserve to be spanked."

"Bastian," I growl.

"Naughty little teases deserve to be spanked, Bastian."

I unleash several smacks in rapid succession. Satisfied, I dip my hand between her thighs.

My little pain-slut's soaking wet.

I lose my mind. Falling to my knees, I shove my face into her pussy. I never eat pussy. Yet I love the taste of her.

Her hips lift, and she thrusts into me.

Greedy and needy. I love how goddamn responsive she is.

I feed two fingers into her, and she wiggles and moans. Yeah, she's going to love my dick.

My tongue and fingers work her over until she comes. Afterward, her body goes limp like a rag doll.

"Don't you dare fucking pass out."

"Oh my God. That was incredible."

"Still with me?"

"Yes."

Blood rushes into my cock. No one has touched her. No one's tested her limits or pushed her boundaries. Yet she chose me. Teased me, tempted me, and fucking offered me the world. *"You can have all my firsts."* I never stood a chance.

And I'm hungry for every innocent inch of her—body, mind, and spirit. "Now you're going to get what you deserve."

She squeals as I haul her over my shoulder and head for our bed.

Our bed. Madonna Mia.

I toss her onto the mattress. She bounces three times before flailing backward, but my clothes are off and I'm on her before she recovers.

Straddling her hips, I allow her time to catch her breath.

Our eyes lock.

I hold up the same two fingers she got off on.

She licks her lips, thinking this will be a repeat performance.

Wrong. I curl my digits beneath the gown's collar, then rip the goddamn gown from neckline to waist.

She freaks. "You tore my wedding dress?"

"I'll buy you another one."

Her eyes grow impossibly wide.

Yeah, baby. Let that sink in.

"Okay," she calmly states. Like she understands what I'm about when I still haven't figured things out. Like she's not the one about to be ruined.

I squeeze her breast.

Her eyes darken, an impossible shade of blue.

God, I'm going to fuck her so good, it'll be like staring into the deepest ocean.

I part her legs with a thigh. "Roll up onto your elbows."

"Why?"

I cock an eyebrow. "So you can watch how a good little girl takes a man's dick."

"Oh," she gasps, and then bites her lip. Hesitant? Worried I'm about to destroy her?

"Can I touch it?"

I curl my fingers over her hand and bring it toward my swollen cock.

She brushes my hand away, and then, taking me in her palm, strokes me hard.

"My hand won't fit around it."

I grit my teeth. She's a fucking natural.

"You feel incredible."

My cock jerks, and she gasps.

"You frightened?"

"Yes and no." Her voice is low, her tone raw with need. "Ever since I saw you in Italy, I've wondered how you'd feel."

I freeze. "What?"

"*Inside me.* I don't mean in my palm."

She's dreamed about me inside her since Italy?

"You on the pill?"

She hesitates, like she dreads answering. Like suiting up even matters at this point. "No."

I always use condoms and never forget to examine them for holes before rolling one on. Not since I was a teenager, after a leaky condom turned me into a father.

I've never been bare inside a woman.

"It jumped."

"What?"

She softly smiles. "Your bull jumped in my hand."

I press my fingers against her folds. She's dripping with excitement.

Wet, and waiting.

Mine.

"Time to make my little cock-slut's dreams come true." I tug her forward and angle her body, my fat crown dragging across her clit.

She shivers.

That's right. My bull is coming, baby. And I'm putting it right where it belongs.

"Anchor your thighs to my hips."

My pulse pounds as she obeys. She's nervous, as she should be. I enjoy rough sex, and mixing pain and pleasure. Eight inches deep and driving home without mercy. Breaking in an innocent like her never held much appeal until now.

Now I'm fucking shaking with anticipation.

But her first time shouldn't be about pain.

I nudge into her entrance.

Fuck. FUCK.

I lean forward and kiss her forehead. "Three shallow strokes, then I'm in. Capisci?"

She nods. Brave little minx.

"And then I'm fucking you."

I push deeper, and she gasps.

Fuck. Fuck. Fuck.

"You're so freaking tight, Alessia. And I can't wait to be inside you." My voice is thick with gravel. "But it's going to hurt, capisci?"

"Please stop worrying," she bursts out, "and fuck me already."

My lips curl. But my smile vanishes after I draw out and slide back in, her walls squeezing around me. Cristo, she feels amazing. No way I'll last long.

"Yes," she pants. "Fill me up, Bastian. Make me yours."

With a flex of my hips, I drive home.

She hisses.

"Holy fuck!" My shout fills the room.

I still, allowing her to adjust. I run my lips across her neck, then kiss the path I created. "Prendi il mio cazzo così bene," I murmur in encouragement.

"I do?" She relaxes.

I nip her neck. "You take my cock like a little rock star." God created her just for me, didn't he? "Mi senti dentro di te?" I demand.

"Yes, Bastian. I feel every inch."

Our eyes connect.

"Can you feel me?" she murmurs.

I almost spill my seed right here and now. But I'm a sick fuck who enjoys testing his limits. "Yeah. Your hot little cunt is taking me so well. Who does it belong to?"

"Sebastiano Beneventi."

"That's right. Alessia Amato is *mine*." I'm a possessive man, but this feels more like obsession.

"Show me," she insists.

I drive home, and my entire body shakes. When I catch my breath, I flex my hips and grind, sinking deeper and deeper. Our lips lock, and her tongue darts inside, mimicking my thrusts and fucking my mouth. I don't kiss, the act more intimate than the scenes I typically play out. But now that we've started, I can't stop.

All sense of time and reason vanishes, and it's just us.

I come hard, her tight passage milking every drop of my seed, on and on—she'll be dripping my come for days. Once I'm completely spent, I still. Then, and only then, do I roll off her.

My hand finds her breast. Even drained, I can't stop touching her.

"That was something."

I know I'm fucked. Yet somehow, I don't care. I roll to my side to face her. "Something?"

"Intense." Her eyes flash. "I rode the bull, didn't I?"

"No. The bull rode you."

She smiles.

Fuck, she's pretty.

I rake my eyes over her. From her flushed face and chest, flat abdomen, and ... *She's still in that damn dress.*

I push off the mattress to stand, then lift her off the bed. "Hold on," I warn, before I shake the gown free.

"My dress," she gasps as I kick it across the room. "It's covered in blood."

Blood and my seed.

I carry her to the bathroom and perch her on the countertop. I clean up first before running a clean washcloth beneath warm water.

She studies my every move. "Aftercare," she finally murmurs.

"Something like that." I tap her thigh. "Let me see."

Heat warms her cheeks, but despite her embarrassment, she parts her thighs.

I tend to her swollen pussy, loving seeing her this way.

Her stomach grumbles as I'm tossing the washcloth into the bin. "Hungry?" Because suddenly, I'm ravenous.

"I can wait."

I lean in. "Your little pussy can't handle another fucking, baby." I pull back, reading disappointment in her expression.

Madonna mia. If she's begging for more now, wait until I've have her tied and helpless beneath me.

"I'll reheat the leftover chicken parmesan." She springs from the counter and sashays out of the bathroom.

I stare into the mirror. *How far am I going to allow this to go?*

I follow her anyway, despite the nagging feeling I'm in over my fucking head now, crushing the ruined wedding dress beneath my heels as I chase after her.

Alessia

WE EAT LEFTOVER CHICKEN PARMESAN, and I wait for the shoe to drop. I'm no longer a virgin. I no longer have a wedding dress. But I am engaged to his son—a fact he'll eventually remind me of. Don Lucchese and the other capos are expecting my wedding to Sandro. Losing my virginity to his father doesn't change anything.

He studies me like a hawk as he devours his food.

I used to be frightened by him.

Now I've never felt more secure or safe.

It's incredible, isn't it? How dumbstruck in love I am? And with each interaction, I fall deeper and deeper for him.

I twirl pasta on a spoon. Good food helps soothe a troubled soul, right? I take a bite—the sauce is nearly perfect. But after having tasted ridiculously exquisite Italian food, I decide a little more sugar and a little less garlic will heighten the flavors.

"You have tomato on your lip."

I raise a napkin to my mouth.

"Don't." He leans in and traces a finger across my lips, drawing the sauce away. I exhale sharply as he licks the tip clean.

His smirk is devastating. "Sweet in every way."

I take another small bite, chewing and swallowing before darting my tongue across the seam of my lips.

His blue eyes darken. In a blink, he's on his feet. "Don't move."

I track his exit, his muscular ass like an Italian sculpture in the flesh. And from the front, he's so much *more*. My lips curve. I'm swollen and sore for a reason, and an enormous one.

He returns with a package.

Excitement fills the air as he removes a shiny steel object shaped like a closed tulip from the packaging. It has a narrow tip, fat middle, and a jeweled knob at the stem's base, bedazzled with the initials B.B.

My lips form a silent O.

Two tubes accompany the package. One is sanitizer, which he uses to clean the new plug.

The second tube is lube.

I promised him all my firsts, and he's wasting no time in claiming them.

With a sweep of a forearm, he clears the countertop, then lifts and sets me on it to face him.

His gaze is intense, and focused on me.

"Show me."

I part my thighs.

"Poor little baby got good and fucked."

His grin is positively wicked. He loves being my first, doesn't he? My heart skips a beat.

He shuffles his stool forward and settles onto it. Without warning, he shoves his face between my thighs and licks my swollen sex.

I weave my fingers through his hair.

"Don't pass out," he warns, just as the room begins to swim.

His arms hook around the back of my knees, and I'm dragged forward. His tongue thrusts deep. It's too much.

"Bastian. Oh, God. Yes."

He slides a wet finger into my back entrance as my orgasm hits.

"Ahh," I cry out, sensation upon sensation stealing my breath away.

He inserts the plug while I'm basking in the afterglow.

I grunt. "I feel full."

"Not as full as you're going to feel." His eyes shimmer. "One day, Alessia, I'll fuck that sweet pussy while you're all plugged up. Make you suck on a goddamn lollipop while I do it, too."

Warmth spreads through me.

"You're perfect in every fucking way."

"*I am?*" I want to ask, but a yawn escapes my lips instead.

He kisses my forehead. "Come on, baby. Let's get some sleep."

I fall asleep in his arms.

But not before he murmurs, "What the hell am I going to do now?"

MY FIRST ACT the next morning is to examine the plug in the bathroom mirror. It's firmly in place, not uncomfortable yet noticeable. As are his initials, sparkling like diamonds on the decorative knob.

I return to my room and dress before heading for the kitchen to make pancakes with homemade peach preserves.

I'm almost to the kitchen when Freido says my name.

"Alessia's too young," he comments.

I clasp my hands, my worries returning front and center.

"Trust me," Bastian replies. "I know what too young is."

New day, new regrets? Is that what this is about? Is he regretting overstepping boundaries?

"This is what you want?" Freido presses.

Silence follows.

"Fuck me blind," Freido exclaims. "Didn't see that coming."

"Just leave the box on the counter," Bastian replies, "and leave me in peace to figure things out."

"I'd say you've already done that."

Too late, I realize where I'm standing, and how this will be perceived.

Freido notices me immediately.

I rush to explain. "I was going to the kitchen to make breakfast ..."

"He's out of his bleeding mind," Freido informs me in a low voice. "Don't let him pressure you into anything, okay?"

"Like what?" My excitement is palpable. Pressure me into doing what, exactly?

Freido snaps his fingers in my face. "Just make decisions based on what's best for you both, okay?"

I nod.

Freido passes by me.

"I love him."

He turns. "You love him."

"Yes."

He rolls his neck. "Does he know?"

"I haven't told him—I'm only figuring it out."

"You're young."

My lips draw tight. "So I heard."

"Then you know he has control issues."

"I like that about him."

He offers me a look like I've lost my mind, then continues down the hallway.

I enter a clean and tidy kitchen. Last night's dishes are cleaned up and the pots and pans back in place. Bastian looks out the window while crunching a cardboard box in his fist. Beautiful, powerful, and *mine*.

"Do pancakes with peach preserves sound good?"

He doesn't answer right away, but prowls across the room and tosses the crumpled box into the trash before approaching me.

He kisses my forehead, and I sigh with pleasure and relief.

"You plugged up like a good girl?" he murmurs, nuzzling my neck.

"Yes."

"Make the pancakes. Then sit on my lap while I feed and finger you."

His expression's downright devious.

Freido's right. He has lost his mind.

But then so have I.

"How long before breakfast is ready?"

"Half hour. Okay?"

He nips my ear, then pulls away. "I'll be in my office."

Oh my God.

This domesticated side of him shatters me. Are we in a relationship now? If so, how will Don Lucchese react? Or does that not matter anymore?

I crack eggs into a bowl. *One day at a time, and perhaps he'll surprise me. Right now, I'll enjoy the breakfast and orgasm he's promised.*

I approach the trash can, and am about to dump empty eggshells inside, when I spot the box. Three words in bold print catch my complete attention: Morning After Pill.

Bastian didn't use a condom.

I'm not on contraceptives.

And the means to prevent a potential pregnancy is in the trash.

"Make decisions best for you both," Freido warned.

A new vision for my future flickers through my mind. Bastian touching my pregnant belly and obsessed with my tender breasts. Little black-haired twins racing around the estate. Boys, who'll thrive better in this world—one where their father is king. Bastian barking orders by day and spanking me inside the Red Room at night.

Me cooking Sunday dinners.

Us, a family.

I stare at the box.

He didn't simply throw it away—he annihilated it.

I dump the eggshells on top.

Humming, I set about making pancakes that'll knock his socks off.

A stack is ready and I'm whipping fresh cream when Bastian begins shouting.

Alarmed, I drop the whisk.

Footsteps echo loudly as men race toward his office.

I follow.

Freido allows me entry into the office, where Bastian paces the room.

"What is it?" I demand. "What's happening?"

It's Freido who responds. "Sandro's been kidnapped."

50

Alessia

I'M SHIVERING, but not because it's cold. It's late, and I'm standing outside Bastian's bedroom, about to force my way inside. What I'll do afterward isn't clear. All I know is I'm tired and overwhelmed by the need to comfort him.

The door handle turns in my grasp.

I quickly enter his dark room before the door can slam in my face. He's sprawled in a chair by the fireplace, and my words get stuck in my throat.

He raises his head at my approach.

"Alessia."

"Are you okay?" I ask.

"How did you get in here?"

I flinch.

"I'm going to have a word with Freido." He furrows his brow, clearly annoyed by my friendship with his top man.

His harsh expression doesn't detract from his appeal. His white dress shirt is unbuttoned, revealing tan skin interrupted by traces of jet-black hair. His legs are stretched out before him, and a hand clasps the other wrist. A black silk tie lies by his bare feet.

I hurry forward and drop to my knees before him.

He rubs his jawline, then curses beneath his breath. "What do you want?"

You. The good and the bad.

Yet offering him sympathy, or pity even, won't work with a proud man like Bastian. Control is his thing, and right now, he's lost it. What I can do is comfort him with my body and distract him with my words.

"I still have the plug in my ass."

His eyes flash.

"I never ... I don't know how to safely remove it."

He stares at me, and I wonder what he reads in my expression. Desperation? Hope? Fear of rejection?

"You should go." His tone is harsh, clipped.

"If that's what you want." I rise, disappointed but not defeated. Not yet. "I'll ask Freido to help me with my predicament."

He springs to his feet. "Like hell you will."

I race toward the door, but he catches me, then pins me against it. "You know just what to say to torment me, don't you?"

I hide my smile.

"Only you can tempt the beast and live to do it another day." He presses into my back so I can feel his erection.

"I want you," I murmur, "that's all."

I dressed to tempt him, wearing a sheer pale blue nightgown with dainty pearls lining the collar and hem, and a thong in the same color, a butterfly-shaped line of pearls on the front and the thin strand evenly dividing his initials in the back.

"Everything is so fucked up right now except for you." He slaps his hand against the plug.

"Oh," I cry out as it drives in deeper.

"The things I want to do to you. Choke you while you come. Blindfold you and bind you to my post. Make you plead for pleasure and beg for pain. But most of all, I want to fuck the innocence out of you."

I whimper.

"But now's not the time." He tugs on the plug as his dismissal hits home. "Relax and breathe," he warns. "Now, count to three."

"One, two ... ah!" And then it's gone.

And so is he, in every way that matters.

"Don't push me away," I beg. "You're upset, and I want to—"

"Upset?" I'm spun around, and he drags my hand to his chest. "Feel that? That's not love or kindness. That's the Beneventi rage pumping through my veins." His nostrils flare, like the raging bull he's nicknamed for. "Upset, you say?" he hisses. "I'm going to murder every motherfucker involved in his kidnapping. If they know what's wise, they'll release him without harm."

"Bastian ..."

"You want to help me? Then go."

No, please.

"Alessia. Fucking go, or I will hurt you. And not in a way you'll enjoy."

He tugs us away from the door, then jerks it open.

I want to tell him he's wrong. There's more burning inside him than anger. The fact he's insisting I go reflects his kindness and concern.

But my bull's been wounded.

And everything reads red.

So I do as he demands, and flee, with the intention of waiting him out.

51

Bastian

HOW THE HELL did this happen?

Last night, my men found Sandro half-conscious in a Brooklyn alley. Trusting no one, I flew him home and had him rushed to Providence Hospital.

Benny's warning plays over in my mind like a sick mantra. I thought we were safe because only the stupidest fuck would dare mess with a Beneventi after what happened to that asshole.

I was right yet wrong. So goddamn wrong.

I unleash my anger once inside Sanro's hospital room, slamming a fists into the wall and sending two nurses scurrying in the opposite direction. "Get a guard posted outside who doesn't reek like fucking sauerkraut," I snarl into my cell phone as the guard in question follows in their footsteps.

I approach the doctor at Sandro's bedside. "How is he?" I demand. On the outside, he looks like hell, but internal injuries could be far worse.

The doctor fumbles with his clipboard. "He has two broken ribs, a fractured nose, and severe swelling on his left side. No internal bleeding detected, but there's a strong likelihood of a concussion."

"Keep him here for the week for further observation."

The doctor hesitates, eyes wide in fear. "We'll do our best. He tore out IV trying to leave, so we've had to restrain him."

"Release him. He'll do as I say."

"Yes, Mr. Beneventi." The doctor hastily unties the restraints and leaves the room. I move closer to assess Sandro myself.

His face is a mess—nose broken, eyes swollen shut. But I can tell he's faking sleep, probably worried I've been informed about his bullshit.

"Open your eyes, Sandro. I know you're awake."

One good eye cracks open.

I grind my teeth in rage. "You okay?"

"I'm sorry I disappointed you."

"You're alive. That's what matters." I drop into the chair beside him, crashing from twenty-four hours of adrenaline. I'm exhausted. So fucking exhausted.

"Emilio Conti is behind this," he confirms the information I received earlier. "He put out hits on both Renzo and me."

I didn't think Conti had the balls. I clearly underestimated the worm.

"My men will take care of him," Sandro says, as if I don't know he disobeyed orders and ventured out during a lockdown, risking his life in the process.

"Leave Conti to me."

"Conti's mine."

He's wide-awake now yet completely delusional. I lean in closer. "You think you can negotiate with me, you little shit?"

"Fine. Whoever finds him first gets to finish him."

I wait, staring him down, but Sandro's stubborn to a fault. Time I change tactics. "Who is she?"

"Who?"

We're playing games now? I slam a fist into the monitor, sending it crashing to the floor. "Your little sidepiece?"

"I'm too busy with the casino—"

"Don't lie. Who's the woman you risked lockdown for? The reason you were dragged off a Brooklyn street, beaten within an inch of your life, and nearly dismembered?"

He should know by now that I'm nothing if not thorough.

"No one important," he lies. "Just a fling."

"Let me get this straight. You left a heavily guarded Soho apartment during a lockdown, for 'no one'?"

"Correct." A hint of defiance laces his response. "A nobody, like sweet little Alessia."

It takes all my control not to wipe that smirk off his swollen lips. He thinks he's found a weakness—and maybe he has—but two can play this game. I sits back and fold my hands on my lap. "Tommaso will be questioned."

His best friend and bodyguard should have done his job. "Tommaso follows my orders," Sandro tries to cover for him.

"His job is to protect you."

"He did what I asked him to do," Sandro grinds out.

Jesus. How can you father one twin who argues every word you say, and another who'd rather poison his veins than deal with you? "That right? And what nonsense was more important than your life? You were snatched off the street. What the hell were you thinking?"

The fight drains out of him. "I fucked up."

"You almost died."

He nods, defeated.

"When you're healed, I'm going to beat the living crap out of you. Capisci?" I've never raised a hand to the twins, though fuck knows I've had reason to.

"I understand." His pride is admirable, but it's also going to get him killed. Where Renzo would laugh off a near-death experience at the hands of an enemy, Sandro will let it fester like an open wound.

I rub my chin and toss him a bone. "You used a goddamn chainsaw?"

"It was a messy kill." He glances at his arms and hands like he expects to see blood. I remember the same feeling after killing Benny —there's something satisfying about being covered in your enemy's blood.

"They tied me to a wooden chair."

"That right?" My men neglected to mention that detail.

"Then left me alone for a coffee break."

"You get what you pay for. Conti's cheap, so of course he's hired dumbasses." I pause, curious. "How'd you get a chainsaw?"

"First, I sharpened a chair leg against the cement floor—like you had us do when we were nine," Sandro explains. "Then I surprised them when they came back. Sure, I could've gone caveman with the chair leg, but why not use modern tools when they're right there?"

My chest swells with something like pride. My sons learned to fight not long after they could walk. They're resourceful little shits.

Thank God.

Though it was God's grace that it wasn't Renzo who'd been taken, or I'd have lost a son. Conti can run, but I'll find him. And when I do, he'll get the same treatment I gave Benny—but worse.

"Your brother would've bare-knuckled it and used the chair leg." I grimace, thinking how reckless he'd be. Fortunately, Sandro's twin excels at one thing. "But they'd have to catch him first."

Sandro swallows hard, then in a low voice, makes a promise. "I'm going to hunt Renzo down and straighten his ass out."

"If you locate him in California and anywhere near that Lombardi girl, make him bleed for disobeying me." No fucking way am I tying my good name to that asshole Lombardi. "Love makes us vulnerable. But vulnerability is a weakness. Capisci?"

He scowls, and it's on the tip of my tongue to demand her name. But I don't. "You'll stay here for the week, then take the jet to Sardinia. I've arranged for additional medical care at a trusted facility." I point a finger at him. "Don't defy me, or I'll burn your goddamn villa to the ground."

He blinks, message received. "I'll check into the damn facility for a few days."

"Recover in Italy until further notice."

The stubborn shit again tries to argue. "Don Lucchese will consider it disrespectful if I don't visit him."

"I'll handle your godfather."

"Tommaso will accompany me," he insists, still trying to save his best friend's ass.

"After I have a word with him." I stand and pin Sandro with a hard look, reminding him that our lives are insignificant—it's the famiglie that counts.

I wait for him to say it. He digs in for a few tense seconds, but then accepts his fate. Our fate—because he's not the only Beneventi making sacrifices. "Prima la famiglia."

"That's right," I softly add. "Family first, always."

"I won't let you down again."

"We'll see, won't we?"

I stay by his bedside long after he drifts off to sleep. Sandro might want revenge, but for me, this is all about respect.

Phone in hand, I issue the order:

Find Emilio Conti.

52

Alessia

WITH EACH PASSING WEEK, Bastian grows more and more distant. It doesn't help that the man behind Sandro's kidnapping has disappeared. Or that Bastian blames himself for underestimating him.

He's obsessed with hunting him down.

Part of me understands why.

Part of me worries rage might be the only emotion he connects with.

It's like being trapped in a cage with a wounded puma, who is either hissing and snarling while pacing around, or locked inside his den.

The guards prevent me from approaching him. To keep me away or keep me safe, or possibly both?

Yet I remain inside the main house and prepare dinner each night, hoping he'll dine with me. At least in this small way, I make my presence felt.

School has begun, and I throw myself into my studies, spending hours in the room off the kitchen. Not that I've abandoned efforts to redirect his attention toward me. By preparing his favorite dishes. By positioning myself where he might notice me.

If he notices, he never acts on it.

I tuck the fresh tomatoes into my apron and straighten, offering my face to the sun. It's a warm September. The garden is flourishing, and the pool is still open. At least the weather's cooperating.

A rumble of voices sends my pulse racing.

I wait until Freido and Bastian are on the path closest to the garden before looking at him.

Our eyes lock.

But Bastian keeps running.

Bastian

THE LITTLE WORM Conti has dug a hole so deep, it's taking longer than anticipated to hunt him down.

I lean against the doorjamb and drink my whiskey while I watch Alessia work. The loyal little Lolita has her head bent, caught up in the online lecture, and is oblivious to my presence.

I should allow her to return to the casita.

She doesn't deserve a life of lockdowns and murder, shady business dealings and being exposed to the darker sides of mafioso life. She's gentle and sweet. Loyal and patient.

And her presence calms me.

I'm a selfish fuck. My men keep her away, yet not too far away.

Basta. I loathe feeling weak, and one more person to care about leaves me even more vulnerable.

I don't *do* vulnerable.

Yet, as I soak in her presence like a hungry beast, I find myself at a loss for what to do.

It'll come to me. It always does.

I force myself to walk away.

AS DAYS PASS, time screws me over.

Conti evades capture.

My patience is worn thin.

And I'm indecisive about whether Alessia should move back into the casita. Out of sight and out of mind, right? I've important business to focus on, and no time for the little mind-stealer.

Problem is, I don't need to see her to be thinking about her.

Her perfume scents the air and stirs my interest. Her happy chatter from her office whenever she's online and in class invites me to pause and listen. Her cooking—fuck, nothing more to say that hasn't already been said.

I stare out the kitchen window at Zoey parading around the pool carefree and topless. Guards stop and gawk, despite my warnings about doing their fucking jobs. I scowl. Alessia's tucked away out of my line of vision. Fuck knows what she's wearing—or if she's bare-breasted like the arsonist.

My temple pounds.

Without thinking, I charge outside and head toward the pool.

"Eyes off the pool," I snap, pointing at the guards patrolling the back. I beefed up security, so maybe these teste di cazzo don't under-stand all the rules yet.

They will.

Once I'm certain the two cockteases by the pool are goddamn clothed.

Zoey, wearing a piece of lint covering her snatch and a wicked grin, is hovering over Alessia's chair as I approach. Alessia's eyes are closed and a beach towel covers her like a blanket. Music drifts from the casita, and nothing alerts them to my presence.

"Say yes," Zoey is insisting.

"I don't know," Alessia replies.

"It'll hurt for like five minutes."

"That's not what's holding me back." Alessia sighs.

"You kidding me? You worried about how the King of Kink might react? News flash ..." Zoey snaps her fingers in the air. "... he'll love it if you pierce your clit."

Madonna mia. I rub the back of my neck. I leave Little Miss

Innocent alone, and this is what she's up to? Deciding to get her motherfucking clit pierced? I'm annoyed, and turned on.

"I'll ask his permission first."

"Permission?" Zoey snorts. "You're either the most patient woman on the planet or a glutton for punishment. You haven't spoken in weeks."

"He has a lot going on," Alessia replies. So loyal. So in trouble if she's naked beneath that towel.

"Yeah, well, like I've said, you're better off with Sandro."

I reach behind Zoey for the remote on the table next to Alessia's chair. With a click of my thumb, the music turns off. Lightning fast, I brush by Zoey and snatch the towel from Alessia's body.

She's wearing a conservative navy one-piece suit.

Dia, am I disappointed? "Beat it," I tell Zoey.

Alessia stares at me aghast.

Breasts swaying, Zoey broadens her stance.

"Don't you have any homes to burn down?" I snap.

"Make up your mind," she snaps right back. "Allow her to marry Sandro and leave her alone. Or don't."

I straighten.

"Stop it, Zoey," Alessia insists.

Who the fuck does she think she's talking to?

Alessia scrambles from the chaise and wedges herself between us.

Marry Sandro? Leave her alone? Or don't? Like she's dictating what I can or can't do?

Alessia presses a palm against my stomach, and I push into her warm touch. "Please don't send her away. She's being a good friend, is all."

I still as her pleading tone washes over me. I miss her soft-spoken manner. Her sweet cries when I fuck her.

"Leave your clit alone. Capisci?"

"Capisci."

"Pool time is over," I thunder, and then stalk off, even more frustrated than before.

54

Alessia

BASTIAN LEAVES me no choice but to handcuff myself to his bedpost.

Waiting for his arrival is torture. Every footstep has me jumping. Every noise garners my intense concentration. How long is he going to ignore me? Does he truly believe nothing's changed?

It's late and I'm half-asleep when the door crashes open.

I know the exact moment he spots me.

"Che cazzo, Freido," he snaps. "Get her out of here."

Footsteps thud just as the moon's pale rays filter into the room and illuminate my naked body.

"I warned her this was a bad—"

The door is slammed closed in his face.

Bastian paces the room. Back and forth. Back and forth.

Calm washes over me. I tossed the handcuff key behind the sofa by the fireplace. I'm not going anywhere. "Please, Bastian. Come to bed."

He stops pacing.

"I want you."

A low curse echoes through the bedroom.

"I don't know what it feels like to climax while a man's inside me."

I gasp as he charges toward the bed. This is what happens when you wave a red flag at a bull.

"You want to be fucked?" He glares down at me.

Okay. Perhaps handcuffing myself to his bed isn't the wisest decision, considering how angry he's been. "Yes. Completely, utterly fucked."

He's already tearing off his clothes.

And then he's on me so fast, my head spins.

He crawls between my thighs and then arches over me, dragging his bulbous tip across my pussy.

His hiss fills the air. "You're dripping wet."

"I told you. I. Want. You."

"You're a little goddamn cocktease," he grunts, his fingers parting me, then invading.

I quiver beneath his touch. "Use me any way you like."

His cock replaces his fingers, and he nudges the fat head just inside my entrance.

This is happening.

Lord, I hope I enjoy this.

"Beg."

Our eyes lock. "Please. Fuck me."

"Tell me how much you missed this."

I blink. Okay ... "I touched myself every night wishing it was your bull inside me."

He thrusts and keeps going until I'm stuffed with his enormous size. I stretch around him, trying to relax while accommodating him.

"Your baby pussy," he pants, "feels even better than last time."

I nod, still struggling.

He kisses my forehead. "My little slut can talk the talk, but can she walk the walk?"

My struggle *amuses* him.

But instead of taunting him, I open up. "You're so big. I'm not sure I'll like it."

His lips curl.

Lord, he's breathtaking.

All signs of the angry man prowling around the estate this week disappear. He's delusional if he believes nothing exists between us.

"But even if I don't, I'll still be yours."

His eyes flash, possessive and hot.

And you're *mine*.

He drops my legs over his arms and sinks in deeper.

I close my eyes.

"Look at me, Alessia."

I snap them back open.

He smirks. "Let me know how you feel afterward."

His hips flex as he withdraws. And then with another smooth movement, he impales me to the hilt. I focus on his face, the way he grits his teeth upon withdrawal, the wonder within his eyes with each thrust forward, the beauty in his expression as he begins to fuck me mercilessly.

And then I forget about his reaction as pain becomes pleasure.

My toes curl and fingers wrap around the metal handcuffs.

It's heaven.

"You love being fucked, don't you?" he whispers in my ear as I strain against the sheets.

"God, yes."

"Any more worries?"

I might get *pregnant*. Because here we are, without protection again. And deep down, the idea thrills me.

"No."

He smirks again. "Hold on, then, while I teach this innocent pussy how to weep in pleasure."

He fucks me in earnest now, picking up speed and rattling the headboard. But when he angles his body just so, and hits a sweet spot I wasn't aware existed, I lose all sense of time and reason. My cries mix with his grunts, his strong body covering my own.

Nothing has ever felt this exquisite—physically speaking. The fact I love Sebastiano Beneventi, and that the signs are there that he shares the same emotion, is extraordinary.

"I'm coming," I gasp.

He slams into me like a man possessed. "Fuck, yeah," he shouts.

We climax together in a symphony of moans and shouts, his hot seed pumping into me as my body milks every last drop.

It's intense.

Incredible.

So much so, I black out.

When I awake, I'm free of the handcuffs but held firmly in place by his warm body.

Exactly where I dreamed I'd be.

55

Alessia

BY THE NEXT EVENING, we're on a private red-eye flight to Italy. Don Lucchese has refused hospice, his struggle with prostate cancer reaching an end.

Though no one was aware the proud old man had cancer.

"Something has to get you in the end," Bastian informed me when I teared up at the news. Yet he's not indifferent to Don Lucchese's struggle. When no one is watching, sadness fills his expression.

Oddly enough, he hasn't warned me about pleasing Don Lucchese. I approached Bastian once, after the flight took off, about how best to respond to wedding questions. But he shut me down with a scowl and proceeded to ignore me. Or pretended to—like I didn't catch his subtle glances from beneath his midnight black eyelashes.

Men fill the seats around us. Traveling with us for moral support, to wish Don Lucchese well, or to protect Bastian?

They occupy time by chatting and playing cards, while Bastian and I work in silence.

Halfway into the flight, I finish my essay. "I need to use the bathroom." I stand and stretch then make my way toward the back of the airplane, where a bigger and more luxurious restroom is located.

I'm washing my hands when the door pushes open.

Bastian arches an eyebrow at me. "The Renaissance masters were kinsters?"

I laugh. "My paper deserves an A+, don't you agree?"

"An A+ with a spanking," he growls, "you dirty little girl."

The air charges between us.

He's not here to use the restroom. Not. At. All. "Can I help you?" I murmur.

"You can." Pause. "Get on your knees."

Lord, he's bossy. I can't scramble to my knees any faster.

He unzips his fly. "Take it out."

I reach inside his pants and curl my fingers over his throbbing warmth. We haven't spoken much since last night. Especially not after the news about Don Lucchese. But instead of leaving me in Rhode Island, Bastian's taken me with him.

I'm about to make certain he's delighted by his decision.

With my free hand, I tug his dress pants to his hips and free his fat erection. Then I stare up at him, and lick my lips.

He growls low in his throat.

"Can I please suck your cock?"

His eyes shimmer. Lord, he loves my submissive side.

"Make it good."

I swirl my tongue across the head before licking him straight to the root.

He shifts forward on his feet.

I relax. *Breathe through the nose, Alessia.*

I feed him into my mouth, his weight on my tongue. Then my head shifts forward and back, each time taking him deeper until I'm crying while gagging on his cock. I keep my eyes open through all this.

Watching him come undone.

Seconds before he climaxes, he tugs my head forward.

A steady stream of come jets into my throat.

"I love how you look when I unload into you. So fucking pleased, like I've given you a gift." He withdraws, and then jerks his cock a few times so the last drops of his essence coat my face.

His eyes say it all. *Mine.*

I wipe a finger across the sticky mess, then lick it off.

His growl rumbles deep before he cleans up and returns to his seat.

Let's see if he can ignore me now, I think, and do the same.

56

Alessia

LIFE IS A SERIES OF JOURNEYS, though we're under the illusion it's only one. Family, education, jobs, marriage, children, love, and death. Each journey shapes you for the next, until it doesn't.

And, as a tired and gaunt Don Lucchese is wheeled into his Tuscany kitchen, his vibrant soul mellowed by cancer, I wonder how many journeys he's lived and if he considers all of them worthwhile.

Because, really, that's all anyone can hope for.

"Alessia," he exclaims, finally spotting me by his gourmet stovetop.

He insisted Bastian and I stay in a guesthouse on his estate. Separate rooms, of course—I'm engaged to Sandro, after all. Not that Bastian leaves me alone. It's difficult to distinguish when one orgasm ends and the next begins. Last night, after we toured Don Lucchese's vineyard, Bastian pinned me down in the dirt between two grape plants and fucked me senseless.

For three days, he's constantly been by my side.

And every day, I fall deeper and deeper in love.

If Don Lucchese weren't so frail, he'd notice. I'm struggling to reconcile the man I met at my engagement announcement and our host.

"If I were your fiancé," he says, "you'd never leave the kitchen."

"Sounds like a dream, Godfather."

His face brightens. He loves when I address him this way. "What are you making me for breakfast?" He waves the nurse away, then rolls himself to the kitchen table, where I set three place settings.

I grin. "Why does it feel like you're keeping us on your estate just so I cook for you?"

"I'm old but nobody's fool," he chuckles. "Of course I am."

"I've made a crostata. Would you like a slice while it's warm?"

"You use cherries? I like cherries."

I shake my head. "No, Godfather. This crostata's filling is Lucchese-grown grapes. I made grape jam, as well."

His eyes fill with tears, and I pause in shock.

"You remind me of a girl I once loved." He dabs his eyes with a napkin. "Still love," he softly adds.

"Dante's mother?" I ask, curious. Love isn't the reason Don Lucchese is feared or respected. He's a dangerous mafioso. But then our relationship is different, isn't it?

"Not that witch. I loved a Napoletana named Lucia. She was beautiful and sweet. We would have married, but ..." He swipes at his tears. "They killed her."

"Who did?"

"The Lucchese brothers. My uncle and father."

I place a hand on the counter to steady myself. "Why?"

"As you know, mafiosi custom is to marry strategically. Power. Money. Prestige. But I resisted, so they eliminated her."

"Because you were to marry Dante's mother."

"Correct."

How horrible. And if this is the expectation ...

I cut a slice of grape crostata with more force than necessary. With a weak smile, I place a plate before Don Lucchese, accompanied by a bowl of fresh whipped cream.

His expression reads pleased as punch.

"I'm sorry for your loss," I finally murmur.

Lightning fast, he grabs my wrist and prevents me from moving away. "You love who you love, Alessia." His tone is filled with so much kindness, I blink back tears.

"Yes, Godfather."

"But in your unique situation, so long as he's a Beneventi, what does it matter?"

My lips part.

He winks.

And then he takes a huge bite on his fork and shoves it into his mouth.

———

Bastian

ON OUR FOURTH night in Italy, I'm summoned to Don Lucchese's bedside.

I dress quickly, without waking Alessia, before being led to the old man's room.

I understand what this is.

It's time.

What I never anticipated is how much I'm dreading his passing. For years, his death represented a new beginning. I worked my ass off to be a worthy choice. I've proven myself time and time again. I sacrificed starting a family and reasoned the twins were enough of a fucking handful—why want more?

But I do. I want it all. The mafiosi kingdom. The control. The power. And *her*.

Alessia.

The little heart-thief.

I scratch the back of my neck. I'm faced with a choice, aren't I? Honor my word or follow my heart?

My father had no honor.

It's the dying old man who made me this way.

Troubled, I enter Don Lucchese's room, only to discover more trouble seated next to his bed. "Dante," I mutter.

"Bastian," he replies.

He's been reporting in from Atlanta as we salvage what we have and rebuild what we must. With the famiglie stock crisis behind us, I'm looking like a fucking hero. Dante, though, remains unfazed by my growing power.

Distrust has wedged a barrier between us. Until I get a credible explanation for why he disappeared, I'll remain suspicious.

"No rush, Bastian," Don Lucchese says. "I might die before your ass hits the seat."

Dai. He hasn't lost his morbid sense of humor, has he?

I pull a chair beside Dante's.

"First, I'll address Dante. You've been a good son. I'm proud of the man you've become."

Dante stiffens in his chair, like he's anticipating what's coming next.

"This Hollywood bullshit is amusing. But if you hope to be taken seriously, stop fucking billionaire's wives and daughters like you're going to run out of pussy, and settle down. In Italy—where your roots are. Am I making myself clear?"

"Yes," Dante grumbles. If he didn't pull the shit he pulled, I'd nudge him in the side and wink.

Don Lucchese shifts in the bed. The nurse hurries over and adjusts his pillow before his focus turns toward me. "Ever since you showed up here unannounced with your two boys in tow, I thought of you as a second son." He pauses, then grumbles, "Do you understand what I'm saying?"

I open my mouth, but no words come out.

Ah, fuck.

"I loved you like a son, capisci?"

"Capisci." My voice is raw, and honest. "You're the father I never had, Don Lucchese."

"I know, boy. I know. Which brings me to this point; I've nominated you as my successor." He wiggles a crooked finger at Dante. "You'll be his second-in-command."

He says this like it's final. But there'll be a second man nominated for the famiglie to vote on.

My guess is it'll be Roberto Ferrara.

Dante leans forward, probably reaching the same conclusion.

But the sly old man is never predictable. My eyes narrow on him. Isn't he unusually joyful for a man on his deathbed?

"There are two conditions, though," he adds.

There it is.

Dante glances my way.

"You"—he points a finger at me—"swear to forgive and protect Dante like a brother."

"Forgive him for what?" I exclaim.

"You"—he jabs the air and addresses Dante—"stop this behind-the-back bullshit you've got going on with Pietro Gallo before Bastian murders you."

I spin toward Dante.

His face drains of color.

The Gallos are one of the Twelve and Italy's oldest and most productive famiglia. They grow pistachios in Sicily and are highly respected by the others. I've never had an issue with their capo, Pietro. I helped him build a global stock portfolio and found investors for his legitimate farming business. What the fuck is Dante Lucchese about? Why the secrecy?

"We'll talk," I snap.

"It's not what you think," he responds in a low voice.

"I don't think anything, yet."

Don Lucchese claps his hands, silencing us. "I've seen a lot in my life. So believe Dante when he says it's not what you think."

The old man knows? What. The. Fuck?

"Now about my second nominee." The old ballbuster's eyes light up. Everything I worked toward hinges on this moment. Who has he chosen? If it's Matteo, I have competition.

Dante and I lock eyes.

Don Lucchese coughs. The nurse wheels over a respirator machine and gives him a hit of oxygen.

My fists clench. He's frail and weak, and fading.

Fuck.

Like me, he despises weakness.

"One phone call," I say after he recovers, "and I can arrange for a woman to make you feel better. If you can still get it up?"

"I can get it up," he grunts. "Which reminds me, Alessia seems content."

I stiffen. *Madonna.* "She's adjusted."

"Sandro's a lucky man."

Dante looks from his father to me.

Fucking terrific.

"That girl is special, Bastian. Soft and gentle. A proud man with too many responsibilities could do worse."

This room is fucking stifling. The nurse better open a window.

"I obviously won't be attending the wedding. But from a man on his deathbed, and from father to son, I've a final wish."

My stomach gut-punches me from inside.

"What is it?"

"Sandro shouldn't be the Beneventi at the end of the aisle. You should be."

I grip the chair as the possibilities within what he's saying race through my mind. Alessia in my bed every night. Her meals in my belly, and hers swollen with my children. Her beautiful face, gorgeous body, kind spirit present in my life—and not because I'm her goddamn father-in-law.

"You should marry her, Bastian," Dante comments.

"She's Sandro's fiancée."

"And?" Dante actually looks puzzled.

"It's a matter of honor." Something *you* don't respect.

"It's a matter of you waking up every day a happy man." Don Lucchese snorts. "Honor reads differently on every man. You, Bastian, never learned to honor yourself first and foremost. Just like all the other stronzi do."

"You honor your word."

"And that's another thing." He waves a crooked finger at me. "You hate disappointing me."

What the fuck? I scowl.

"You heard me."

Is it true? Is Sandro even more of a chip off the ol' block than I expected? He hates disappointing me the same way I hate disappointing Don Lucchese? We Beneventi men are proud. We're control freaks, admittedly—even Renzo, though he expresses it differently.

"I fucking loathe disappointing you," I admit.

"Well, if you don't marry Alessia, you will. And I'll haunt you from the grave for it."

Suddenly, everything feels lighter.

"Someone better ask me who else I nominated before I drop dead with unexpressed glee."

Dante and I make eye contact once more. "Who is Bastian's competition?"

The old man cackles.

"Benny Manocchio."

We stare in stunned surprise.

He covers his mouth with his hand. "Oops, I'm bad. Guess, in my weakened state, I forgot to remove a dead man from the ballot."

THE OLD MAN is dead by morning.

I take a walk out into his vineyard, and do what I never do—I cry.

57

I STAND NEXT to Sandro at Don Lucchese's grave. Dangerous men surround us, and not for the first time do I wonder if a Turkish prison might be a safer place. No one dares touch me—not with their new capo di tutti capi dominating our universe.

Early this morning, the Ten assembled with Don Lucchese's lawyers. The nominees were read, votes were cast, and Bastian assumed power. Like Don Lucchese, he demanded the others sign a new terms of succession contract. "Democratic bullshit," he informed Sandro and me on the drive to the old man's gravesite. "The plush stock portfolios I presented just before the vote will keep them docile, obedient, and rich."

I nuzzled against him as he stared out the window for the duration of the ride, and comforted him with my body. Without a word, he tossed an arm around my shoulders and pulled me in tight, though Sandro's mouthed "What the fuck?" echoed loudly around the backseat. My fiancé shook his head, then looked out the other window, so much like his father that I almost liked him.

I'm thrilled for Bastian, I truly am. But a persistent thought destroys my own happiness. Do I get what I want, too?

Sandro nudges me in the side, forcing my attention onto him. "First impressions count."

We stand side by side as mafiosi in expensive black suits toss dirt onto Don Lucchese's coffin. Bastian's on the opposite side and engulfed by his men while Sandro and I wait our turn.

The threat of rain hangs over the funeral procession, the air thick with humidity. I'm light-headed, the events of the last few days taking their toll.

"With that sad face," Sandro continues, "no one will believe we're the happy couple."

I offer up a weak smile.

"I won't disappoint him again."

I search his tight expression. "You never disappoint him."

He grunts in disagreement.

Although my inclination is to reassure him, I don't. Now is not the place or time. Like Sandro said, everyone around us expects a happy couple. "Family first."

Sandro nods. "That's right."

"Soon-to-be *husband*," I say loudly, and take his hand.

He scowls, then quickly corrects himself. "*Wife.*"

We're still holding hands when our time comes to pay our respects. Sandro approaches the grave first, while I withdraw a napkin from my pocket and unwrap it. Fresh tears fall as reality sets in. I liked my godfather, despite who he was and despite the circumstances.

I love Bastian, despite everything, despite my broken heart.

I approach Don Lucchese's grave, then sprinkle the napkin's contents onto his casket. "Rest in peace, Godfather."

"What the hell was that?" Sandro demands once we resume our positions.

"Chocolate biscotti. His favorite."

Sandro's expression softens. "You're too good for any of us."

I catch sight of Bastian as the circle surrounding him parts. Even at this somber occasion, his sex appeal is undeniable. Tall and handsome in a dark suit that complements his features. Graceful in the way he scratches his neck and shakes his head. A man in full control of himself, and those around him. He overshadows these men in every way, doesn't he? So big and commanding in nature. Is it surprising they respect him? Maseratis line the cemetery while men line up to speak with him. He's boardroom executive, criminal mastermind, and ruthless killer all in one.

"Wipe your eyes." Sandro hands me a tissue.

"Thank you."

The sermon concludes, and Bastian gestures for us.

We both step forward.

"Not you. Just me."

"Oh," I utter, crushed. Why would my father-in-law include me in his business?

Sandro hesitates. "I murdered Emilio Conti, the man who kidnapped me. They're going to want a recap of the gory details, something my father likely doesn't want you to hear. Capisci?"

"I understand." A shiver races up my spine. This is the world I live in, yet I still struggle with how these men can kill someone like it's part of their job description.

"Be right back, *wife*," Sandro calls out as soon as he reaches the group, drawing everyone's attention. Acting very much like Renzo would act in this situation.

With a scowl, Bastian's eyes brush over me before he turns back to the group.

My old nervousness returns. I'm still shy around most people, though not the Beneventi men. Not Bastian—I'm bold as brass in his company and bed. But everything's changing, and nothing about my future's clear.

I'm what, exactly?

Fresh air might relieve my sadness. I retreat in the opposite direction of the procession, passing the first car in a long line of them—a cherry red Maserati that costs a fortune—to climb a small hill with a tall shady tree at the top.

Halfway there, I notice a young woman standing beneath it.

I wave.

She doesn't wave back.

She's gorgeous, with deep red hair and a model-like figure. Dante's girlfriend? Models and actresses love him.

"I'm hoping there's a breeze up here," I softly say as I approach her.

For several awkward seconds, her beautiful green eyes fixate on my hand before she raises them.

I fall back, shocked by her tormented expression.

"You're engaged to Alessandro?" she demands.

"Excuse me?"

"Or are you already married? He called you *wife*."

"Not yet." I stiffen. "I'm his fiancée."

She drops like a rag doll to her knees.

No. No. No. No. No. What has Sandro done? "Are you okay?" I fall to the ground beside her and lightly touch her arm.

She shakes her head. Not only is this beautiful creature involved with Sandro, she loves him.

And I ruined it.

No, wait. Sandro ruined it. How could he not tell her he's engaged? "Are you okay?"

"For how long?" she chokes out.

"Months."

She draws in a breath. "This summer?"

"Yes."

She wobbles to her feet, and I rise with her. "He's an asshole for not telling you."

"Yes," she mutters. "He is."

"I dislike him," I admit. "And he loathes me, if it makes you feel better ..."

"It doesn't. What I feel is ..." She stares off into the distance.

"Lost?" I blurt.

"Yes."

What can I say? I'm lost, too? What reassurances can I offer her? What does it matter who I love, if the outcome breaks everyone but

Bastian's cold heart? "I'm sorry," I whisper. Because I am. For her. For Sandro. For myself.

"I'll be going now." She spins and hurries away in the opposite direction.

I want to run after her. But family first, right?

My emotions are all over the place, and I draw in a few calming breaths. Because tears are best shed when no one is watching. Once composed, I retrace my path.

Except as I pass by the red Maserati, a door hangs open, though mourners are still assembled around Don Lucchese's grave.

"Angel."

I stumble. "Renzo?"

A hand appears, and he waves to me.

With a glance over my shoulder, I approach the vehicle.

Renzo slides over on the seat, then pats the cushion.

I climb inside. "Oh my God. What? How?"

He smirks. "Why did I break into Matteo Lombardi's car?"

He looks much better than when we last met. Less gaunt. More muscular. And his eyes are clear. "What are you doing here?" I murmur.

"Don Lucchese was my godfather."

Sadness weighs down his voice. "Sorry for your loss, Renzo."

"How's my father handling his death?"

I sigh. "He hides his emotions well, but he loved the old man."

"I know." His handsome face sobers. "And you? Are you okay?"

"No."

All the air goes out of him.

"I love your father," I blurt.

Renzo shakes his head. "Jesus, Alessia. I was afraid this might happen."

"You knew?"

"Not that you'd fall in love. But I had a feeling my father wouldn't be able to resist you once he got to know you." He frowns. "Hold up. You're still engaged to Sandro?"

"Yes."

"But you're ... um ... involved with my old man."

"Fucking him? Yes. All the time, actually ..."

Renzo's eyes become saucers.

I laugh. My admission shocks his fine sensibilities?

I change the subject. "You look good. Healthy. Rehab worked."

"Not rehab—my fuckhead brother is what did it. Tied me to a bed and told me to sweat it out. Not even Sergeant Dickwad is that cruel."

Is this what Sandro's been up to in Italy—other than breaking hearts?

"So it worked?"

Renzo sighs. "Am I abusing? No. Am I an addict who is temporarily clean? Yes. Is there a possibility I'll slip up? Every fucking day."

"Then come home."

His eyebrows rise. "To my brother's designer digs in Soho? No thank you."

I instantly sober. "No," I murmur. "I meant Rhode Island."

My heart sinks.

Renzo, seeing my distress, tugs me into a hug. "My father's fucking possessive. No way is he letting you go. Capisci?"

"Capisci," I softly reply.

"Will you give him a message?" He releases his hold.

"Of course."

"Tell him to call off his men. I'll handle my shit at my own pace and time."

"He loves you, Renzo."

"Tell him I love him, too." He flashes a smile. "You, too."

"I better get back before he notices I'm gone."

"Alessia. Trust me when I tell you, he noticed the second you left his side."

I wish it were true.

But this is reality I'm living in, not some contrived fantasy.

I climb out of the car.

"Give me a few minutes to disappear before you tell him, will you?"

I nod, because it'll take a few minutes to make it to Bastian's side.

"Oh, and Alessia?"

I glance back at him. So broken, yet on the mend. So tormented, though he gets off on it, doesn't he?

His eyes fill with mischief.

"I'm going to enjoy calling you Mom."

I'm drunk, sprawled on the hotel room floor beside an equally inebriated Sandro. Unlikely allies, even unlikelier friends. But stranger things have happened, right?

It's nearing eleven. Bastian left the funeral with a few other capos, but not before ordering Sandro to bring me here and book a room. His words hit like a final toll, marking the end of our time together.

On the way, I mentioned the redhead I spoke to. Sandro's reaction? Devastation, plain as day. He might still be a world-class A-hole, but there's a heart beating somewhere in that chest of his.

The booze was his idea. Staying in his room was mine.

He raises his whiskey glass to my wine bottle. "Here's to Renzo, running wild and free." I told him about our encounter, though Sandro wasn't surprised his brother showed up at their godfather's funeral. What threw him was hearing that Renzo and I met in the backseat of Matteo Lombardi's Maserati.

"Wild, free, and sober," I add, clinking my bottle against his glass.

"Sober. A state I don't want to be in right now."

I nudge an empty bottle with my foot, watching it roll away. Two more full ones sit nearby, waiting for their turn. "Neither do I."

We keep drinking, and Sandro makes another call to his men—

probably the hundredth by now. I glance at the clock just as often, anxiety gnawing at me. Where is he?

"He's never committed to a woman before," Sandro says abruptly, breaking the silence. "Having two heirs to carry on the Beneventi name without marrying gave him the freedom to do whatever the fuck he wants."

I stare into my wine, feeling like I'm swallowing something far more bitter than the alcohol.

"If you really love him," Sandro continues, his tone flat, "you'll need to teach him how to love a woman. Because I'm not sure he's capable of it."

I look at Sandro, feeling utterly lost.

"I said too much."

No kidding.

"Are you in love?" I ask, thinking about how he bolted from the limousine earlier, racing back to the cemetery only to find the redhead gone. Since then, he's been tight-lipped about his girlfriend.

He snorts. "Me? In love?"

My lips twitch. Now he sounds more like the heartless fiancé I've come to know—and hate.

But then he mutters, "Maybe." His tone carries a weight that makes it impossible not to feel his pain. It's easy, since my pain mirrors his.

I roll onto my side, studying him. "That's a yes."

"It's complicated."

"Isn't it always?" I pause, guilt tugging at me. "I'm sorry. She asked, and I just answered honestly. I didn't know."

"Forget it. My men will find her."

He downs his whiskey in one swift gulp.

"Sandro, what are we going to do?" I ask, my words slightly slurred.

"I don't know. When my father hauled you back to Rhode Island, I thought everything would sort itself out. But now... I'm not so sure."

I bite my bottom lip, hesitating. "He's at a club right now, celebrating, isn't he?"

Sandro offers a slight nod.

"And he probably has a trio of women at his beck and call."

"It's likely. But he'll be more concerned with what's happening back here."

My eyebrows raise. "How so?"

"On paper, a wedding seems perfect. But I bet he loses his fucking mind at the thought of me putting my dirty hands on you."

"You mean sex?"

"Fucking." He grins a sinister grin. "No way is he immune to the idea of us consummating our marriage, especially knowing my tastes run toward hardcore."

"So we tell him no. Next time he mentions the wedding, we refuse to go through with it. What's the worst he'll do? Lock us in the dungeon?"

Sandro takes a long drink, considering my words.

I lift the wine bottle to my lips and take a deep sip.

"You ever tell Sebastiano Beneventi no?" Sandro asks after a moment.

"Yes. And he ended up eating takeout most nights."

Sandro chuckles, a sound so rare it catches me off guard. In that moment, he almost seems more like Renzo than the Sandro I know. "Bet that pissed him off. He loves your cooking."

Loves my cooking, but not me.

"You really aren't afraid of him, are you?"

"It's more that I trust him not to hurt me. At least, not in ways I don't want him to."

Sandro coughs, and I burst into uncontrollable laughter. What a prude—and a hypocrite. Thanks to Zoey, I know all too well about Sandro's "dirty hands". He's all about dominating women in the bedroom. That poor redhead should count herself lucky she escaped. "We should practice," I finally say.

"Practice? Fuck no. He'd kill me if I actually touched you like that."

"Not that kind of practice," I clarify. "Let's practice saying no. Pretend you're Bastian. Ask me something about the wedding."

Sandro's growl is immediate. "Did you make a fucking wedding list yet?"

My lips part in surprise—he sounds just like Bastian.

"Well?" Sandro flips his wrist as if checking the time. "I haven't got all goddamn day."

"No."

That felt good.

"What do you mean, no?" he demands, his voice seething with irritation.

I shrug. "No list."

"Wow, you do have a backbone after all."

"Your turn." I press my lips together, doing my best Bastian impression. "Did you find a suitable church, one with walls that won't crumble in horror at my presence?"

"No."

I arch an eyebrow. "No?"

Sandro straightens and strikes a menacing pose. "No."

I tap his glass with my wine bottle. "No."

"Everyone around me thinks I'm a control-freak. So why is it, when it comes to my father, I'm always the obedient son?" His voice carries a hint of frustration, tinged with disappointment in himself.

I laugh. "You clearly enjoy exerting control over others, and you're a jerk—though a loyal one. But remember, your father is your capo. Just like everyone else, you have to follow his orders."

A loud thud against the door jolts us and moments later, it swings open with sudden force. Bastian stumbles in, slamming the door in the doorman's face before staggering toward us. "You didn't book her a room," he snarls, his fury aimed at Sandro.

"She's spending the evening with her fiancé," Sandro replies calmly.

"And you"—Bastian jabs a finger in my direction—"were supposed to be alone and waiting." Either he's as drunk as we are, or I'm seeing double, because there seem to be two of him glaring at me.

I notch my chin. "But instead I'm with my fiancée."

"Not anymore." Bastian plucks me up into his arms.

"Everything went well?" Sandro asks, unfazed.

"Yes. Better than expected, even."

"Good."

I'm pulled in close and despite my confusion, despite my worries, I melt into him.

"You're both drunk."

We don't bother replying—there's no need.

"Fuck it," he grumbles. "Let's get this over with. We need to discuss the wedding."

"No," Sandro and I say in unison.

"What the fuck do you mean, no?"

"No wedding," Sandro states firmly.

I feel Bastian tense around me. "I want you and your brother there."

"No," I hiss. "There won't be a wedding."

Sandro grins, and I wink at him. We did it.

"We'll spend a few more days in Rome," Bastian informs me, "and you can shop for a new wedding dress."

"What happened to the old one?" Sandro asks, still smiling. Odd. But then, he's far from an average Joe.

"He ruined it when—"

Before I can finish, Bastian bounces me in the air. I grab his shoulders for fear of falling.

"You fucking love her." It's not a question but a statement from Sandro.

"Of course I love her."

What? Wait. The room starts to spin.

"I love three people in this world: you, your asshole brother, and her." Bastian kisses my forehead. "I never break my word. But I love her so fucking hard, and I'm tired of pretending otherwise."

His admission flips my world upside down.

He loves me.

Sebastiano Beneventi loves me.

"I love you, too, Bastian," I declare fiercely.

His lips claim mine in a passionate kiss. Behind us, I hear Sandro mutter, "Thank fuck."

Before I can fully grasp it, I'm leaving one Beneventi fiancé behind and being swept away by another.

58

Bastian

"WHERE ARE YOU TAKING ME?"

She's seated beside me in the backseat, blindfolded and at my mercy.

I waited until noon to wake the little drunkard, then commanded her to take two aspirin and eat the continental breakfast I'd ordered to soak up the wine. While she obeyed, I showed her the dress I purchased and wanted her to wear. Pink, ankle-length and collarbone high, and ultraconservative. I paired it with the sluttiest black lace underwear I could find.

She loved everything.

Hangover dealt with, I escorted her to the car, then blindfolded her once we settled inside.

Why? Because once my mind is made up, shit happens.

We arrive at our destination midafternoon. "What's this about, Bastian?" she breathlessly demands. "Are you bringing me to a club?"

Kink club, she means.

Days ago, I was balls deep and whispering dirty promises in her ear. The curious little kinkster can't wait to visit her first sex club.

But first things first.

I pay the security detail at the entrance before leading her inside the vacant space. "It smells like incense," she stammers.

My lips curl. The little sensualist's senses are piqued. *Just you wait, baby, because I'm about to blow your mind.*

Our steps echo across the marble floor until we reach our destination. Grabbing her hips, I lift and position her on a marble-columned banister before climbing over it. I want nothing to obstruct the view.

"Count to three, then open your eyes. Capisci?"

"Capisci," she eagerly replies.

I release the blindfold, then drop onto one knee.

Her eyes grow to the size of saucers when she opens them. "*Ecstasy of Saint Teresa?*" She draws in a breath. "You took me to the Santa Maria della Vittoria chapel? I thought, because you blindfolded me ..."

"Another time, baby. I promise."

"Lord, she's beautiful, isn't she?" she asks, enthralled by the sculpture.

On her perch, wearing a pink dress and a wondrous expression, I know in my heart I'm a lucky man. I withdraw the diamond and emerald ring from my pocket, and softly murmur, "Beyond compare." Then I wait for her to fully comprehend what this is about.

Several minutes tick by before she drags her eyes away from the statue. When she spies the ring, her fingers curl around the banister to steady herself.

"Alessia Amato, will you marry me?"

Silence fills the chapel.

She flings herself at me, and I fall backward with her on top. "Yes, Bastian. Oh my God. Yes."

Kisses rain down across my face.

I laugh, roll into a seated position, and grab her hand. "Let's see if it fits." I slide the ring into place, claiming her as fucking *mine*.

She holds it up to the light. "It's perfect."

I roll us over and straddle her. Then, I kiss her.

Her arms wind behind my neck, and she arches into me as our tongues glide together. With Alessia, I can never get enough.

I lift off her and unzip my pants.

"What are you doing?" she whispers.

"I'm going to fuck my fiancée six ways to Sunday ..." I jab my

thumb over my shoulder at Saint Teresa on the pedestal above us. "...
until the same expression falls across her beautiful face." I reach
beneath her dress, tear off her sexy underwear, line my cock up and
then drive into her so hard, she glides several inches across the marble
floor.

"Oh God, Bastian," she cries out. Loving my aggressiveness.
Loving me, in every way.

I pound into her. She wiggles and moans, on sensory overload as
her gaze wanders from the statue to the frescoes to my face. Her tight
cunt grips me like a vise, and soon, we're a series of dirty words,
curses, and throaty moans. "I'm never forgetting this moment," she
pants in my ear.

"Hey," I bark, earning her complete attention. "I love you."

Her smile is ecstasy. If I were a fucking sculptor, I'd capture her
expression so I could stare at her beautiful face every day. Place my
masterpiece inside my great room as a reminder to stop being a dick
and to cherish the three little ballbusters, who I love to death.

But Alessia will be my wife now.

I can stare at her until my heart bleeds.

"I love you, too, Bastian," she moans, then shatters beneath me.

Mine, I think, emptying into her. *Forever and always.*

EPILOGUE

Alessia

"You'd tell me if Sebastiano Beneventi is forcing you into marrying him, right?" my sister exclaims.

Zoey snorts. "Well, duh. Check out her baby bump. He knocked her up so fast, The Flash and Shazam are eating his dust."

"Shazam?" Sienna looks to me for an explanation.

I brush away Zoey's hand, and fix the botched job she's done with my lopsided veil. We're tucked inside a vestibule at St. Mary's Church in Rhode Island. A small stone church with beautiful stained-glass windows and walls thick enough to support the blackened hearts of the men in attendance.

And the heart of the man waiting for me at the altar.

My husband.

The father of the baby I carry.

We learned we're expecting about a month after our return from Rome. Bastian insists we conceived during our naughty hookup inside the Santa Maria della Vittoria chapel. The doctor has all but confirmed it, yet I think the man's terrified to say otherwise. Fate played a role in my and Bastian's relationship, after all. We may not have met while visiting the chapel, but our little bean, Teresa, bonds us as a family.

As for us marrying at the Tavern on the Green, Bastian insisted Sandro cancel the venue and pay the subsequent cancellation fee after Sandro gloated about knowing his father would never him, or any other man, claim me.

There's a scuffle outside the door.

Zoey hurries toward the commotion and flings the door open.

Sandro stands there, clutching his jaw.

But the man cupping his own chin next to him is who I race toward. "Renzo, you're here. He's going to be so happy."

"I'm escorting her down the aisle," Sandro states.

"Not if you can't walk," Renzo replies, and sweeps his foot behind his brother's leg, then shoves him, sending him toppling backward.

"And to think," Zoey mutters, "I slept with both of them."

Everyone stops to glare at her.

"Years ago," she stammers. "Both times were totally forgettable."

Lord, Sandro and Renzo look distraught.

"Tell him, Alessia," Sandro insists. "I'm—"

"No."

Sandro pauses, then grumbles, "That's your new favorite word now, isn't it?"

"Both of you can escort me. Your father will love that."

Renzo smirks. "Yes, Mom."

"You better get moving," Sienna says. "Unless you changed your mind ..."

I sigh. I understand her reservations—she did escape the country, fearing for her life. But I wish she'd trust my judgment. Wish she'd be happy for me. But *I* trust my own judgment, and I'm happier for it.

And secure.

And loved, deeply.

And satisfied, on so many levels.

I grin.

The music begins.

I laugh when Sandro and Renzo offer me their elbows at the same time.

Bastian

The moment my little bride appears, I know deep down, I'm truly, utterly fucked. She's so beautiful, it hurts. Aside from my sons and now baby Teresa, I've never loved someone this hard.

Two men escort her. Men—not boys. Sandro, who has finally grown a set of balls, and Renzo, who has lost some of his anger and is walking, not stumbling, alongside Alessia.

The future of the Beneventi famiglia walks toward me.

And I take a rare moment to appreciate how lucky I am.

The famiglie are in attendance: a smirking Luca Ricci, still my closest ally; an expressionless Xavier Moretti, whip smart and taking it all in; Dante Lucchese, my right hand and, quite possibly, my biggest enemy; and a smug-faced Matteo Lombardi, whose gambling addiction's becoming a disgrace to the famiglie. His daughter, Elia Seraphina Lombardi, has accompanied him. Trouble in fucking pink high heels, and all of it is directed at Renzo.

He better handle his bullshit *after* the ceremony.

My attention skips over the lesser men. Everyone's tight-lipped now after one man thought he'd gossip about me at my fucking wedding. I had him beaten, not killed—believing it's bad luck to order someone killed from inside a church. The beating silenced the gossip.

Governor Amato sits with his head bowed. Disappointed Alessia didn't ask him to escort her down the aisle? Has the bastardo realized he's been a shit father? Or is he disappointed his role is as observer and not participant?

My eyes shift back to Alessia, who ever so slowly makes her way toward me. Her wedding gown is conservative, with tiny pearl buttons leading up from her waist to her neck. I'm going to slice each fucking button off with the tip of my knife later on while she stands perfectly still, like a good little wife. Then, kiss her belly before licking up her sweet nectar I know I'm going to find.

Her ass is pink beneath the gown.

And God damn me, if I don't grow hard at the thought.

It's difficult to believe she's a kinky little mama-to-be.

Or that her presence calms me in ways I never realized I'd been missing.

But as the priest begins the sermon, and she slips her hand into mine, I believe that with our love and her by my side, anything is possible.

THE END

Sandro's story, DIRTY MAFIA SINNER, is next!
Here's a quick taste of my bossy, super kinky, a-hole hero.

Never in my life have I been so reckless.

I glance over my shoulder at the stranger as we climb the stairs to my fourth-floor walkup. Random acts are not my thing, and I'm shocked I invited him in.

My friends back home joked how my house was the nicest in town, yet they hardly saw the inside. I had my reasons for keeping my family life private. But the truth is I'm great at being the shoulder others cry on yet struggle asking for help myself. Not that this stopped the Big-Hearts-with-Big-Mouths back in Marietta politely inquiring about my mental condition after "The Tragedy," believing talking about what happened will fix me.

Just for a little while, I want to give no fucks. Tonight, every fiber within me is awake. And, if the man behind me gets off on playing with broken things, guess what? Tonight's his lucky night.

"All these apartments are vacant?" His gravelly tone breaks the silence and echoes through the stairwell.

"Yes. My unit was the first one renovated. The rest are under construction."

"You live alone in the building?" Lord, his voice is sexy, even while laced with disapproval.

"My best friend was supposed to be my roommate." We reach the top-floor landing, and I find my key. "But she moved in with her boyfriend. I've only been in New York City for a week and haven't had the time to find another roommate."

We fall quiet as I unlock the door. Then we step inside and into the kitchen, and I flip on the light.

"This is the lock?"

My lips draw tight. Ciro's LLC owns the building and was renovating it as a flip, up until C&C Enterprises won the casino contract. Progress has slowed, yet the workers completing the renovations still show up sporadically for a few hours' work. I requested a better lock, but Ciro dismissed my concerns, reminding me about the expensive, high-tech keypad and the overpriced security cameras installed in the main entrance. "No place safer in Brooklyn," he informed me, blowing me off.

"That's the lock," I reply, a bit unnerved by the stranger's unwavering regard.

"The construction crew all women?"

"All women? No."

"You can't be that stupid."

The insult shocks me like a blast of ice water in the face. *You wanted to feel something, Riley. And he delivered.* I wait for my anger to surface. Because he's correct, a five-year-old could pick the lock.

His eyes bore into me as he leans casually against the door, radiating a heady combination of arrogance, power, and danger. My wildly thumping heart competes with the warning bells in my mind. I should feel insulted and demand he leave. But I won't. The tension between us crackles, powerful enough to dissolve his harsh words and strip away my common sense.

"You're right," I murmur, and he blinks in surprise. "The lock needs replacing."

His blue eyes are like the deepest sea, turbulent and unrelenting, dragging me into uncharted territory, as he studies me. But there's no warning when he prowls forward, forcing me to step backward until I'm against the bathroom door, facing the entry. He places a hand to my right and draws in close, caging me. His head tips, and I gasp as his warm tongue touches below my ear. He smells like lemon and spice. Looks like a wet dream. And everything about him feels ... *right.*

I must be losing my mind.

My lips part with a small gasp as he licks a trail across my jawline. "Why did you invite me inside?" he growls. A shiver races up my spine at his husky tone.

"You know why," I whisper.

"You want me to fuck you." Statement, not question.

I nod. Except how do I tell him it's not just that? How do I invite a complete stranger—even one so shockingly handsome—to over-power me with sensation, play with each and every shattered piece within me, and make me feel alive?

His eyebrows pinch as he reads my expression.

"Please," I beg.

He cups the back of my neck and holds me still while ever so slowly drawing a finger, like a knife blade, across my throat. To strike fear? To intimidate? To force me to squirm and push him off me?

It's a dangerous game we're playing. Even so, excitement licks up my spine as I act on instinct alone and tilt back my head, offering him my throat.

His grin catches me by surprise. Arrogant. Dangerous. Sexy beyond words.

His thumbs press against my throat. "Ever orgasm like this?"

Wide-eyed, I shake my head.

"Oxygen restriction heightens the pleasure."

I'm at a loss for words. Don't most men steal a kiss or grab ass as part of foreplay? Lean into it with charm and intent? "Erotic asphyxi-ation," I murmur. "The brain releases endorphins and adrenaline, causing a drug-like high."

His eyes pierce me, and my body warms beneath the intense scrutiny. Finally, he steps back. Loss sweeps over me, but it's temporary.

"Take off your dress."

My hands shake, yet I manage to reach behind me and unzip my black dress. It slides down my body and pools at my ankles. Leaving me in a flimsy lace bra and matching thong with a triangular patch that barely covers my sex.

"Holy fuck."

His hungry gaze rakes over me while I stand frozen and he looks his fill. His reaction is reassuring, and Lord knows I need more than a flash of his wicked grin to counter the fact I'm slightly terrified.

He removes his belt and unbuttons his pants. Wow, is this really happening? Before I can change my mind, he's spinning me around and pushing me belly-first into the door. My heart beats against the wooden panel. Rat-tat-tat. Rat-tat-tat. Every pulse is dialed into him.

My arms are pulled back, and expensive leather wraps around my wrists.

"Wait," I protest, reality crashing in. Oh God. He's binding my wrists. What was I thinking, relinquishing control to a complete stranger?

He nudges a thigh between mine, spreading them. "Stop fighting what we both want."

"And what's that?" I squeak.

"Your surrender."

Dirty Mafia Kingdom

Dark mafia romance

Dirty Mafia King

Dirty Mafia Sinner

Dirty Mafia Torment

Dirty Mafia Lover

Deadliest Lies Novels

Dark contemporary with *a lot* of suspense

Rogue

Mercenary

Hit Man

Player

Liar

Bastard

Worth the Fight Series

Sexy contemporary sports romance

Knock Out

Tap Out

Out for The Count

ABOUT THE AUTHOR

Michele Mannon has been writing romance since her first publication in 2012. A multiple recipient of Romantic Times Magazine's prestigious TOP PICKS award, Michele's books always pack a punch, leaving readers laughing out loud or swooning and biting their fingernails at all the appropriate times. Her books have been sold in print, digitally, and on Audible.

She loves the darker shades in romance; the anti-heroes and villains, the angst mixed with a heavy dose of unexpected.

Michele lives on a mountain overlooking the Delaware River, where she can be found with a glass of Riesling in her hand and a laptop on her lap. On occasion, she posts on TikTok @authormichelemannon

For more news and updates, visit her website - michelemannon.com or connect on social media @authormichelemannon